BOULDER CITY LIBRARY

3 14

D0484173

J   Jacobson, Jennifer
JAC   Richard

Dollar kids

THE
DOLLAR
KIDS

THE DOLLAR KIDS

JENNIFER RICHARD JACOBSON

ILLUSTRATED BY RYAN ANDREWS

CANDLEWICK PRESS

This is a work of fiction. Names, characters, places, and incidents are either products of the author's imagination or, if real, are used fictitiously.

Text copyright © 2018 by Jennifer Richard Jacobson
Illustrations copyright © 2018 by Ryan Andrews

All rights reserved. No part of this book may be reproduced, transmitted, or stored in an information retrieval system in any form or by any means, graphic, electronic, or mechanical, including photocopying, taping, and recording, without prior written permission from the publisher.

First edition 2018

Library of Congress Catalog Card Number pending
ISBN 978-0-7636-9474-6

18 19 20 21 22 23 LSC 10 9 8 7 6 5 4 3 2 1

Printed in Crawfordsville, IN, U.S.A.

This book was typeset in Berkeley Old Style.
The illustrations were done in pencil and digital watercolor.

Candlewick Press
99 Dover Street
Somerville, Massachusetts 02144

visit us at www.candlewick.com

For Holly, who loves the residents of Millville
(old and new) as much as I do
J. R. J.

For Yamaga, and the house that could have been
R. A.

ABE'S BEEN GONE A LONG TIME.

HE'S PROBABLY GIVING GEORGIO AN EARFUL. MAYBE I CAN FINISH GLOBBER DOG BEFORE HE RETURNS.

LOWEN...

WHAT? WHAT IS IT?

WHAT'S WRONG?

THERE'S BEEN A TERRIBLE ACCIDENT.

A... A RANDOM SHOOTING AT GEORGIO'S.

ABE WAS THERE.

THE TWIZZLERS!

HE'S OK, RIGHT?

NO, SWEETIE.

HE'S DEAD.

HE'S ONE OF FOUR CHILDREN DEAD.

1.

MARCH

Lowen was an artist. At three, he drew big fat heads with spindly arms and legs. At four, he drew vehicles: trucks and buses, but mostly police cars with lights on top. (He already knew to surround the lights with sunrays to indicate flashing.) By his sixth birthday, he preferred drawing people and animals (especially giraffes) in action. And by eight, he'd draw pretty much anything on demand.

But from eight to eleven, things changed. Lowen spent every spare moment drawing comics. He loved the way a simple line (an arrow for a nose, for example) was all that was needed to convey the whole of a person. And how you hardly needed any words at all if the panel was drawn well. Whereas a picture or a portrait shows you everything, comics let you imagine other worlds filled with action and victory. Comics promised stories.

When Abe died, part of Lowen died, too. For months he couldn't sketch anything at all. He'd tried to return to the comics he'd been working on, but the minute he picked up the pencil, Abe's voice—with imagined comments, questions, and suggestions—cut through his brain and strangled his heart.

It wasn't until months later, while lying in bed—casting about for ways to keep himself awake to avoid the nightmares—that he began to picture a new comic. Panel by panel he imagined the day Abe was killed. The panels came clearly, logically, like a movie in his mind, without extra thoughts or voices. While his older brother, Clem, was at basketball practice the next day, Lowen stole to their room and began to draw the comics he'd imagined.

From then on, it was the only thing he'd allow himself to draw, and then, only privately. He'd chosen a new sketchbook (he always got one or two as birthday gifts) for the Abe comics, as he'd come to think of them, and he stored them between the mattress and the box spring at the end of his bed.

He didn't tell anyone about them. How could he? He couldn't admit that he had been the one to send Abe to the store: not to his parents, not to his brother and sister, not to Mrs. Siskin (Abe's mother), not to the counselor who insisted on playing a gazillion games of Battleship to earn his trust. When you can't trust yourself to do the right thing, you certainly can't trust others.

The comics helped. He no longer felt choked by the guilt. But they did nothing to ease the sadness that quivered in his gut like a venomous snake, ready to spring at any moment. He turned himself into one of his comic book zombies so as not to wake the slithering thing that nested inside him, drifting through his classes, zoning out during lunch and recess.

And then he discovered the dollar houses.

He'd gone down to the lobby to retrieve the mail and there was Dad's *New Yorker* magazine. His father had canceled his subscription years ago, but they kept on sending it anyway, which made the magazine seem mysterious and fun. Out of habit, he flipped through the magazine, searching for the cartoons (cartoons that he often didn't understand, but liked studying anyway), and his eyes rested on the title of a brief article: *Homes for Sale, One Dollar (and Heaps of Sweat)*. Such a thing seemed impossible, so when he finally reached the fourth floor (elevator broken again), he'd perched on the couch and read the whole thing. Apparently, lots of cities had tried this plan — and now a little town called Millville was doing the same. They were selling five completely rundown houses for one dollar each.

He couldn't tell much about the town from the article, just that it had been a mill town, the mill had shut down, and now the town was trying to save itself by bringing in new businesses and increasing the number of kids in their school. No matter. It seemed like an inviting place. It seemed like the kind of place that had never heard of the shooting at Georgio's Grocery.

It seemed like a way out.

If they moved, he wouldn't have to walk past the Siskins' door every day. He would no longer be tricked into thinking that Abe was going to pop out at any minute. He would no longer have to hear Mrs. Siskin crying.

His mum always said that you might not get what you want in life, but you often get what you need. The opportunity to buy a house for a dollar seemed like life was giving the Grovers exactly what they needed at the very moment they needed it.

Even Mum had to agree. She'd longed for a house since she moved from a cottage in Cornwall, England, to live in the U.S. But here in Flintlock, a house was out of reach. Even a condo cost way more than they could afford. That, and she was tired of working as an assistant chef at Sonny's, where her boss was never sunny. If they moved to Millville, they could not only afford an entire house (one dollar!), but she could open her own restaurant in one of the many vacant storefronts. Rent in the

Millville business district, she discovered, was dirt cheap. She wouldn't open a fancy restaurant; people in Millville were going through tough times and probably couldn't afford things like beef Wellington (despite the fact that Mum made the best). She'd create what she called a take-out shop—food-truck fare without the truck! Suddenly the move seemed perfect.

And his father? His big dream was bringing medical care to an underserved area. (*Underserved*, Lowen had learned, was often another word for "poor.") Sure, as a physician's assistant he had to be supervised by a full doctor, but how hard would it be to find a doctor to work with? His other big dream was to restore a home in need of love. Shazam! Two dreams in one.

Clem was surprisingly open to the idea. As a three-season athlete who didn't care for sitting on the bench, he reasoned that he'd get more playing time at a small school. It seemed to Lowen that it took no time at all for Clem to jump from *more playing time* to *high-school star.*

His sister, Anneth—who was also older than Lowen, but younger than Clem—was the lone holdout. "I don't want to move to some Podunk town away from everyone and everything I love," she said. By *everyone* she meant her best friend, Megan.

Despite Anneth's objections, the Grovers decided to apply. After all, there was no sense in arguing when their chances of acceptance were as likely as winning the lottery.

Lowen had looked over Mum's shoulder as she wrote of her desire for an affordable house—her two sons were older now and needed rooms of their own, and she longed for a useful kitchen and an herb garden in the backyard. Then she'd paused and asked, "Is it OK if I tell them about Abe?"

No! That was the last thing he wanted her to do. He wanted to move where no one had heard of Abe, where no one would identify him as a friend of one of those kids who got shot. But in the end she convinced him that telling the story of the random shooting might make their application stronger. If they were to have any hope of getting a dollar house, they needed to stand out from the hundreds or even thousands of other applications.

"We'll ask them to keep the information confidential," Mum said.

After racing to the mailbox every day after school; after saying a thousand prayers, even though, as someone who didn't attend church, he wasn't quite sure he was doing it correctly (or whether he was calling attention to his deservingness of punishment instead); after listening to Anneth tell him over and over that she was sorry about Abe, but really, they had all known him and the world did not revolve around Prince Lowen; after not drawing a single thing (not even a new Abe comic), their answer came in the form of a phone call.

Ms. Duffey, a Millville town councillor (and the town librarian), called to congratulate them. They were being offered a house for one dollar.

There was such surprise, such enormous delight when Mum shared the news around the family table, that Anneth didn't even bother to state her case.

They had done it! Their application had been accepted!

There was one small catch, though: there would be a lottery to determine which family got which dollar house. The Grovers had pored over the pictures online, and their hearts were set on the only four-bedroom house among them, even though it was hard to tell how big the rooms were or where the four bedrooms were located. But they'd know more when they actually saw the houses on moving day. As Mum cautioned, "Pictures can be deceiving. We shouldn't settle on any one house till we've had a chance to see them all in person."

2.

END OF JUNE

To Lowen, the five-hour drive from Flintlock to Millville seemed like an eternity.

Clem drove most of the way, in a borrowed royal-blue Toyota Camry. Now that they were moving to the country, he was determined to get his driver's license. And since the Grovers didn't own a car (absolutely no need for one in the city, Dad always said), the trip gave him the opportunity to practice. Most of the ride sounded like this:

Dad: There's a car coming up on your left.

Clem: I see it, Dad.

Dad: You're slipping too far to the right. Careful!

Clem: Dad, *relax*!

Lowen was squashed in the backseat between Mum, who was all elbows as she tried to complete the paperwork for the house lottery, and Anneth, who kept sighing (that is, when she wasn't texting Megan) and moving her butt from side to side to remind him that he had slipped off his allotted four inches of padding in the center. If he were to draw a thought bubble over her head, it would read, *You have robbed me of my entire life!*

"Slow down, Clem!" Dad said. "You just passed it!"

"Passed what?" Clem snapped. He'd reached peak frustration.

Dad turned to look out the rear window. "Millville," he said.

"Just now?" Mum asked.

"Mill was on the left, shops and houses on the right," said Dad. "Just like we read online."

Anneth glanced back. "That was it?"

Following instructions, Clem turned the car around in a Dollar Mart parking lot and rolled slowly back down Highway 27. They passed a home with a large TV dish attached to its front porch roof, and another where a woman in a bright-blue bathrobe was watering the flowers hanging from her mailbox. She lifted her arm to wave, but then let it drop when she didn't recognize them.

"Pull over here," Dad said, and they parked on the same road they'd been traveling since they left the interstate, the same road that was, for less than a half mile, Millville's Main Street. The family tumbled out of the sedan and onto the cracked sidewalk.

"Megan is not going to believe this," Anneth said as she videoed their first view of the businesses across the street.

It was indeed the same village that they had seen online. But what the photos on the town website or on Google Maps didn't show was the incredible . . . What was the word Lowen was looking for? *Downtroddenness.* Former stores and businesses were boarded up. And even those that were still in business—Roger's Market, Donna Marie's Antiques, and the Pub—were all in desperate need of paint. The spotty patches of grass in front of the stores needed mowing; the garbage needed picking up. The only things that weren't battered were the American flags that waved from the telephone poles.

"Let's walk," said Dad, reaching his hand out to Mum, who squinted at the buildings in front of her—the same way Lowen sometimes squinted when he was drawing and needed a different focus.

Lowen didn't budge. "What about the houses? The lottery starts in less than two hours and we haven't seen any of them."

"We've got some time," said Dad, pulling Mom along the sidewalk. "And I think we'd better explore. I know we came to a consensus, but once we've really seen this town, we might want to rethink our crazy plan."

Anneth brightened. *"Really?"*

No! Lowen thought. He caught up. "Where will your shop be, Mum?"

"Yeah," said Clem. "Which building will have the sign that reads THE CORNISH EATERY?"

Lowen shot his brother a look of gratitude, a look that Clem acknowledged with a wink.

After much deliberation, Mum had decided to open a Cornish pasty shop like the one her parents had owned back in England. Cornish pasties were little hand pies—like turnovers, but savory instead of sweet. "I doubt the locals will have heard of pasties," she admitted. "But they're the very definition of comfort food, and that seems like a safe bet for a town where most people are down on their luck." She arranged to rent space in the same building as a breakfast restaurant called the Busy Bee. It had faded red siding and looked like one of those square buildings with a flat roof in old Western towns—the kind of structure that would have swinging saloon doors. The Busy Bee was shut up for the afternoon, and the entire building was dark. The air smelled of burned grease.

Mum's shoulders slumped.

"It just needs some love, Mum," Lowen said with more enthusiasm than he felt.

Mum smiled at him. "Some?" she quipped, and then added, "Everything looks so bleak."

The Grovers walked a few more blocks past a small post office, a cinder-block municipal building, and a little brick library before they reached Handy Hardware and the end of Main Street. This spot afforded them the best view of the mill, or what used to be a mill. Here again, what had looked proud and shiny on the website now looked decrepit. It was an enormous tangle of boxy structures, pipes, and vaporless smokestacks—a breathless giant. Behind the mill ran the Grand River, which had a kind of wet wool smell. A faded sign painted on a silo read ALWAYS BE CAREFUL. STOP ACCIDENTS BEFORE THEY STOP YOU. The snake deep in Lowen's gut twitched its tail.

The entire town had been built to keep that mill running, and now it was gone. It was gone and, apparently, so were most of the people.

"Wow," Clem said, turning back toward the town. "No shawarma, no movie theater—"

"Shawarma?" Anneth interrupted. "There isn't even a pizza place! And no clothing stores, either," she added.

Clem nodded. "No concert venue. No skate shop."

Was he siding with Anneth now?

A woman and her three daughters approached them from across the street. Two of the girls were clearly younger than Lowen, but the oldest one, who wore red high-tops and had her dark hair pulled back in a ponytail, seemed about his age.

"Excuse me," the woman asked. "Do you know where we might get some lunch?"

Dad laughed. "Look at that! We're already passing for locals!" He explained that they weren't yet familiar with the town. Turned out, both families had come for the lottery. The Doshis were moving from a very small apartment in a big city with poor schools. At least that's what Lowen caught from standing outside the circle while trying not to look at the girl who was trying not to look at him. Thought bubble above both their heads: *Awkward*.

"Is there one house you're hoping for?" Mrs. Doshi asked Mum.

The one with four bedrooms, Lowen thought. He knew he wasn't supposed to make up his mind till they'd seen the houses in person, but he was tired of sharing a room with the always sloppy, frequently stinking Clem. He practically gagged after each of Clem's games—especially a basketball game.

Mum shook her head. "We haven't had a chance to see them yet."

"You're British!"

Mum smiled. "And here I thought I was sounding

more like a Yank every day! Do *you* have a house in mind?"

"We do." Mrs. Doshi smiled. "But I don't want to influence you!"

Dad started to ask questions about the homes, but the youngest Doshi, whom the sisters had called Meera, reminded her mother that she was *starving,* and Lowen used that moment to send the message that he was impatient to see the houses, and the two families broke off with the promise to see each other at the lottery. The girl, the one who was about his age, gave him a little nod like they were already buds, and that made him feel kind of, well, woolly-headed.

As soon as the other family had popped into Roger's Market, Clem said, "Too bad there isn't a Cornish eatery in town. I bet that Meera would have liked her own little pie."

Mum laughed. "Let's go find our dream house."

Lowen asked if he could hold the photocopy of the hand-sketched map the town had provided and direct them from dollar house to dollar house. It wasn't hard; all of the houses were built on the hill behind Main Street. Whereas the streets back in industrial Flintlock meandered (paved cow paths, Dad called them), the streets in Millville were rolled out in a perfect grid. Those streets that climbed up from Main Street were named after trees: Cedar, Birch, Beech, Maple, Spruce, and Elm. The streets that crossed them were named after landmarks: Park, Church, Monument, School, and Forest.

"Practical people, these Millvillians," Dad said.

They passed a dingy used-car garage as they headed up Maple.

Anneth dragged herself up the hill. "This place is worse than I thought," she said much too loudly.

Lowen looked around to make sure that there was no one on the street within earshot, but there was no one on the streets, period.

Truth be told, he had to revise his picture of Millville, too—something he'd done several times already. When Mum (who had done the Internet research) told him it was a rural town, he pictured majestic trees, green moss, and waterfalls . . . just like the valley in Bone, one of his favorite graphic novel series—only without the monsters. Then later, when Dad (who had been doing some research of his own) declared that the houses were not spread out like farmhouses in the country but were actually clustered, he pictured the kinds of homes that were shown in TV commercials—homes with sparkling glass doors that led to big backyards with swimming pools. He'd held on to this fantasy for a week or two before he peered over

Mum's shoulder when she was doing some additional investigating and realized he still had it wrong. ("I think you're picturing suburbs," Mum had said, "but there's no city near this town.") In fact, the houses were more like city houses in that they were fairly close together, each with its own small patch of yard.

As the Grovers climbed toward the first house, two boys passed them on bicycles. One zigzagged from the left side of the street to the right on a bike that was too small for him.

Mum sighed. "No helmets?"

Two blocks up, they reached the park. It was a grassy space with a bandstand in the center, but no trees or duck ponds or running trails. The two boys had thrown down their bikes near the bandstand and were patting a dog that seemed to be wandering on its own.

Clem stopped and nodded to their right. "There's one!" he said. "That's a dollar house."

"Easy to spot," said Anneth, "despite the fact that every single house on these streets looks the same." She started to take pictures, but Dad told her to put her phone away. People lived in those homes.

Anneth was right. The houses around the perimeter of the block-wide park were all the same type. If Lowen were to sketch one, he'd begin with the roofline. Each one had a triangular roof, just like the ones little kids make when drawing a house. Below the roofline were two windows. Below the two windows was a porch roof. Some of the houses had an open porch; others had a three-season room with windows. Most were a faded grayish white. And maybe because the windows had lost their shine, or maybe because the porches drooped, or perhaps because they all had funny additions to the backs or sides, Lowen thought of them as granny houses.

"They're mill houses," Dad said. "Probably all built by one or two builders at the same time the mill was being constructed."

"They're all the same design, but if you look closely, each one is unique," Mum said. "Look at those two houses. The one on the right has windows that are close together, like a picture window. The house on the left has windows that are far apart—"

Like eyes, said a familiar voice in Lowen's head. *Spooky eyes.* Abe's voice. Lowen shook his head to dismiss it.

"But the dollar house is clearly the *most* different," said Anneth, who let the house do the rest of the talking for her.

It was a total wreck. What once was grass was now a tangle of weeds. The wooden front steps had gaping holes. The gray paint peeled, and in some places there was bare wood with visible rot. Shingles were curling off the roof. Toward the back was a garage; the door was partially open and crooked. No doubt it was stuck.

Lowen imagined the child who might have lived in the house years ago. He pictured him dropping his bike on the lawn and racing inside while the tires still spun. He saw him sitting on the open front porch, munching on a cold cherry Popsicle, watching people go by. For a moment he thought, *I could be that kid.*

But then he glanced at the tall grass and the sagging porch and he felt tired. Perhaps he couldn't be that kid. Perhaps he was already too old.

"We knew the houses wouldn't be pretty," Dad said.

Mum used her fingers to pull her dark hair off her face. "Yes, but I didn't think they would be so *depressing*. How are we going to meet the requirement with you still in Flintlock?"

Dad was the only family member who had not come prepared to stay in Millville that night. He and Mum agreed that it would be better if he didn't give up his job at the hospital right away. For the first three months or so, he'd keep making money back in the city—money that could go toward home repairs. As Mum reminded them often, all applicants for dollar houses had to have at least three kids (to keep Millville Central School running) *and* agree to upgrade and maintain their house for both safety and appearance. Each house had been inspected and came with a long list of changes that had to be made within one year, or the final sale would not occur.

Of course they met the first requirement (though only because Mum and Dad refused to let Anneth stay back in the city with Dad), but the enormity of the second requirement was sinking in.

The front door opened. "Hello!" called a round, beaky woman who reminded Lowen of a hen. She introduced herself as Mrs. Corbeau, owner and chef of the Busy Bee. "Cutting it a bit close, aren't you? We lock up in ten minutes."

"Ten minutes?" Mum asked.

"Yes. It's in the instructions. The houses are available for viewing until one o'clock."

Mum and Dad exchanged a look. How had they missed that? "But the lottery doesn't start until two."

"True," said the woman. "But we do need lunch before the lottery begins, you know. The other families arrived early this morning." Mrs. Corbeau eyed Mum closely. "You're the woman who's opening the pastry shop, aren't you?"

"It's actually a *pasty* shop—"

Dad stepped forward. "Surely there's a way you could let us view the homes. After all, it's a big decision."

"Sorry. The rules are the rules. Next time I suggest you read your instructions more closely."

Mum shot them an apologetic look.

"You better come in," said the woman. "Stop wasting your ten minutes. At least you can see this house. The others don't look that different. Not really."

"What about the one with four bedrooms?" Clem asked.

The woman waved her hand as if it were of little consequence. "Just picture this one with another bedroom tacked on somewhere."

The Grover family stepped up onto the open porch and through the front door. To the left was a living room with a filthy green carpet and stained and torn flowery wallpaper. Thought bubble above Anneth's head: *Gross!*

Lowen had to agree. A dark dining room with once fussy but now tattered curtains served as the connector to a crumbling kitchen with pink cabinets. He pictured the woman who might have cooked in this kitchen when it was first built—someone with rosy cheeks and strawberry-blond hair swirled upward like whipped cream. She wore a pink apron and baked raspberry cupcakes topped with pink icing. Where had she gone?

Today, the pink paint had worn off most of the doors. The room smelled distinctly of cat litter.

Mrs. Corbeau led the way upstairs and bustled them through three bedrooms and a bath.

When they returned to the lower floor, the woman placed her hand on Lowen's shoulder (no doubt she would have put her hand on his head if he weren't so tall for his age) and said to him, "Won't it be lovely for your family to have your very own home? One away from the big city? And how fortunate that Millville is selling this to you for only one dollar!"

Had she read the application? Was this her way of telling him she knew his story? Whether she had or not, Lowen knew that what she was expecting at this moment was a thank-you . . . and that confused him. All he could do was nod.

Then she pushed them all out the front door and said, "The lottery starts promptly at two at Central School. Don't miss that!"

3.

MOMENTS LATER . . .

As they watched Mrs. Corbeau walk away, the reality of what the Grovers were doing seeped in. They would be starting over in a new town—a town that offered none of the old comforts of Flintlock. Not only that, they'd be responsible for fixing up a revolting house—something that seemed fun while poring over online pictures, but not so fun when standing in the middle of a moldy, run-down, cat-litter-smelling dump.

Anneth looked at Dad expectantly.

"We'd lose the money we put down on the shop," Dad said.

Mum nodded. "And, according to the lease, six months' more rent."

Dad scrunched his face the way he always did when he was dealing with a potentially bad situation. "Not to mention all the equipment you ordered."

Anneth jumped in. "You can return it, can't you?"

Mum and Dad shared a look. Lowen pictured their combined thought bubble: *Maybe we could just cut our losses. . . .*

Suddenly Lowen knew that as dismal as this town looked, as hard as fixing up a dollar house would be, he did not want to drive back to Flintlock, where absolutely nothing would have changed. "We've come all this way. Let's at least go through with the lottery," he said. "Maybe we'll get lucky and get the four-bedroom house. And maybe it won't be in as rough shape as this one. Besides," he said, and turned to his dad, "you're always talking about how rewarding it would be to fix up a home 'in need of love.' We can't give up without even trying."

Mum smiled at him and Dad pulled him into a hug. "Lowen's right. When did this family lose its sense of adventure?"

Clem, who was busy watching a group of teenagers that had gathered on the other side of the park, shrugged.

Anneth glared at Lowen. "Whatever the prince wants," she said.

The Grovers raced around town to look at the exterior of the remaining four houses. Both 29 Cedar and 18 Pine had very small lots (no room for an herb garden), and 32 Elm was the farthest distance from school and Mum's shop.

Their quick tour was reinforcing their original assumption—the four-bedroom would be the best for them.

"There it is!" Lowen said as they started to climb Beech Street. It was a yellow house built around the same time as the others, and as Lowen had hoped, the porch was open—no windows, no screens. But whereas the other houses had just two windows above the porch roofline, the Grovers' house had two smaller windows above those.

"Maybe the fourth bedroom is on the third floor," Clem said. "I call it!"

"The houses next door—at least the one on the corner—look nice," said Mum. It looked better cared for than any of the other homes they'd seen so far. It was nicely painted, and the lawn was manicured. Flowers hung from the porch.

"But what if everyone wants this house?" asked Anneth. "What if we get a high number and the four-bedroom is the first to go?"

What Anneth said was true. The odds were against getting the one and only house they wanted. They decided that rather than climbing all the way up to 11 Beech, they'd head to the library to check out the interior of the houses one last time and make a list.

Unfortunately, the library closed at noon on Saturdays. Anneth (who had retrieved her laptop from the car) found that she could still get online without a password while on the granite steps. So they sat right there and did their best to examine pictures that took a long time loading.

A couple heated disagreements ensued over which was nastier: fake brick paneling or torn wallpaper? Cracked bathtub or greasy grime at the edges of a curling linoleum floor? A duct-taped window or a hole in the wall? They decided on the houses in this order:

1) 11 Beech Street: Four bedrooms, two bathrooms
2) 18 Pine Street: Rooms painted in neon yellow, orange, and hot pink; cracked tub
3) 32 Elm Street: A dark house with grape leaves carved into the kitchen cupboards and fake brick paneling on the walls
4) 4 Maple Street: Horrible carpet, torn wallpaper, and dirty-litter-box smell
5) 29 Cedar Street: Heaps of ugly furniture and garbage bags filled with who-knew-what left in every room (Why didn't they clean them out before taking the pictures?)

Then they headed up to the school to seal their fate.

Lowen expected the school to look much like the six elementary schools in Flintlock: tall, imposing structures with cement steps leading to many heavy doors. Instead, this one, located at the very top of the hill, was a squat, one-story brick building with windows that presumably snaked around all sides. He was going into sixth grade, Anneth eighth, and Clem was going to be a junior in high school, but they'd all be attending classes in this one building.

Outside, congregating around the gym doors, were small groups of people of all ages, chatting. For a moment Lowen thought they were other families come to participate in the lottery, but the crowd was too big. Too big and too familiar with one another. It took another moment for Lowen to realize that unlike any group in Flintlock, there were no faces of color. He wondered how the Doshis felt about that.

When they entered the gym, Lowen braced himself for more disrepair, but unlike the gym in his old school—a multipurpose room that had a rolling wooden floor with a faded painted bear in the center, and frayed basketball nets—this one had a bright polished floor, a massive digital scoreboard, and walls lined with championship banners. He caught a whiff of new varnish. Clearly, here in Millville, sports were king. Clem would be happy about that.

The Grovers wove their way to the front of the gym where risers had been set up to create a platform. There were five easels on the stage; each one held a poster board with the floor plan and photographs of a house. The plans intrigued him, but Lowen wasn't ready to be quite so visible.

"I'll let them know we're here," Mum said, stepping up to talk to someone official.

Dad led the rest of the family toward rows of folding chairs where the Doshis and a few other families—who looked considerably more nervous than the people hanging out by the door—were mingling. Before they reached them, though, Clem broke off and headed in his own direction.

Mrs. Doshi smiled. "Nice to see you again!"

A small woman turned toward Dad and held out her hand. "Eden Kelling, from Wichita. This is my wife, Kate," she said, introducing a taller woman with short blond hair. "And our rug rats are around here somewhere." Eden looked around the gym with an unconcerned smile.

"All the way from Kansas?" Dad asked.

Eden nodded. "I flew commercial planes out of Eisenhower; now I'll fly hunters and fishermen from the Granger into the more remote territories. Kate—"

Just then, Kate reached down to grab a speedy toddler.

31

"Kate, otherwise known as the woman with three arms," Eden kidded, "is a computer programmer and can work from anywhere."

"I'm also something of an amateur contractor," Kate added, tickling the little boy she held in her arms and making him giggle. "I'm looking forward getting my hands dirty!"

"And who are these guys?" Dad asked, crouching to stop a matching toddler from doing a face-plant in front of him.

"This is Logan," Kate said, "and that's Ben. Our other son, Mason, is over there."

Lowen followed her gaze and spotted his brother on the other side of the gym. Clem had already found a bunch of kids his own age. Mostly Millville kids, he guessed, though one of them must be Mason. They were staring at the championship sports banners that lined the ceiling and laughing. No doubt Clem had thought of something funny to say.

"How do you tell them apart?" Anneth asked.

Lowen turned back to the Kellings. His sister had a point: the toddlers were identical.

"It was almost impossible when they were babies," Kate said, "but we've gotten so that we can pretty reliably tell which is which."

"And if that fails, Logan has a small scar above his left eyebrow." Eden laughed. "The silver lining of having such rambunctious toddlers!"

Anneth leaned in to see.

As Dad introduced himself to the Greys, who were from Honolulu, Lowen's heart sank. The Greys were a family of *six*. They had two parents, three kids, and one grandfather. No doubt they also wanted the house with four bedrooms. Lowen felt irrationally resentful of them, even though they seemed nice enough; why would anyone move from *Hawaii* to a small town thousands of miles away that routinely dropped below zero degrees in the winter?

"Do you feel like a lab rat?" someone asked. It was the oldest Doshi girl, the one in the red high-tops. Suddenly she was standing next to him.

"What?" Lowen asked.

She bounced on her heels. "It's like we're pawns in a behavioral experiment, you know?"

Lowen's brain scrambled for a response, but he'd had no practice in talking about behavioral experiments, and even less practice talking to girls.

Thankfully, a man in shorts and hiking boots stepped in from behind. "You must be Lowen Grover and Samina Doshi, right?"

"Sami," the girl said. "Everyone calls me Sami."

"I'm Coach Walker," he said. "We're sure glad you're here. I'm looking forward to both of you participating on our sports teams."

"I'm in," Sami said. "Do you have a forward on your girls' soccer team?"

"Coed team," Coach corrected. "Around here schools are small; middle-school boys and girls play together. But the forward position is open; I'll be eager to see what you bring."

"Are you the soccer coach *and* the basketball coach?" Sami asked.

"Middle- and high-school soccer, basketball, and baseball."

"What, no football?" Lowen kidded.

"No football," Coach said seriously. "Too risky. Our enrollment is so small that most of our athletes play three seasons. I don't want my players injured before basketball season."

"Well, my brother, Clem, plays all those things," Lowen said. "He's over there, if you want to talk to him."

"What about you?" Coach asked. "Which sports do you play?"

"I'm not really into sports," Lowen admitted, aware of Sami watching him closely.

34

"Well, you will be soon!" Coach said enthusiastically. "Without everyone's participation, we won't have teams. We're counting on you, Lowen."

Lowen's brain raced for a reason to refuse: *I have a very rare and serious heart condition. My left foot is actually situated where my right foot should be. I break out in hives the size of golf balls when I play sports. . . .*

But Coach didn't seem to expect a response. "And now if you'll excuse me," he said, "I've got to get this lottery started." He crossed the gym and hopped up on the staging, then took his place behind a table.

Lowen was left feeling on the hook with Coach and wondering how he was going to weasel out of this whole "we need you" sports thing. He made the mistake of glancing at Sami, who seemed to take this as an invitation to talk. But before she could get a word out, a screech of microphone interference drew everyone's attention to the three people seated on the stage.

An older man, with a stern face and dressed more formally than Coach or the woman seated at his other side, wiped his brow and leaned forward to speak directly into a microphone. "We'll begin," he said.

Those that were still standing moved toward seats. Lowen sat down beside Dad and Anneth in the last row of folding chairs. Mum joined them. She had a big stack of papers in her hands. "I just signed our life away," she said.

"No turning back now," Dad kidded.

Anneth popped up from her texting. "But, Daddy, you said—"

The older man continued. "I'm Douglas Avery," he said into the mic, "president of the town council. To my right is town councillor and librarian Barbara Duffey, and to my left is Coach—ah, I mean selectman Bo Walker."

Chuckles burst from the bleachers, now filled by the people who were once near the front door.

"I had no idea that this was going to be such a public event," Mum whispered. "I thought choosing a house would be a private affair."

Lowen recalled Sami's comment about this being a *behavioral experiment*. Maybe she wasn't so far off.

Mr. Avery continued: "We'd like to welcome our five new families to Millville. If you could stand up when I call your name . . . the Doshis. The Greys. The Grovers. The Kellings. And last but not least, the Muñozes." (The Muñozes appeared to have only two kids, but the rules definitely specified three. Lowen hoped that there was a third girl somewhere, one around Anneth's age, since everyone else seemed younger or older. A new friend would make a big difference in Anneth's willingness to give Millville a try.) Each family stood in turn, and the crowd applauded politely. Clem raced over to join his family in a clownish way, and he got the laugh he anticipated. "What fine, *diverse* families," Mr. Avery said. Lowen tried to shoot Clem and Anneth a look, but Anneth had her nose in her phone, and Clem seemed to be looking anywhere but at him.

"We'll begin with a short film that presents the origins of our great town."

The lights dimmed and the movie began. It had an old-timey sound.

"They converted an old reel movie to digital," Clem whispered as he slipped in next to them.

A deep voice narrated the film: "The proximity to the Grand River and the abundant forests made Millville the ideal location for a paper mill. Construction included a dam and power development, a grinder room, and a hydroelectric station." The narrator went on to talk about how many machines were purchased to run the mill.

The movie then switched from mill pride to the construction of homes, the digging of wells, the building of a school, and the establishment of a town government. Fire equipment was purchased (and later an ambulance and a police car), and a cemetery was established. By 1927 the town had lots of other businesses, too: a men's clothing store, a car dealership, a hotel and restaurant, a shoe-repair shop, a jewelry store, a milliner (which Mum said was a hat store), a barbershop, and an ice-cream parlor. There were two grocery stores. It seemed like the whole town had popped up practically overnight. In every scene there were smiling, happy families. People were greeting one another on the streets, watching children perform at the bandstand, sitting on their front porches with sparklers.

The movie ended with happy high-school students taking off their graduation gowns and entering the mill—a place where promotions and prosperity were guaranteed.

"You hate to think of what the founders would think of their booming town now," Dad remarked.

The townspeople in the bleachers clapped when the lights came back on, and Councillor Duffey outlined the procedure for the lottery: Families would be called in the order their application had been received. When called, one member from the family would come forward and choose a number from a hat. Number 1 would have first choice of a house; number 2 would have second choice; and so on. After signing a lease, families could move into their house that afternoon.

The Greys, from Hawaii, were the first to choose a number. They sent their youngest child, a smiley four-year-old boy named Lagi, to the front of the gym. He stood on tiptoes to reach into the hat and pulled out an envelope. He was then directed to stand right where he was and wait until all of the families had drawn their envelopes before opening his. He couldn't stop grinning; clearly, Lagi thought this was fun. But Lowen didn't want fun; he didn't want suspense. He wanted this part of the lottery to go as quickly as possible.

Because of the cute factor, or because it was simply easier to follow suit, Mrs. Doshi sent her youngest, Meera, to choose an envelope.

When the Grovers were called third, Clem said, "I'll go!" but Dad stopped him. "Lowen can handle this," he said.

Lowen froze. Not only did he not want all of these faces looking at him, but he didn't want the responsibility of choosing. What if he selected a terrible number? Unfortunately faces were already turned to him, expecting him to rise, and refusing to go would only bring more attention. He stood, walked to the stage, reached into the hat, and grabbed the first envelope he touched. He felt like a giant standing next to the other kids. He locked eyes with a spot on the floor like it was his long-lost friend.

The Kellings went next, and sent up Mason, which made Lowen feel a little better. The Muñozes were the last to go. They sent up their younger son.

Finally the kids were told to open their envelopes. Lowen tore open the seal and stared down at the number 4. Not great, but at least it wasn't number 5.

"A house is a house," Mum said when Lowen came back to his chair. "We'll make it ours."

The Muñoz family had drawn number 1. Lowen held his breath as Mr. Muñoz glanced at the easels on the stage. Finally, he said, "We'll take thirty-two Elm." The house with the fake brick paneling. There was still no sign of a third Muñoz kid. Perhaps this family had somehow gotten the requirement for three children waived. Perhaps the smaller house suited them better.

The Kelling family chose the house with all the DayGlo rooms. Yes! Of course! The twins could easily share a room.

Even though he knew better, a small drop of hope rippled inside Lowen. Maybe, by some weird luck, they'd still get the four-bedroom house.

"Rena's next," said Mum. Rena was Mrs. Doshi.

"They'll take the four-bedroom for sure," Clem muttered.

But they didn't. Rena and the girls seemed very happy to get the house with all the junk in it. In fact, it looked like the jam-packed house had been their first choice. Lowen and Clem couldn't help themselves; they did a little happy dance. The four-bedroom would be theirs!

40

"People have different tastes," said Mum. "Looks like this lottery is working out in everyone's favor."

Lowen couldn't believe his family's luck.

When their name was called, the Grovers walked to the front of the gym and examined the poster-board displays of the two remaining houses: 11 Beech Street and 4 Maple. The four-bedroom house and the stinky house that they'd toured earlier in the day. They lingered over the picture of the four-bedroom for a few moments, knowing that the house would be theirs.

The house had a tiny addition and a detached garage. The addition made the house look like a bird with one broken wing.

Mum glanced over at the Grey family—all six of them. Mrs. Grey looked distraught. She pulled Lagi up onto her lap.

Clem and Lowen exchanged a quick glance of horror. Mum was about to pass on the only house that would allow them to get out from under each other's stuff and annoying habits.

"Mum," said Clem, trying to use his mature voice, his voice of reason. "Remember that you are moving your family a million miles away from everything and everyone we know and love. You *owe* it to us to pick the four-bedroom house."

Yikes, thought Lowen. How could Clem be so smart about some things, but so clueless when it came to others? Mum couldn't stand claims of entitlement.

It was in that moment that Mrs. Grey, possibly reading Mum's mind, put Lagi down and tiptoed toward the stage. Mum squatted so they could talk privately.

There was a look of apprehension on Mr. Avery's face, and rumblings from the audience. Mrs. Corbeau, the woman who had showed them the stinky house, stood up in the bleachers.

"If you're sure," Lowen heard Mum whisper to Mrs. Grey.

Mrs. Grey nodded gratefully. Lowen's heart dropped.

Mum turned to Mr. Avery. "We'll take the house on Beech Street."

The Grovers looked at one another, stunned. But Mum just smiled. For whatever reason, it seemed that the Greys didn't want the four-bedroom house. They were happy with the stinky house on the park.

The Grovers moved in for a group hug.

"I'm going to find the restroom," Lowen said.

As he searched for one up and down the locker-lined hallway, thinking about the lottery, he felt as if his family had dodged a bullet. *Another* bullet.

The snake lifted its head. What should have been a

moment of happiness was not. Lowen doubted that he'd ever feel a pure sense of gladness again. How could he feel happy when he was here and Abe was dead?

Closer to the center of the building, he heard music—music that was simultaneously jarring and soothing, like the first bite of vanilla ice cream over warm apple crisp, or stepping outside on an icy winter's night and looking up to see a sky full of stars. He felt a swelling sensation deep inside his body.

He followed the music until he found the source: a girl, likely the fifth Muñoz, playing the cello. Her dark hair hung over her face. Sunlight streamed through the windows, across her cheek, and danced on her bow hand. For a moment, Lowen wanted nothing more than to sketch that hand.

The girl stopped playing and looked up at him. He could see now that she was older than he was, probably more like Clem's age, but it didn't stop his heart from scrambling up to his throat.

"Is it over?" she asked.

The song? Did she mean the song? Or perhaps she meant his staring?

"The lottery?" she clarified. "Is it over?"

"Oh," said Lowen. "Yeah. Yes. Yes, it's over. Are you a Muñoz?"

She nodded. "Luna Muñoz."

"You got thirty-two Elm. The one with the carved grape leaves," he said, guessing that she would be pleased.

Luna shrugged. "They're all the same." She began packing up her cello.

That's when Lowen heard his name being called. "I better go," he said. "Your playing—it was crazy. I mean beautiful. Crazy beautiful." Lowen never talked to girls, and now he'd spoken to two in one day.

Luna smiled, and when she did, her eyes smiled, too.

Just then Clem burst into the room. "Hey, Low, we're lea—" He stopped cold. Apparently you didn't need to hear Luna's music to see that she was, well, special.

"You play the cello," Clem said, reaching over to carry her case for her. "Cool. I'm Clem, Clem Grover. Do you live here in Millville?"

Lowen trailed behind, listening to his brother talk to Luna, and acknowledged two things: for the first time he was *not* grateful that his more outgoing older brother had taken over a conversation, and at this moment his blood was no longer frozen in his veins. Listening to Luna's music, he had felt something other than sadness or worry. It wasn't gladness, certainly. But he had felt . . . what?

Alive.

4.

THAT AFTERNOON . . .

As soon as the Grovers exited the gym, Mum pulled out
the key to their very own house and waved it in the air.

"May I see it, Mum?" Anneth asked.

"It's just a key," Mum said.

"I know, but I want to take a picture."

"I want to see it next," Lowen said. It was, as Mum
said, just a key. But he cradled it in his hands when it was
his turn to hold it. Unlike the apartment key he carried
back home, this one felt magical. It was the key to a new
kingdom, a new life.

The Grovers decided to leave the car at the school
and walk to their very own house near the corner of
Beech and Monument.

"Home of the Grovers!" Dad called out as they
approached. Close up, they could see that it was in the
same disrepair as all of the others. The front yard had a
small patch of unmowed grass that was mostly dandelions

and a cracked cement walkway that led to partially rotted front steps. It was easy to imagine teams of insects munching away in the dank, soft wood of those steps. Laying eggs that would turn into larvae. Little worms.

On one end of the porch were two rusted chairs. A scraggly bush with light-yellow flowers (honeysuckle, Mum said) grew up over the railing at that end. The overbearing scent of the flowers reminded Lowen of floral air fresheners that were intended to mask bad smells but instead mixed with them to make lingering, headachy odors.

As Mum stepped gingerly up the steps and tried to turn the key in the door, Clem slipped around back.

While the others waited, clouds of little black flies swarmed around Lowen's head and dove for his eyes. He looked down at a fly settling on his arm and smooshed one, then another. They were tiny and easy to kill, but there seemed to be hundreds. No, make that *thousands*. Maybe wishing for no screens wasn't such a good idea.

"Hurry up, Mum!" Anneth cried, flapping her arms around her face. "We're being eaten alive!"

"You're not going to believe this," Clem said, swatting as he returned, "but there's nothing behind us but a parking lot — paved with newly painted lines."

Dad took the key from Mum. "There must be a business nearby."

"I suppose," said Clem.

"Augh!" Dad said, battling flies while trying to open the door. "Let's try the back door."

They walked around the house. A grassy driveway led to a single detached garage. Beside the garage was a weedy yard with a rotating clothesline. A small picket fence had once been erected to mark the end of the yard and the beginning of the lot, but it was mostly flat on the ground now.

The parking lot took the space of two housing lots. Their next-door neighbor's garage abutted one end of the parking lot, which seemed a strange layout.

"Look," said Clem. "A basketball hoop!" Sure enough, a basketball hoop (a now crooked basketball hoop) had been erected on a pole at one end of the pavement.

"Do you suppose this lot belongs to our neighbor?" Dad pointed to the house next to theirs, the one with the nice front lawn.

It was at that moment that an ambulance quietly pulled into the parking lot.

"Oh, dear," said Mum. "I hope our neighbor isn't ill."

Two men jumped out of the ambulance and came around to the back, where they opened wide doors. One of the men hopped into the rear. Moments later, a gurney emerged and was gently lowered out of the vehicle. Lowen couldn't quite tell from where he stood, but it seemed as if there was a body on the gurney—though what he could see of it was covered with a sheet. The paramedics wheeled the gurney into the garage that faced the parking lot.

Mum and Dad looked at each other with instant recognition—recognition and fear.

"Someone home from the hospital?" Anneth asked.

Dad hightailed it around the house back to Beech Street, with Mum close behind.

"What's going on?" Clem asked as the three kids raced around the corner.

Mum and Dad stood in front of the home next to theirs.

"Lovely," Mum said in her most sarcastic voice.

"Impossible," said Dad. "Someone should have prevented this."

It wasn't until that moment that Lowen saw a small, discreet sign that read FIELD'S FUNERAL HOME.

No wonder the other families didn't choose the four-bedroom house! They'd all had a chance to visit the homes. No one wanted the four-bedroom house because it was *next to a funeral home*! The person on the gurney? That person was *dead*.

Dad shook his head. "It's not too late to back out," he said. "The officials would have to understand. Like

I said, they never should have let this happen. You told them . . ."

Mum sighed; her shoulders drooped. "Some things just aren't meant to be." She sounded as if she'd traveled a million miles only to arrive back where she started.

"Damn," said Clem, and for once no one told him to watch his language.

Lowen's family hadn't dodged a bullet after all.

Come on, Lowen. It was the voice . . . Abe's voice. *Dead is just dead. I should know.*

The snake rose up. He turned to his family. "I want to live here. I want to live at eleven Beech Street."

It only seemed right that Lowen should be reminded every day that dead is dead.

It's what he deserved.

5.

MOMENTS LATER . . .

Of course it wasn't as easy as that. Mum and Dad had to ask him a million more times if he thought he'd be OK living next door to a funeral home, and then they talked among themselves, and then they asked him again.

In the meantime, Clem practiced air jump shots and Anneth wildly texted messages to Megan that Lowen guessed were variations of Guess what! We might be coming back to Flintlock!

Finally he overheard Dad say something to the effect of *Well, death is a part of life,* and the next thing they knew they were going around to the back door to see if their key would fit there.

It did.

The back door led them through a musty mudroom lined with coat hooks, and then into the kitchen. The kitchen cabinets had doors, but they were ill-fitting, crooked. Two of the cupboard doors had come off altogether, leaving only hinges. One lower cupboard was covered with a broken sheet of trellis—a door replacement, probably intended to keep out a dog or a cat or possibly something wilder than that. The floor was a patchwork of bare wood and linoleum. Although it was clear that someone thought the floor should be changed, Lowen couldn't tell in which direction they were headed.

"It's a bit of an albatross, isn't it?" Mum said. She opened one of the top cabinets and the handle came off in her fingers.

"There's duct tape on the oven door," Clem said.

"And a hole where the dishwasher should be!" said Anneth.

"Who needs a dishwasher when you have three kids?" joked Dad.

"Very funny," said Anneth.

"In all seriousness, though," said Dad, "you guys are going to have to roll up your sleeves and help us get this work done. Your mother and I can't do it alone."

Clem looked at his father skeptically. "This is *your* dream project, Dad," he said, heading out of the kitchen, presumably to find his room. "The three of us will have school—and sports."

Not me. I won't have sports, thought Lowen. He was still determined to get out of that obligation somehow, despite the coach's declaration. Not that he'd be any good with the house repairs, either.

While Mum and Dad began discussing priorities for the kitchen, Anneth and Lowen wandered through the rest of the house. It had the same layout as the one they'd visited. They passed through the dining room, which had water spots on the ceiling and floor, to the living room, which was small but had large windows that looked out on the porch. One of the windows, the one on the side of the house, had cracks patched with duct tape. The staircase to the second floor was at one end of the living room.

Anneth made Lowen climb the narrow staircase first. It was dark, and you couldn't help thinking of the ghosts that might be lurking upstairs.

"Clem?" Lowen called.

There was no answer.

The stairs climbed to a second-floor hall and then turned and narrowed, leading to the third floor. The hall on the second floor was short, with three bedrooms and a bathroom coming off it. The bathroom had black grunge growing on the walls, and several of the shower tiles had fallen off.

The largest bedroom at the front of the house also had its own bathroom with a toilet and sink. They knew without asking that this bedroom would go to Mum and Dad.

The other two bedrooms were both small and very dark. The cobalt-blue one had a single sloping wall and a window that looked out to the backyard. The forest-green one was longer and narrower and had two sloping walls and a window that looked out at the funeral home. The closet in that room was small and missing a door.

"You can have that one," Anneth said, pointing to the green room.

Lowen wasn't surprised by her lack of sympathy. She was making it very clear that she was done babying him. He wanted to live here; he could look out at a place where they embalmed bodies.

What did it matter?

He could hear Clem banging around above their heads and decided to investigate the fourth bedroom. The curved stairway was steep, and he found himself using his hands as well as his feet to crawl up. He didn't get far before he reached an open trapdoor. "I'm coming up!" he announced.

"You have my *permission* to come up," Clem clarified.

He entered a room that had no doubt been the attic at one time. Bare and patchy wallboard had been screwed to the steeply pitched walls. There were two small windows at the front of the room and one larger window at the back. Dad and Clem were looking out the back window at the fire escape when Mum called up, "Is it safe?"

"It looks fine," Dad called to Mum. Then he addressed Clem. "But no sneaking out in the middle of the night!"

Clem turned and muttered, "Yeah, Dad. 'Cause that's the kind of kid I am."

It seemed like everything Dad said annoyed Clem these days.

Dad and Mum walked back to get the car while the kids sat on the floor of their new living room, munching on the last of the car snacks that Mum had in her handbag.

"I doubt our old furniture will look right in here," said Anneth, reaching for the carrots.

"Yeah," said Clem. "But we won't have to worry about the elevator constantly breaking and having to trudge up four flights."

"Or Mrs. Finlay banging on our floor with her broom whenever we're having fun," said Lowen.

Anneth laughed. "Or the landlord always suggesting that he's going to turn our apartment into two upscale condominiums."

Lowen was happy to see his sister smiling. "Or the smells of Limburger cheese coming from across the hall," he added, but he no sooner said it than he realized that the odor had come from Abe's apartment and that it had been a long time since they'd smelled anything at all in the hallway.

The listing stopped.

It took less than ten minutes for Mum and Dad to return with the car, and less than that to unpack it. Everyone, except Dad, had brought one small bag of clothes, toiletries, a sleeping bag (Mum had to buy hers at the local Goodwill), and an air mattress. Dad, who had already contacted the movers to give them the official address, would drive the borrowed car back to the city that night. The rest of their belongings (except for the few things Dad needed at home) would arrive on Monday.

Wanting his first night in the new house to be a happy one, Lowen took his time in deciding where to place his air mattress. He tried putting it under the window, but he felt too claustrophobic under the eaves (and too close to the dead). Instead he chose the opposite wall, closest to the center of the house. He placed the two Bones books and another graphic novel that he'd read on the long car ride to Millville next to his mattress. His pajamas he hung on a hook in the open closet. He noticed a hole by the baseboard of the closet and hoped that it wasn't home to a rat—especially since he was sleeping on the floor.

He had just placed his bag with his extra clothes and toothbrush in front of the hole when he heard knocking on the back door. Unfortunately, he didn't have a window that looked out in that direction.

"It's that group of kids you were talking to in the gym, Clem," Anneth said, her voice echoing in the empty house.

Clem practically slid down the first set of stairs, leaped down the second, and called out, "Toodles!"

"Wait!" Mum yelled. "Find out where you're headed and tell us, and then say good-bye to your father before you go."

A familiar, but nevertheless acute, sadness began to settle over Lowen. As long as he was with his entire family, as long as they had the promise of winning a new house, as long as they had discovery ahead of them, he'd been OK. But now Clem was racing off with new friends, something he almost never did from the apartment (his friends were spread out all over the city), and Dad was leaving to go home to Flintlock without them. Truth be told, Lowen hadn't really faced the fact that they wouldn't be living as a family now that his father would live three hundred miles away, alone in their former home, maybe for months.

Clem gave Dad a quick hug, assured him that he'd do his part to help Mum, and then was out the door.

"Daddy, please take me back to Flintlock with you!" Anneth cried. "I can't stay here in this horrible house without you or Megan or the places I know."

Dad pulled Anneth into his arms. Then he glanced up at Lowen, saw him waging his own battle with tears, and pulled him into the hug. Mum wrapped her arms around them all. "We are still a family," she said. "We still have each other, our old friends, our happy memories."

"And new adventures on top of that," said Dad, with perhaps more enthusiasm than he felt. "We can't be afraid of change."

"But I don't want change!" Anneth cried.

"We know that, Annie," Dad said. "Mum and I don't want you to think we're not listening to your needs, too. If you truly can't be happy here, we promise we'll reassess. For now, try to think of this as summer camp. See how it goes."

Too tired to continue the familiar battle, Anneth nodded.

Then Dad,

and the royal-blue Camry,

drove off.

6.

THE NEXT MORNING . . .

While Clem slept late (Clem always slept late), Mum suggested that she and Lowen and Anneth walk down to Dollar Mart for cheap household items and nonperishables: toilet paper, paper towels, pasta, rice, cereal. Then they'd go to Roger's Market for perishables: milk, eggs, fruits and vegetables, which were likely to be more expensive in a small market but fresher, too.

"I'm starving," Lowen said, reminding his mother that they hadn't had a proper dinner the night before.

"We'll stop at the Busy Bee for breakfast," Mum said, "and check out our building mates."

Whereas Mum's shop was going to be a take-out place, the Busy Bee had around ten tables and a small bar. A sign at the door advised them to seat themselves; they settled into the one remaining booth on the side of the room. As they did, the noise level dropped to whispers and all heads turned their way. If Dad were there, he'd probably wave to the onlookers or introduce the family to the people at the closest table. But that wasn't Mum's way. She dropped her eyes to the menu, willing others to be polite and look away. Anneth pulled out her phone and began texting. Lowen reached to examine the bee-shaped salt and pepper shakers and wished for a moment that he hadn't complained about being hungry.

A man and woman came in and, noticing that there were no booths left, resigned themselves to a center table. It didn't make sense, but Lowen felt like his family had sat down where they didn't belong.

He didn't think it could get more awkward, but then the Doshis walked in and it did. Rena, all smiles, came directly over to their table, the three girls following. "Good morning! How was your first night in your new house?" she said, her voice sounding loud in the hushed space.

"Jolly," Mum said. "Though things will be nicer when our furniture arrives."

Ack. Why did Mum always revert to her snobbier-sounding Briticisms when she was nervous? Could they possibly stand out more?

"The girls slept like babies. Especially Hema," Rena said. "Must have been all the exercise we got yesterday."

Mum laughed. "These hills will take some getting used to."

Excuse me, Lowen wanted to say. *These hills just happen to be home to everyone sitting around us. Could we stop working so hard to be outsiders?* He looked at Anneth for some moral support, but she was apparently reporting the scene to Megan back home.

By this time, no one was trying to hide their stares.

"Come with me," Sami said to her sisters, suddenly taking charge. She led the girls over to the remaining table in the center of the room, pushed their chairs in closer, and began softly reading from the menu.

Rena was chatting with Mum about the lack of an exercise studio in town (eye rolls from the crowd) and the fact that she was probably going to have to purchase a latte machine to get by, when, thankfully, their meal finally came and Rena headed to her own table. Sami, Lowen couldn't help noticing, had ordered for all of them.

Fortunately, unlike the Busy Bee, Dollar Mart had only one other customer, a young woman in shorts and flip-flops, combing the aisles. On the left side of the store was stuff like kitchen utensils, bedding, school supplies, and games. On the right were groceries. Anneth started to get a cart, but Mum reminded them that anything purchased had to be carried home, so it would be better if each of them took a basket and filled it only partway.

"We should have done this when Dad was here," Anneth said. "Then we wouldn't have to carry everything back up the hill."

"Dad had a five-hour drive ahead of him," Mum said. "Ten hours is a lot of car time in one day. I didn't want him to get sleepy. Besides, we're not going to be able to afford to buy a car till the shop is turning a reliable profit, so this is something we're going to have to get used to."

"Clem should be helping," Anneth said.

"We'll go later in the day next time," Mum said. She led them down an aisle, all business. "But we need to stock up on a few essentials." She reached for paper cups and plates.

"What?" Lowen exclaimed. Mum hated to waste trees.

"I have no choice," she said defensively. "The dishes don't arrive till Monday. Is this the smallest package here?" she asked, holding up a package of cups.

"This one's smaller," Anneth said, pulling a package of red cups off the shelf.

"Yes, but plastic. Worse." Mum tossed the paper cups and plates in her basket.

"Do you want these paper towels?" Lowen asked.

"Are they recycled paper?"

Lowen looked at the packaging. "I don't think so."

"Then no paper towels," Mum said. "Go to the kitchen aisle and get us two new dish towels and a sponge."

Anneth followed Lowen to the kitchen aisle. They knew exactly which towels to get: the ones with pictures of violets. It was Mum's favorite flower.

When they returned to the food aisles, Mum was chatting with the Kellings, the ones with twins. Apparently Mason was babysitting while they were shopping. As Lowen stood staring at soda his mother would never let them buy, he overheard Eden tell Mum that they had considered purchasing a dollar house in many different cities—Detroit, Buffalo, and Gary—but they wanted to raise their kids in a small town, so they were thrilled to be accepted here in Millville.

"Small towns have their advantages," said Mum agreeably. "But I had forgotten how . . ."

Lowen knew she was fishing for the best word.

"I'd forgotten how *curious* small-town folk can be."

Eden nodded. "But they chose us, right? And we're a very diverse group. So they must be accepting."

"You would think," Mum said, but she didn't sound so sure.

When the women finally said their good-byes, the Grovers returned to the task at hand.

As it turned out, Dollar Mart carried none of their

usual brands. They only had white pasta, not whole wheat, and white rice, not brown. They only had sugary cereals, not the low-sugar cereals that Mum insisted on at home. All of the choices of granola bars contained corn syrup. Mum's voice rose with each new frustration.

"Find the anchovy paste," Mum barked.

Lowen and Anneth gave each other a look of horror. Sure, they knew that their mother made a great bow-tie pasta with anchovy paste, but they also knew that there was no way that Dollar Mart would carry such a thing.

"Go on," Mum said as she frowned at the label on a can of soup.

"We'll get it dreckly," said Anneth. It was one of Mum's Cornish sayings, which sounds like directly, but sort of means "Yeah, right."

Mum snapped her head up at Anneth and then caught her own foolishness. She couldn't help but laugh. "Cheeky! Guess I was being a bit unrealistic, huh?"

"Maybe Dad could bring some," Lowen said, trying to be helpful.

Mum ruffled his short dark hair. "What was I thinking?" she said. "Where is my adventurous attitude? Here," she said, handing Anneth a box of alphabet pasta to put in her basket, "these look fun." From there she added easy-boil white rice ("Why not make things easier in the beginning?") and a box of Froot Loops. The granola bars contained not only corn syrup but chocolate as well.

Mum seemed to be enjoying herself as much as Lowen and Anneth, and in the end, she reached for a big bag of Cheetos. "Let's shock Clem," she said with a big grin. And then to Anneth, "Go get us a container of Breyers Chocolate Truffle, too."

The young woman had finished shopping moments before them and was standing at the only open register. She glanced their way just as Anneth added the carton of ice cream to her very full basket.

"Hey, Charlotte. How are the little ones?" the clerk, an older woman with long gray hair, asked her.

The young woman—Charlotte, apparently—dug in her purse for a handful of crumpled bills. "They're fine. They've got swimming lessons this morning. Gives me a chance to get something done." She smoothed out the bills and began counting them. "How's Louisa?"

The clerk began bagging the groceries. "She's good. She misses Millville, but she doesn't miss the stress of being out of work."

"Don't I know it," Charlotte said as the clerk bagged the last item. She stared at the total. "You know, Sally, I don't think I'll take the popcorn after all. That bag leaves more seeds in the bottom than it pops."

"No problem," Sally said, and she deducted the price from the total.

"And take out the cereal—the kids complain that the generic puffed wheat tastes like cardboard."

For a moment, Lowen was annoyed. Why not make these decisions *before* she got in line?

"You know, I have to agree with them," the clerk said as she ran the cereal back over the scanner, deducting the price. Charlotte counted her bills again and frowned.

That's when he got it: it wasn't that Charlotte didn't want the items—it was that she didn't have enough money to pay for everything. He glanced at their baskets at the same moment Charlotte did.

Lowen wished they hadn't tossed in so much junk in the end. He could tell that Mum was uncomfortable, too.

"Let's skip these, too," said Charlotte, as she handed back a bag of potatoes.

That's when Mum jumped in. "Put those potatoes on my bill," she said.

The woman stared at Mum. Hard. Color rose up to her face. "That's not necessary," she said gruffly. "I have plenty of potatoes at home. I don't know what I was thinking."

"Of course," said the clerk, and completed the transaction.

After Charlotte paid, she turned back to Mum. "Thanks, though," she said grudgingly, and then she and her cart were gone.

Sally, the clerk, rang up the Grovers without any of the same friendliness she'd shown Charlotte.

"Well, that was awkward," said Anneth as they left the store.

"It was my fault," said Mum. "I was trying to help, but I just ended up embarrassing her — and myself."

They had filled far more bags than they had intended to and would have to be more careful at their next stop. Mum kept reminding them to stay off the road as they walked the highway back to Roger's Market.

Like the building Mum was renting for her restaurant, Roger's was small and wooden. It was light green and in need of paint. A sign affixed to the side read HOT COFFEE, NACHO CHIPS, ICE CREAM, PENNY CANDY. Mum and Anneth began to cross the small parking lot out front, but Lowen froze. The market looked dark to him, menacing. No doubt there'd be some sort of bell, just like the bell at Georgio's, announcing their arrival. All eyes would be on them.

"I'll stand out here," he said. "And watch the bags."

Mum looked down at all the bags they were carrying. "That sounds like a good plan," she said. "Anneth, why don't you stay with Lowen. I'll just get some vegetables for a sauté and milk for breakfast. I won't be long."

Anneth started to object, but then realized it was an opportunity to check her phone. As far as Lowen could tell, it hadn't buzzed in a while.

Mum was true to her word and came back only a few minutes after she went in, but Lowen's heart had raced the entire time she was inside.

"Are you OK?" she asked him when they were reunited. "You don't look well."

Lowen shrugged. He wanted her obsessive observation of him to stop. "I'm just hungry again," he said, which wasn't entirely true but true enough.

As they finished trudging up the three blocks on Beech Street, they spotted a group of people standing by their front porch.

"There you are!" shouted a short woman wearing an oversize flannel shirt. If Lowen were going to make a cartoon of her, he'd draw droopy eyelids behind large, round eyeglasses. "We couldn't imagine where you went off to! And with your door locked!"

Hadn't Clem heard them knocking?

"We're the Welcome Wagon!"

Neighbors from both sides of the road had brought them food to eat. The short woman led them all through the back door, right into the Grovers' kitchen, and set the food down on the kitchen counter. They introduced themselves, told how long they'd lived in Millville (although as far as Lowen could tell, most of them had been born here), and exclaimed at how pretty Anneth was ("Dark hair and freckles just like her mother!"), how tall Lowen was for his age ("And would you look at those hazel eyes and dark eyelashes!"), and how exotic Mum's accent was.

Mum invited them all to stay (despite the fact that they had no furniture *or* real dishes), but thankfully they declined. "We'll let you get settled," they said with promises to have the family over to dinner at their homes sometime soon.

One tall woman with black hair pulled back in a severe bun hung back. "You've been to Dollar Mart," she said, observing the bags set down on the floor.

"Oh, yes," said Mum cheerfully. "As we've discovered, there's not much you can't buy there."

The woman shook her head. "Don't shop at Dollar Mart for groceries," she scolded. "If you do, you'll put Roger's out of business. Roger may be dead and gone, but that market keeps his children and their families here in this town. It keeps them clothed and fed."

Lowen waited to see how his mother would reply. Though her English accent tended to delight, her English ways sometimes caused her to be a bit too direct. A bit, well, like this woman standing across from her.

But Mum didn't have a chance to respond before the woman leaned over and said more warmly, "But you know all about hard times. And now look! You have a home for only a single dollar!"

Confusion crossed Mum's face.

"Don't you worry," the woman said. "We'll do our best to continue helping *you* out, too."

Mum looked a bit taken aback (thought bubble: *Help us out?*), but she quickly recovered. She thanked the woman and said she would try to give as much business to Roger's as she could.

"Why does everyone seem to think we're poor?" Lowen asked, once the Welcome Wagon had gone.

Mum laughed good-naturedly. "Well, after we open the take-out, and after we pour every last cent we've saved into fixing up this house, we might well be." Then she grew more serious. "I think some folks just assume that we can't afford to pay more than one dollar for a house—that we came here because we're down on our luck or desperate. They're not factoring in all of the money needed for repairs, or the money we're investing in starting up our businesses. Here we thought we were doing *them* the favor by moving here and investing in their town, but clearly some of the locals think that *we're* the ones in need of help!"

This thought didn't seem to sit well with Mum, who sounded short-tempered when she directed them where to put the groceries away: "Milk, juice, and seltzer water go on the top shelf of the fridge. Condiments on the door."

Just like it was back in Flintlock, thought Lowen, but he didn't point this out. The Welcome Wagon had not, in fact, made things easier for Mum, and he sensed that what she needed most at this moment was to be in full charge of the situation.

"Go wake your brother, Lowen," Mum said.

Fine with him. He climbed all the way up to the third floor only to find that Clem wasn't in bed at all. Where had he gone? Certainly he would have left a note. Nothing upstairs.

By the time he returned to the kitchen, Clem was back, eating a handful of Froot Loops and showing Mum the note he had left on the counter—the one hidden under a casserole dish. *Gone to find my buds,* the note read.

They'd been in Millville less than twenty-four hours and Clem had not only found friends, but had adopted their language. Back home he had "comrades." Here, apparently, he had "buds."

Mum served them heaping platefuls of American chop suey (still warm) with fluffy white rolls. It was a meal that their dad sometimes cooked at home, but this one was deliciously saltier.

Even though Lowen missed Dad, he found he was actually enjoying himself, eating a warm meal prepared by someone else in a kitchen owned by his family—even if it *was* pretty run-down.

And he remained relaxed until he bit into one of the big fudgy brownies that Mr. and Mrs. Field had brought them, the same Field as Field's Funeral Home, and Clem said, "Do you think these moist chocolaty brownies are made with human blood?"

7.

TWO DAYS LATER . . .

Their belongings arrived as planned. In addition to
the boxes of clothes, books, and Legos (which Lowen
still messed with from time to time) was a carton of
his old sketchbooks that he'd purposefully left behind
in Flintlock. He had intended for the box to stay in the
apartment for as long as Dad stayed in the apartment.
But here it was now with a note from Dad written in
marker: *Lowen, thought you might miss these.*

He did miss them. Before the shooting, he'd spent
every free moment drawing comics. That box Dad sent
held about two years of Lowen's work. Still, he couldn't
bring himself to open it.

He couldn't hide the box in his closet (too small),
so he carried it out to the garage where Mum was storing things that either "didn't work in this house" or that
she couldn't deal with yet. Climbing over boxes marked

TEXTBOOKS and TAX RETURNS, he tucked it far in a corner. Then he placed another box labeled KNITS on top.

Lowen hoped that not looking at the box would put an end to his missing, but it turned out that he still thought about it. It was the same way with the funeral home. Even though he absolutely refused to look out his window, he couldn't keep his mind off the place on his first night. Lying there, staring up at the dingy ceiling, he'd wondered about the body they'd seen going into the home. Where had it gone precisely? To what room? Would there be a funeral service next door? Would a black hearse come to take the body to one of the churches they'd seen in town, or to the cemetery? (His knowledge of hearses came from reading graphic novels. He'd never actually attended a funeral. Not even Abe's. His parents had wanted him to, but he'd refused, and thankfully they didn't make him.)

The next day Mum gathered them in the kitchen and listed the things that needed to be done. She divided the tasks into three categories:

1) Chores to ready the house for the furniture: *Scrub windows, floors, walls, and bathrooms; toss remaining curtains; tear up old linoleum and carpet.*

2) Jobs that must be accomplished before the final inspection: *Replace front steps, porch, and siding wherever rotten; repair windows, wallboard, bathroom tiles, kitchen cupboards, and oven door; eradicate mold from the bathrooms; paint exterior.*

3) Projects we'd like to do (someday!): *Enlarge and remodel the kitchen; create an herb garden in the backyard; restore the hardwood floors; give all of the rooms fresh paint.*

"Anything else?" Mum asked.

Anneth shrugged (thought bubble: *Count me out*) and Mum turned to Lowen and handed him the pad and pen. He couldn't think of any practical needs, so he tried to think of something else to add to the wish list: a tree house? A tire swing? A hammock? Then he remembered that they had only one tree in the backyard and it was a flimsy evergreen. Not even a decent Christmas tree. Nevertheless, his fingers began to move the pen over the corner of the pad. A doodled circle turned into a face. Anneth's face. He drew piercing eyes.

Make her eyebrows go up. Abe's voice. Lowen quickly scratched out the doodle.

When he looked up, their next-door neighbor on Anneth's side, the short woman who they learned was Mrs. Manzo, waved from her kitchen window.

He added a fourth category to the list: *Things to buy.* Below that he wrote *window shades.*

Lowen spent the rest of the day washing windows (being almost tall enough to reach the tops), helping Mum pull up the remaining linoleum in the kitchen, and scrubbing his bedroom floor. That night he wondered how many bodies might be stored next door. Perhaps all the tiny black flies around their house had something to do with the bodies.

The next day, Lowen pulled up stubborn, deeply rooted dandelion weeds in the front yard, helped unpack boxes, and rearranged furniture until Mum shouted, "We're done!"

The modern furniture that had occupied their living room in Flintlock looked out of place in this tired, worn house. Mum stood back to survey their work and huffed, "Someday, it will all come together."

That night, he fell into bed, too exhausted to do more than wonder if the body they'd seen had been a man's or woman's. . . .

While Clem and Anneth waited the next day for the arrival of a stackable washer and dryer (and instructions on where to install it in the mudroom), Lowen accompanied his mother to her shop. Mum suggested they take a route they hadn't walked previously, so they went down one block to Church and followed it west for two blocks. Lowen took stock of each house they passed. Sure, the Albatross (as they'd taken to calling their house) was in pretty bad shape, but so were the other homes in town. Many had sagging roofs, chipped paint, and front porch railings that looked like smiles with missing teeth. The front steps of two of the homes had grown so rotten they'd had to be removed. In both cases, the detached steps remained off to the side on the overgrown front lawns.

But one house in particular, on the corner of Church and Cedar, stood out from all the others; not because the house was so dilapidated—just the opposite. It seemed untouched by the town's bad luck. The stately white house (which was even grander than Field's Funeral Home) sat slightly higher than the others around it. Its lawn and shrubs were trimmed, and several flower gardens were bursting with color. There was a little wishing well in the backyard, and a decorative windmill that was lit by early morning sun. Lowen was staring at the windmill as it slowly turned in the whispery breeze when an older man came out the front door to retrieve his newspaper. It was the selectman from the lottery: Mr. Avery. He glanced at the two of them, gave the tiniest nod of the head, and then disappeared inside.

"I bet all of the houses were that well-kempt at one time," Mum said.

It was easy to imagine.

They turned left on Cedar, which brought them directly to Mum's shop. She placed her load of cleaning supplies down on the sidewalk and searched for the key in her handbag.

"You could just finish the job," Lowen quipped, nodding at the starburst of broken glass on the door. No doubt a decent shove would send the glass tinkling to the ground.

Mum frowned. "I'll start a list of repairs for the landlord."

"Good morning, you two," said the hennish woman who had shown them the house on the first day, the one who owned the Busy Bee. She appeared to be returning from an errand.

"Good morning, Mrs. Corbeau," said Mum. "How was the breakfast crowd this morning?"

"A little slower than we're used to in July. We're thinking of making some changes."

"Change can be exciting," said Mum. "I'll be eager to hear what they are."

There were many boarded-up storefronts on Main Street in Millville, each of which Mum could've rented for a song. But Mum purposely chose the space next to the Busy Bee. She had read that it's better to be clustered with other thriving businesses—even other restaurants—than try to operate on a block where there are boarded-up storefronts. When folks went to the Busy Bee, they'd be reminded that Millville had a new lunch shop in town.

That's what Cornish pasties were intended for: lunch. When Lowen and his siblings were little, Mum made the small tarts with steak, potato, onion, and sometimes (when she could find it) rutabaga. The small circular pie dough would be folded over the filling and then, at the place where the two halves met, pinched to make a handle. This, too, was a Cornwall tradition. Backalong, as Mum would say, Cornish miners had taken the pasties to work with them. The handle allowed them to eat most of the tart without getting the coal grime in their mouths. As the kids got older, Mum started experimenting. She made lamb and mint, pork and apple, and vegetarian curry pasties. That's what she planned to do in Millville. She'd start with the traditional pie and then introduce others.

When Mum pushed open the broken door of her shop, glass fell to the ground.

"Top of the list," she said.

She reached for the switch and clicked on the light, but the place still looked dark. It took a minute for Lowen's eyes to adjust before he could make out the table in front, the counter in the middle, and the big restaurant-size oven in the back. The room obviously hadn't been used for a very long time. There was dirt, accumulated grease, and cobwebs. It smelled sour—and a little fishy.

Mum gave a little laugh when he mentioned this. "Good nose. It used to be a seafood store."

Lowen looked at his mother. Despite the little laugh, she sounded depressed.

"A bigger window, in the front—that's what you need," Lowen said optimistically. "So people will feel invited."

She nodded. "Brilliant," she said faintly. "We'll add that to the list, too."

Lowen grabbed the broom from her hands and began moving it around. He was getting used to cleaning up, and sweeping seemed the easiest way to start.

Mum grabbed a rag and went to the large sink in the back to wet it. The faucet groaned. "No water," she said, giving a great sigh and resting her arms on the sides of the sink.

"Why did it close?"

"What's that?" And then, "Oh, the fish shop. I don't know. Perhaps I should have found out." Her head dropped. "I did research, but I also let my imagination get away from me. I dreamed a place, then made what I discovered online fit my dream."

Lowen stopped sweeping. "Is it nothing like you thought?"

Mum closed her eyes. Shook her head. "Maybe I wanted to go back in time."

"But it can still work? Right? You can still have your restaurant. We can still have a house."

She opened her eyes and smiled at him. "That's right." She grabbed a bucket and said she'd be right back. She was going next door for some water.

Back in Flintlock, Lowen had done very little deep cleaning. Oh, sure, he'd picked up his room when told (that is, until he watched Clem shove everything under the bed and he started doing the same), and once a week it would be his turn to wash the pots, but that was it. Since he'd moved to Millville, all he'd done was chores. Yet it was so much more satisfying. Each time they washed and scrubbed and swept, the place looked transformed.

After a morning's worth of work, Mum's shop looked much better, more welcoming. She'd opened the door and the three small windows and rays of sunshine—not to mention an earthy breeze from the Grand River—began to slip in.

When Lowen and Mum lifted and centered the table, Mum said, "It's a bit like playing Wendy Houses, isn't it?"

Lowen smiled. That's what Mum had called pretend play when she was a girl.

That night Mum suggested to Lowen and Anneth (who had done two loads of laundry in the new washer and dryer) that they walk down to Roger's for an ice cream. Lowen knew that he couldn't avoid walking into Roger's forever. If he did, his mother would surely be searching for a grief therapist again. So instead, he pre-occupied himself with the kinds of ice cream they might have: Creamsicles, Nutty Buddy cones, ice-cream sandwiches, Chipwiches . . .

When they passed the park, Lowen saw his brother with a group of Millville kids, Mason, and Luna.

Something stirred deep inside of Lowen. It wasn't the snake this time. It was a longing and a bit of fear mixed together. Like preparing to jump from the high dive at the pool. He wondered if Clem felt the same thing when he stood in that group and talked with Luna.

Clem gave the tiniest of nods as they passed.

When they got to Roger's, Lowen stuck as close to Mum and Anneth as he could without it being obvious. He picked out a Blue Bunny caramel chocolate bar from the freezer and handed it to Mum. He knew Roger's probably had candy right next to the counter, but he was going to avoid looking at it. So instead, he made a point of checking out the bulletin board in the front of the store and read about a church supper, a generator for sale, and carpentry services.

He felt relieved and even a little proud leaving the store. He'd faced one of his fears, which seemed like a pretty good start to "addressing his anxiety," as the therapist constantly said. Maybe he wouldn't even think about the dead body next door that night. Maybe, he wouldn't think about anything unpleasant at all.

After watching reruns of a talent competition show, he said good night to Mum and Anneth. He texted Dad good night and had received a Sleep well, son in return. He thought of texting Clem, but that seemed lame.

Then he climbed the dark stairway, turned into his dimly lit room, and stopped dead—

A boy was sitting on the edge of his bed.

8.

THAT NIGHT . . .

His first thought when he saw the boy was *Abe*.

His rapid-firing second thought was that this boy—who was obviously older than Abe—was a ghost from the funeral home next door.

The boy (or the ghost of a boy) leaned forward on his elbows. "How do you like my room?"

"Your room?" Lowen managed to say.

"Yup." The kid stood and walked over to where Lowen was standing. Lowen jumped aside, but all the kid did was flip the light switch.

Not a ghost, then.

The boy had a buzz cut and wore a tattered T-shirt with camo pants. He drifted over to the closet and peered inside. Lowen's duffel bag was there. Was this kid a thief? Was he looking for something to steal?

"My grandfather is a town councillor."

Coach? Not likely. "Mr. Avery?" Anyway, what did that have to do with anything?

He nodded. "I live with him. But this is my family's house. My father built the dormer in this room. That's what you call the addition. A dormer. It makes the room longer."

Lowen wanted to say, "It *was* your family's house, and get out of *my* closet," but he felt less certain of these facts.

The kid picked up one of Lowen's Bone books and leafed through it. "How tall are you?"

"Five foot six," Lowen practically shouted, hoping Mum or Anneth might hear him and come investigate. What did this kid want?

"I'm Dylan Firebrand," the kid said. "People call this the Firebrand House."

"Lowen Grover," Lowen replied. He was tempted to add, "And we call this house the Albatross," but he didn't think Dylan would appreciate the joke.

"I know," Dylan said. "You're in the sixth grade like me." And with that, he brushed past Lowen, clunked down the stairwell, and went out the front door. The door none of them had used yet. Neither Mum nor Anneth seemed to notice him at all—almost like he *was* a ghost.

Lowen took a deep breath, though it didn't stop his heart from trying to break out of his rib cage.

He thought of going downstairs, telling Mum what had just happened, but he remembered her feelings of defeat earlier today. He didn't want to add one more worry. So he said nothing and crawled into bed. But a good deal of time passed before he stopped lying there with his eyes open, convinced that people were drifting in and out of his room.

Lowen figured he wouldn't see Dylan Firebrand again until they landed in the same classroom in September.

That wasn't the case by a long shot.

The next morning when Lowen stumbled down to breakfast, Dylan was lolling in the kitchen talking to Mum. She was pouring him a paper cup of juice. "Look who's here," she said.

Lowen didn't know if Mum meant him or Dylan. Either way, she seemed pleased.

Lowen knew that his mother wished he had more friends. It used to worry her that he mostly spent time with Abe, who was so much younger than he was. He'd tried to explain that he had plenty of friends at school. It's just that he didn't like having friends over. When friends came to your house, you had to entertain them: figure out their interests, keep them busy. In his precious spare time, Lowen wanted to do the things *he* loved best. Alone. He'd hoped that she would take the hint and realize that he probably didn't love having Abe hanging around, but she never did, and he couldn't bring himself to say it outright. It just felt too mean.

Lowen poured himself a cup of juice and waited for Dylan to ask him more questions, but mostly Dylan talked to Mum. He told her where his mother had kept her pots and pans, how the refrigerator light would come back on if you jiggled the bulb, that they never bothered to lock the front door—which was probably why it had been stuck, after being locked for so many months—and that trash was picked up on Thursdays.

Lowen reached into a box of oatmeal squares (which Mum had found at Roger's, and which had unfortunately replaced the marshmallow cereal), pulled out a handful, and headed out the door.

"Where are you going?" Mum called.

"To explore," Lowen replied. "I need a break from cleaning."

"Why don't you and Dy—"

Lowen didn't slow down to listen. He had no interest in befriending Dylan Firebrand. He'd probably give Lowen all kinds of advice about where best to place things in his room. It was just too weird. And let's face it, Dylan was probably better off without his friendship.

He decided to walk farther up Beech Street instead of down toward town. A scruffy man in jeans and slippers (slippers that Lowen would turn into big hairy things if he were to draw them) stepped out of a home badly in need of repair and paused to talk to Lowen on his way to get his newspaper.

"You're one of those Dollar Kids, aren't you?"

"I guess, yeah."

"So where's your family from?"

"Flintlock."

"Crazy city, man! I could never live in one of those crime-infested places. Sure is nice and peaceful here in Millville, isn't it?"

Lowen just nodded and kept moving. He had never thought of Flintlock as crime-infested before; the shooting at Georgio's had been the only really violent crime he'd heard about. He wondered again how much people knew about him.

When Lowen crossed School Street, he noticed a public playground and went to investigate. A worn picnic table occupied the only shade. Sprawled across the spotty grass were a metal swing set with three swings, a wooden teeter-totter, a tall metal slide, and one of those merry-go-rounds that turned only when pushed. The merry-go-round had faded, paint-chipped animals for seats: a rabbit, a duck, a rooster, a lamb. It made him wish that he were younger. That was the problem with being eleven: you didn't belong with the teenagers skateboarding on the paved paths by the bandstand, and you were too old to ride the merry-go-round—even though it still looked fun. He'd pick the duck.

Behind the playground was a fenced-in pool. An instructor was standing in the shallow end of the pool, giving some kids slightly younger than Lowen a swim lesson. The kids were sitting on the edge of the pool, their feet dangling. Lowen shivered. It seemed awfully early to have to get into that cool blue water. One boy glanced up at Lowen and then whispered to the kid beside him. Now both were looking his way. Lowen sped up.

He walked west on School and back down Maple, where he recognized the Grey kids out in their front yard. The three kids were playing a game where they kept reciting, *"Mr. Fox, Mr. Fox."*

Lagi came running over to him on the sidewalk. "What's your name?" he asked.

Lowen told him, and the little boy said, "I'm Lagi. That's Lily, and that's Wanda."

The two girls joined them.

"Do you want to play Mr. Fox?" asked Wanda, who Lowen guessed was in third or fourth grade. "I'm it."

"Please, please, please!" said Lily, who was probably two years younger than her sister, and wearing butterfly wings.

"Please, please, please!" Lagi repeated.

The two younger kids grabbed on to his hands and tried pulling him into the yard. Lowen smiled and recalled a time when Abe had begged him in a similar manner. The snake climbed. "I have to get home. My mum's expecting me," he said.

He took the longest route back he could think of, hoping that Dylan would have moved on. As he approached 11 Beech, he noticed two bags by the front porch. One had boys' clothes; the other contained a tablecloth, a wooden bowl, and some Tupperware. He had no idea who had dropped them off or what it meant.

"The Welcome Wagon again?" Anneth asked, when he deposited the bags inside. Fortunately, Dylan was nowhere in sight.

"Maybe," said Mum. "But I have a sneaky suspicion it has more to do with the folks in this town viewing us all as quite needy."

"What do we do with all this junk?" asked Clem, who had finally gotten out of bed.

Mum shot him a chastising look. "I guess we accept their generosity," she said, looking for a place to store the bowl.

"But aren't we here to help *them*?" asked Lowen. "You know, bring in more people, more businesses . . . that sort of thing?"

"We're here to help each other," said Mum. "I'm sure they realize that."

9.

EARLY JULY

The appearance of mysterious things continued to occur. They never saw the person or persons who left the items, which made them feel watched.

Some of the things were useful. Anneth claimed a box of buttons and used them to decorate the sleeves of a jean jacket. Mum picked wildflowers to fill a bud vase, which she set on the dining room table. They placed the random assortment of loose magnets on the refrigerator.

Other things the Grovers had no use for: dented shades, Jell-O molds, bed ruffles, steak knives, needle-point pictures. Most of these things Mum packed up in their empty boxes and stored in the garage. She would have sent them home with Dad on one of his trips back to the city (to drop off at Goodwill), but she worried that they might be loans.

One day a card table appeared on their lawn. (It went to the garage.) Another day they came home from a trip to the market to find a large corduroy recliner. "Can we keep this?" Clem asked, already testing it out. "It's super comfy."

"And super ugly," said Dad, who was up for the weekend. But, after a family discussion, they moved it into the living room for fear that the donor's feelings would be hurt if they didn't. Mum's shop would be opening soon and they couldn't afford to hurt anyone's feelings.

Dylan's appearances were also a regular occurrence. He came around at least once a day. He never knocked. He just traipsed in, helped himself to a granola bar from the cupboard or a slice of cheese and a bit of turkey from the fridge, and then stretched out on the floor to watch TV. It didn't matter if Clem was watching a baseball game or if Anneth was watching reruns of a fashion show, he'd prop himself up on his elbows and stare at the TV until someone clicked it off. If the TV wasn't on when he arrived, he plopped down on the couch or in the corduroy recliner (if it wasn't occupied by Clem) and listened to the conversation going on around him. Clem and Anneth usually acknowledged him in some way—sometimes with just a nod, sometimes with questions about Millville.

Clem: How far do you have to drive for tacos?

Anneth: Why is the Internet service in Millville so ridiculously slow?

Clem: Are any of these spiders around here poisonous? Can you get malaria from the mosquitoes? And what are those little black droppings in the corners of my room?

Anneth: Why does everyone say hi when they don't even know me?

Clem: Why do most people in town drive trucks?

There were questions that Lowen wanted to ask: How many teachers will we have in sixth grade? Are they nice? Who are the popular kids? Can you sit anywhere you want in the lunchroom? Stuff like that.

And he was also curious about Dylan. How come he lived with his grandfather? Did his parents live with Mr. Avery, too? Was Mr. Avery as strict as he seemed? But he wouldn't allow himself to ask.

As it turned out, Dylan didn't seem to care whether Lowen talked to him or not. In fact, he seemed to prefer the company of Clem and Anneth.

Which should have made Lowen feel relieved; after all, he wasn't looking for a friend. But it didn't. It made him feel shunned—and slightly paranoid. Dylan's grandfather was town councillor. Had he told Dylan about Abe? Had he told Dylan to stay away from Lowen? Or could Dylan just tell that as far as friends were concerned, Lowen wasn't worth the effort?

Mum, Anneth, and Clem seemed amused by Dylan's presence and kept referring to him as "Lowen's new friend," which irritated Lowen to no end. Couldn't they see that Dylan spent all his time talking to everyone in the family *but* him? Besides, a friend was someone you looked forward to seeing. It wasn't someone who barged into your home—and your life—without permission.

First Abe, and now Dylan.

Lowen took to helping Mum at the restaurant first thing in the morning so he could leave the house before Dylan arrived.

On the second Monday of July, Lowen pulled himself out of bed, wolfed down his breakfast, and then grabbed some old rags and a roll of parchment paper.

"You're good to come to the shop with me," Mum said.

"It's fun," said Lowen, who was telling the truth. He and Anneth used to play restaurant when they were younger; now his mother was creating the real thing.

Because the landlord was in charge of the repairs, the shop was transforming at a decent pace. He had put in a large front window at Mum's request, and he'd hired an electrician to put in some extra lighting. "He's tired of having this place empty," Mum had said. "He wants us to succeed, too."

"So what should we do today?" Lowen asked, plopping the supplies down on the table.

"Let's paint these grimy walls," Mum said. She went over to her handbag resting on the table and took out two twenty-dollar bills. "Go down to the hardware store and buy paint."

"What color?"

"You pick. I trust your artistic judgment."

Lowen smiled. One of his favorite things to do in the entire world was to buy art supplies. This wasn't exactly that, but the thought of looking at paint chips with all those shades and combinations of reds and yellows and blues made his heart skip.

"What about brushes and rollers and stuff?"

Mum thought for a moment, then shook her head and grabbed her handbag. "While you're at the hardware store, I'm going out to do a little borrowing."

Handy Hardware was the most crowded store Lowen had ever been in, but not crowded with people — crowded with things. Maybe, with so many stores in town closed, boarded up, Handy Hardware was attempting to sell everything a Millvillian could need. There were tools resting against toboggans, fishing rods leaning up against flyswatters. The place was a mess.

"May I help you?" asked a skinny man with pointy

shoulders, pointy elbows, and a pointy nose. He'd make a great comic book character.

Lowen didn't want to be helped. He wanted to spend time studying all of the paint chips, making comparisons. But not answering seemed rude. "I need to buy paint," he said.

"Watercolors, acrylic, spray paint?" said the clerk.

"House paint. Or, in this case, store paint."

"Ah," said the man. "Which store you painting?"

"My mother is opening a lunch restaurant next to the Busy Bee."

"You don't say," said the man. "Right next door?"

Lowen nodded.

"Interior or exterior?"

It took Lowen a moment to realize that the man was asking about the paint again. "Interior," he said.

"We used to have a lunch place here in town," said the clerk as he led Lowen down a zigzaggy aisle. "But then everyone started taking their lunches to work. Of course, there are a lot fewer people working in town now than there used to be."

Lowen knew this. Mum had discovered this when she did research. But, as she pointed out, if Millville was going to make a comeback—and they seemed to want to make a comeback—they would need some new shops on Main Street.

They arrived at the interior paint section. "The custom colors and the most popular colors are 'bout thirty-seven dollars a gallon," the man said. "But this color here . . ." He pulled a paint can from the top shelf and wiped the dust off the lid with his apron. "This color, um, *Blue Ambrosia,* is on sale for sixteen dollars a gallon."

Blue Ambrosia? The can didn't show the color. But it sure sounded pretty. Besides, you couldn't beat the price. Mum would be proud that he'd economized. He'd take two.

His mother wasn't alone when he got back to the store. Sami was standing in the middle of the store with her mother.

"You look surprised to see us, Lowen," said Rena, smiling. "Your mother came by to borrow painting equipment, and since the younger girls were playing at the Greys', and Sami and I had just run out of things to unpack, she picked up two helpers to boot!"

"Mom can't set up her business until the loan is approved," Sami said. "She's going to open a handmade pet clothing store—one with grooming services."

Rena nodded. "The pet industry is one of the fastest growing industries in this country."

Mum smiled. "People do seem to love their animals."

"Do you have a pet?" Sami asked Lowen.

Lowen shook his head. "My dad's allergic," he said, putting one can down and handing the other to Mum.

She lifted the cover of the can with a screwdriver and revealed a dark metallic blue.

"I thought it would be a lighter color," Lowen said. "The word *Ambrosia* makes me think of something fluffy."

"I kind of like it," said Mum. "It's surprising. Totally unexpected." She lifted the can to pour the paint into a tray.

"No!" said Sami. "You can't use blue!"

"Why?" Mum and Lowen asked simultaneously.

"This is going to be a restaurant, right?" said Sami. "The color blue suppresses the appetite!"

"B. F. Skinner?" Rena asked her daughter, while giving Mum a slightly apologetic smile.

"I studied Skinner in school!" said Mum. "He worked with rats!"

"And pigeons," Sami said, smiling.

"His theories help explain our behavior," Mum said to Lowen, to fill him in.

"Right," said Sami, "but I'm not talking about *his* theories." She gave her mother a look. "I'm talking about color psychology. Foods that are blue have gone bad or are poisonous," said Sami, "so our brains learned a long time ago to avoid them."

"What about blueberries?" Lowen pointed out.

"Name another one," said Sami, folding her arms. She waited.

He racked his brain. Lowen could tell that his mother and Rena were trying to come up with some, too. All were unsuccessful.

Mum looked at Rena.

"She wants to be a psychologist," Rena said. "That is, after she's played for the U.S. soccer team. My ambitious daughter."

Mum gave Sami an approving look. Then she put the can down and put the cover back on. "Do you think Handy Hardware will take this back?" she asked Lowen.

Lowen shrugged.

"Who sold it to you?" asked Rena.

He described the clerk.

"Mr. Corbeau," Rena said.

"Related to the woman who owns the Busy Bee?" asked Mum.

Rena nodded. "Husband."

"Sami," said Mum, "what color makes a person ravenously hungry?"

"Red," said Sami without hesitating.

"Here you go," said Mum, handing the cans back to Lowen. "You know what to do."

"I'll go with you," said Sami, taking one of the cans from Lowen. "If the red is too pink, it will have the same effect as blue. Pink makes us think of gross stuff, like raw meat and artificial preservatives."

Lowen wasn't thinking about color psychology as they walked together. He was worried about returning the open can of paint. "What are we going to say?" he asked as they approached the hardware store. "What if Mr. Corbeau won't let us return it? It was opened. And it was on sale. Sometimes things on sale can't be returned, right?"

Sami kept walking.

Lowen swatted a mosquito that was biting his neck and looked over at her. Did she even hear his question?

Just as they arrived at Handy Hardware, Sami said, "Be confident. And don't even say the word *return*. Say 'My mother thought the color of this paint was unusual and she was wondering if you had something similar in red.' Trust me, people who work in hardware stores love to solve other people's problems. They're great at it! So instead of thinking of how he's going to turn you down, he'll be wondering which cans of red paint he wants to get rid of."

Lowen's head was spinning. No way could he remember all that.

"You're back!" said Mr. Corbeau to Lowen.

"This was a cool color," Lowen said, "but it's not, well, it's not quite right."

Sami stepped in. "Do you have a red that would be equally unique?"

"*Equally unique,* you say." Mr. Corbeau looked a bit wary, but like Sami predicted, he couldn't resist the search. "Put that open can on the counter and let's see what we can find."

He walked down the aisle and back up the ladder.

Lowen was giving Sami a doubtful look when Mr. Corbeau said, "I have exactly what you're looking for."

Lowen took the can from Mr. Corbeau and used the bottom of his T-shirt to wipe the greasy dust from the lid.

The label read RIVAL ROSE.

"Could you show us the color?" Sami asked.

Boy, this girl is brave, thought Lowen. *Or bossy.* He wasn't sure which.

For a moment, Mr. Corbeau stared at Sami, and then he began to loosen the lid of the can. "Your family's Indian, right?" he asked her.

"My parents are," she said.

"India. I suppose that's where all our jobs have gone."

Sami bit her lip. "That's not really the case, you know. Besides, I'm American, and we came here because my mom needed a better job, too."

Brave, thought Lowen. Definitely brave.

Mr. Corbeau looked at Sami sideways. Then he went back to working the lid. "Guess there's nothing more American than needing a job."

The lid popped off.

Lowen leaned over to check out the paint color. It reminded him of strawberry Twizzlers. He felt a quick quivering of the snake inside him, but he pushed the unpleasant memory away. He looked to Sami to see what she thought of the color.

"We'll take it," she said.

10.

THAT SAME DAY . . .

Mum, Rena, Sami, and Lowen spent the morning painting the walls of the Cornish Eatery. Rena told Mum more
about her pet-grooming store. "I'm especially excited
about the clothing," Rena said. "I have designs for all
seasons, but around here there's got to be a demand for
warm coats and insulated boots."

The winters in Millville were supposed to be pretty epic.
Lowen recalled more than a few headlines about record-
breaking snowfalls when they'd researched the town.

"You should see the outfits she's made," Sami added.
"They're much better than the ones in stores."

"Well, they caught on with my friends at home,"
Rena said.

"You're too modest, Mom," Sami said. "She's a real
artist."

Rena came over and kissed the top of Sami's head.
"My daughter is my biggest cheerleader. The men in my
life? Not so much."

Lowen could tell from Sami's expression that she thought her mother was oversharing. "You don't need a man, Mom," Sami said. "You just need more confidence."

"Yes, well, all the confidence in the world isn't going to make your dad more reliable," Rena quipped. "Sami never knows when she's going to get a phone call from her dad," she explained with disgust in her voice.

"He texts sometimes," Sami said. "And maybe he'd be in touch more often if he didn't have to call *your* cell phone."

Lowen pretended to be absorbed in painting. He wondered if Sami missed her dad as much as he was beginning to miss his.

By afternoon the color had done the trick: Lowen was famished! He hoped that Clem and Anneth had remembered to go to Roger's for groceries.

"Which route home today?" Mum asked as they locked up.

Lowen chose Cedar to Church to Beech so he could walk past the Millville First Baptist Church. The minister changed the marquee often, and he usually wrote something funny.

Last week it read *God answers knee-mail*.

Today it read *Free trip to Heaven — details inside*.

Which didn't strike Lowen as funny at all. He looked at his mother to see if she'd read it, too, but her mind appeared to be elsewhere.

Free trip to Heaven. Right. The snake slithered between his ribs. Right after the shooting, people talked a lot about Abe being in heaven. But when Lowen was in fourth grade, a kid had told him that there was a pause between living and the afterlife—limbo, she called it—where a person's life was reviewed. If God was in your heart, you went to heaven. If not, hell.

As they walked, Lowen tried to push the Abe thoughts away, but his mind began to play the next story in his Abe comics. . . .

"What is it, honey?" Mum asked, pulling him out of his fantasy.

"Nothing," said Lowen.

"Thinking about Abe again?" She was too good at noticing.

Lowen shrugged.

"Do you think it's been easier here? Less sad?"

He blasted a rock from the toe of his sneaker to the other side of the road. Why talk about it? No one knows where Abe is now. Just because he imagined limbo doesn't mean it exists.

They turned onto Beech Street and heard Clem's and Anneth's voices through the open windows. They were yelling.

Both Mum and Lowen broke into a jog.

Anneth was trapped in her room. Apparently she had gone in to Skype in privacy with Megan, and when she tried to come out again, the door was stuck. The knob wouldn't turn.

Clem was barreling into the door, the way cops on TV do when they're breaking down doors.

"Stop it, Clem!" Mum shouted. "You'll hurt yourself."

Clem gave the door one more bang.

Anneth screamed and then returned to talking on the phone. Lowen could tell by the shrillness of her voice that she was talking to Dad.

Mum rattled the glass doorknob. "What is it with the hardware in this house?"

"Maybe some butter would help," said Lowen, who as a little kid had once gotten his finger stuck in the bathtub faucet and his mother had come to the rescue with butter.

"Dad says to take the door off the hinges," Anneth shouted through the door.

Just then Mr. Field came charging up the stairs, dressed in a three-piece suit. "Please!" he begged. "We're having visiting hours next door. We can't have yelling and banging. You've got to think of the mourners."

Mum apologized to Mr. Field and told Anneth to freak out as quietly as possible.

As Mr. Field turned to go down the stairs, he paused to let Coach come up. (Didn't anyone in this town ever knock?) Dylan waited at the base of the stairs. He must have been here when Anneth discovered she was trapped and gone for help.

"Hey, Lowen," Coach said as he passed him. "Have you been practicing your mad soccer skills?"

Lowen grunted a noncommittal sound—a response, but not an answer.

Mum looked relieved to see Coach. "Can you help me take this door off its hinges?"

Coach took a moment to investigate the door. He shook his head. "Won't work." He explained that the doorknob had a metal mechanism that was stuck in the wooden door casing. "You need a locksmith," he said.

Anneth shrieked. "How long is that going to take?"

"That's enough screaming, Anneth," said Mum. "We can hear you just fine through the door." She turned to Coach. "Don't tell me: the nearest locksmith is forty miles away."

"I'm guessing that would be true," said Coach. "But seeing how this is an emergency, he might come in a day or two."

Another screech from Anneth was followed by loud organ music from the funeral home next door.

Mum groaned. It was a familiar groan. It was the groan she made every time she learned that the thing she needed was forty miles away.

"You folks have a ladder?" Coach asked.

Mum shook her head. "Why?"

Coach smiled broadly. "When God closes a door, He opens . . ."

"A window!" Mum finished. "Of course."

"You'll still need a locksmith to fix the door," Coach pointed out. "But at least this way we can get her out sooner rather than later."

Mum went downstairs to call a locksmith in Ranger, and Coach and Clem left to borrow a ladder. Dylan had disappeared to who-knows-where. Lowen felt weird leaving Anneth all alone, so he sat outside her door and tried to talk to her.

"So . . . what are you doing?"

"Nothing. Just like I've done for the past three weeks," she added. She sounded far away, like she was sitting on her bed. "Because there's absolutely nothing to do here."

He wanted to say, *You could help Mum with the shop,* but he knew better. If Mum's restaurant was a success, Anneth would be trapped in Millville forever.

"What's Megan doing this summer?"

There was a pause and then: "Hanging out at the pool at the Y," Anneth said, her voice sadder.

Lowen didn't really like Megan. She was pushy and opinionated and Anneth always acted differently around her, as though she didn't have any opinions of her own. But his sister obviously missed her. "I'm sorry that you had to leave your best friend," he said, and meant it.

Anneth didn't respond. At least she wasn't yelling at him that this was all his fault.

"You know," said Lowen, "there's an outdoor pool in Millville. It's public."

"What, and just show up?" said Anneth. "Without knowing a soul?" She had moved off her bed and was sitting beside him on the other side of the door. The door rattled when she leaned on it.

She had a point.

"What would Megan do if she were the new one in town?" asked Lowen.

Anneth sighed. "The same thing she's doing right now back home. She'd find a new best friend."

Lowen was almost disappointed when Coach arrived with the ladder. Anneth was talking to him, *really* talking to him. It might have been the first time since the family decided to buy a dollar house. He reluctantly left his post at her door and went around to the back to watch the rescue of Anneth.

He was not alone. After they paid their last respects to the deceased next door, the curious wandered into the Grovers' backyard to see what the screaming had been about.

"Fire?" a man with a mustache kidded.

"The girl's trapped in her bedroom," said Mrs. Manzo, who had come bustling out of the house next door and stood as if she had a supervisory position.

Lowen stood with Mum near the base of the ladder.

Clem walked over to him and draped his arm over Lowen's shoulder.

"Hey, Shrimp," he said.

"Hey," said Lowen.

"Welcome to the Grover Family Circus," Clem muttered, and for a moment Lowen felt like his brother's confidant. Yes, their family might appear weird, but it was *their* family. Lowen searched his brain for something witty to say in response, but before anything came to mind (as if anything clever *would* come to mind), he spotted a group of older girls standing on the other side of the lawn, watching Clem.

Oh. So Clem's arm around him was part of the show. Still, it felt nice.

"Come out the window backward," instructed Coach, who had gone up the ladder to guide Anneth.

Clem moved over to help Lowen hold the ladder, keeping it steady.

"My legs are shaking!" Anneth shouted, and Lowen wished he could help her. He knew that she would be entirely mortified when she reached the bottom and turned around to face the crowd that was forming.

Fortunately, she didn't have to face the crowd all alone. The minute her foot touched the ground, two girls her age wobbled over in heels to claim her as their own.

"Your belt is so cool; did you make it?" one of the girls asked.

The other girl grabbed Anneth's hand and examined her nails. "Where did you find mint-green nail polish?" she asked.

Before Coach left, Lowen summoned the courage to speak to him. "Coach, about soccer . . ."

"What's up?" Coach asked.

"Would it be possible to be the scorekeeper for the team or something?"

"I'm afraid not. I really need you to be on the team. Without you, we don't have enough registered players to be in the league."

"Trust me, you don't want me on your team. I don't even know the rules!"

Coach adjusted the brim of his baseball cap. "You know, other cities sell houses for a dollar, but they don't require that families have three kids. We do. And you know why? So we can keep our school open and our sports teams running—and, hopefully, winning. I voted for your family over all of the other applicants because I knew you kids could help us do that."

Lowen nodded, trying to remember any question on the application that suggested he could do such a thing. And then he remembered a section that asked about their family's interests. Mum had given consideration to all of their interests and had listed "sports." What she didn't say was that Clem played sports, Anneth liked running in gym, and the rest of them watched Clem. He tried to think of what to say without sounding as if Mum had lied.

"We have to work as a team, Lowen. You need to give it your best try." Coach called Clem over. "Clem, I'd like you to help me," he said.

"Sure, Coach. What do you need?" Lowen could tell that Clem really liked Coach. That he wanted to come through for him.

"I want you to teach your brother to play soccer."

"Lowen?"

"Do you have another brother?" Coach asked.

"Anneth's not so bad," Clem said.

"I promised her the last spot on cross-country. It's Lowen I want you to focus some extra time on."

"Sure thing, Coach," he said. Thought bubble above Clem's head: *This stinks.*

That evening, they sat at the small kitchen table while Mum cooked and Anneth retold the experience of descending the ladder. "Wait till I tell Megan!"

"Mrs. Grover?" It was Dylan. He'd been standing nearby as usual, offering to be Mum's taste-tester, listening but not saying a word. He pointed to the glass doorknob that the locksmith, who arrived hours after Anneth's rescue, had replaced. "Do you mind if I keep that?"

Mum laughed. "Of course not. Consider it yours."

"Thanks, Mrs. Grover," he said. He grabbed the knob and sprinted out the door.

Clem raised his eyebrows at Lowen—another rare moment of solidarity.

The moment made Lowen feel a little better about Clem's reaction to Coach. "Clem," he said, "can we play some soccer after dinner?"

"Sorry, dude," Clem said, leaning back so his chair balanced on two legs. He only called Lowen "dude" when he was trying to get him to do—or in this case not to do—something. "I've got plans."

"Clem, I'm sure you could help your brother out," Mum said. "Give him some tips."

Clem dropped his chair back to the floor. "Ask Dylan," snapped Clem. "He'll teach you." And with that, Clem left to go upstairs. "Clem!" Mum shouted after him.

"Forget it," Lowen said.

"You could look at videos online," suggested Anneth. "You can learn anything online."

Lowen gave her a weak smile. A minute ago he couldn't wait for supper. Now he had lost his appetite.

Sure, Clem didn't spend time with him very often, but he always assumed that it was because he was busy with homework and sports and stuff. It never occurred to Lowen that his brother didn't like hanging out with him.

"I'll talk to him," said Mum.

"No, don't," Lowen said adamantly. The last thing he needed was for Clem to start calling him Prince Lowen as well.

And as it turned out, Anneth was right: there were tons of videos on how to play soccer. There were videos that taught the techniques of dribbling, passing, and running. There were videos that taught the responsibilities of the positions and the rules. Sure, there were times when Lowen got sidetracked by videos on how to draw a soccer player in action, but for the most part he was learning the game. With each video he watched, he felt faster, smarter, more graceful.

He couldn't wait to show Clem just how good he could be.

11.

MID-AUGUST

After food processors and a warming tray had been purchased . . . after the plumbing was turned on, repaired, and turned on again (a process that took almost two weeks) . . . after the building inspector and the food inspector had given Mum the go-ahead . . . opening day for the Cornish Eatery was set for August 13.

The entire Grover family would need to work at the shop until Mum had a sense of how many pasties she would need to make each day. If there turned out to be an enormous demand for the meat pies, Mum would try to hire someone in town to help out—hopefully Rena. (The bank had refused Rena the loan for her pet-grooming/clothing store. As Sami told it, the bank manager had said, "Ms. Doshi, if you're going to establish a successful business, you have to understand people in these parts. None of us would be caught dead putting a coat on our dog or cat—especially during these hard times.")

So now Rena was trying to come up with a new way to make a living.

Things seemed to be moving along swimmingly by opening day.

Clem was using the food processors to mix extra pasty dough. Anneth was rolling dough into flats and placing them into the refrigerator to chill. Lowen and Sami, who was often at the shop when her mother was, too, were cutting potatoes and onions for the filling. Dad was cutting the steak and moving cooked pasties from the oven to the warmer. Mum was layering new meat pies: onion, potato, meat; and Rena (being a vegetarian—all the Doshis were) was layering vegetarian pies: onion, potato, carrot, and mushroom. Then both women crimped the edges and popped the pasties into the oven. The whole room smelled of buttery piecrust and roasted onions.

Sami, as directed, propped open the front door to let some of the heat—and the delicious aroma of the pasties—escape. "Whoa," she said. "Why is there such a long line at the Busy Bee?"

Mum, who was adjusting the drink selections in the glass cooler (not that they needed any adjusting), said, "Go check it out, Lowen, and report back." Lowen finished up writing the definition of *pasty* on their chalkboard, then slid off his chair and walked out front. Sami followed.

Just like Sami said, there was a long line of Millvillians outside the Busy Bee. Some, like Mr. Avery and the plumber who had worked on the shop, Lowen recognized. Others he didn't.

It didn't make sense. Sure, there was often a crowd of people early in the morning. The quilters, the Knights, the bird-watchers, the town council, and the poets all chose to have their meetings over breakfast at the Busy Bee. They often popped their heads into Mum's shop to see how she was progressing, and most seemed excited about the new lunch shop opening soon.

But the Busy Bee closed at 10:30 a.m. It was nearly 11:00 now.

Sami pointed to a standing sign next to the long line. It read, THE BUSY BEE NOW SERVES LUNCH. FREE MACARONI AND CHEESE TODAY!

Lowen quickly turned so no one in line could see his reaction. He ran back into their shop, shut the door behind him, and exploded: "They're serving lunch now!"

"And offering free food," Sami added. "*Comfort* food."

Everyone huddled around Mum, who slowly collapsed into one of the two chairs around the table in front.

"It doesn't make sense," Rena said.

Mum shook her head as if to shake away a bad dream. "Why would Mrs. Corbeau do this?"

"The scarcity principle," said Sami.

Everyone turned to look at her.

"The what?" asked Anneth.

"The scarcity principle. It brings out competition. Mrs. Corbeau likely believes that there is a limited number of dollars that can be spent on eating out in this town. She's afraid that you'll take money from her. Therefore, she's going to compete with you directly by offering lunch."

Clem looked at Sami.

"Online psychology class," she said.

"Sure," said Rena bitterly. "They want families to move into Millville so *they* can make a living, so *they* can keep their school and their sports teams running, so *they* can look out their windows and see something prettier than the foreclosed houses. But how do they think this is going to work if they won't help *us* make a living, too?"

"I'll go next door and talk to them," Dad said.

"No, don't, Weaver. It's up to me to show them that this little town will be better off if we have two good restaurants."

"How are you going to do that?" asked Lowen.

"I don't know," Mum said, getting to her feet. "But the first step is to serve the bloody best pasties we can make!"

* * *

During the first two hours, the other new families popped in to congratulate the Grovers and to celebrate the opening. Even though the Cornish Eatery was technically a take-out shop, and there was only one table in the front, everyone ate their first pasties on the premises, making the opening feel more like a party. Some of the little kids sat right down on the floor.

The Greys, who thoughtfully brought an extra oscillating fan to counter the rising summer temperatures, raved about the pies. "I'll have to find a way to sneak out during my lunch break to stock up on these pasty pies," Mr. Grey said. Mr. Grey was actually Dr. Grey—a veterinarian—and he planned to open a veterinary office in town. When Rena told him about her failed business plan, Dr. Grey suggested she try selling some of her wares in his office.

Kate Kelling brought the toddlers and Mason. Eden had already started her job as a seaplane pilot, flying fishermen into the more remote lakes. "But I'll take one of these meat pasties to go," Kate said, wiping one of the twin's faces with a napkin. "Eden will love it!" After eating two pasties, Mason convinced Clem to go off with him to play in a pickup soccer game.

Lowen hoped Clem had noticed all the effort he was putting into watching videos and would invite him—but that didn't happen.

That's OK, thought Lowen. Because the only new family that hadn't arrived yet was the Muñoz family, and if Luna showed up and Clem wasn't around, well, that was certainly all right with him.

Unfortunately that didn't happen either. Only Mr. Muñoz (who was a freelance journalist) and the other two kids (Mateo and Diego) came in. After Mum told them that pasties are even better reheated the next day, they bought a half dozen to go.

Despite the unexpected competition from the Busy Bee, opening day was lively, and celebratory, and fun.

The second day was different.

The food was prepared, the restaurant was prepped, but then the Grovers waited.

And waited.

And waited.

Mum wiped the counters over and over again. Anneth checked the napkin holders, but they were still quite full. Lowen swept the floor while sweat rolled down his back, despite the stale breeze provided by the fan.

Only one customer came that afternoon, and that was Dylan. He showed up a half hour before closing and paid for his pasty in nickels. All nickels. Then he sat at the table and scarfed down his pasty, telling Mum that her pie was the best food he'd ever tasted. "And my gram was a good cook," he added.

By that time, the embarrassment of having no other customers, of having stood around for so long and watched first concern and then feelings of rejection grow in his mother's eyes, made Lowen irritable. So did Dylan's method of payment. Obviously Dylan was using his hard-earned money. His generosity should have made Lowen feel warmly toward him. But it didn't. If possible, Lowen felt even more wary of this kid.

12.

TWO DAYS LATER . . .

On the third day, two Millville girls came by the restaurant. They were the same girls who had stood at the base of the ladder when Anneth had been trapped. Mum tied her apron tighter, thinking that they had come for pasties, but it turned out that they had come to say hi to Anneth and show her their green nail polish.

"Corrine found it online," said one.

Corrine held her hand out to compare the color of her nails to Anneth's. "Yours is prettier," she said.

"I mixed this color myself," said Anneth.

"I didn't know you could do that!" said Corrine.

"Yeah, mixing makes some awesome colors. But your color is cool, too."

That was the sort of thing that Anneth would say to Megan even if it weren't true, thought Lowen as he tried to give the impression that he (and the Cornish Eatery) was incredibly busy.

"It's OK," said Corrine, "but you're the trendsetter."

Anneth laughed. And just like that they were admiring Anneth's DIY headband, and the bow she'd attached to her T-shirt, and then the two girls were pulling Anneth out of the shop and off to Dollar Mart to see if the store carried anything they could use to upstyle their tired wardrobes.

Mum sighed, and then, noticing Lowen noticing her, put on her hopeful face.

Unfortunately, hope didn't help. The only other person to enter the shop that afternoon was Sami, who came to see if Lowen wanted to go to the pool with her.

The *No* was out of Lowen's mouth before Sami could finish her sentence.

"I insist!" Mum said to Lowen. "It's summer. You should be outside."

Being sought out by Sami made him nervous. He wanted to say, *Look, you don't get it. I'm a lousy friend. No, make that a* dangerous *friend.*

But it seemed like staying in the empty shop with Mum would only make it worse for her. If he left, she could stop faking cheeriness.

So, twenty minutes later, he and Sami were standing outside the chain-link fence at the town pool, towels in hand.

"Sorry, kids," the lifeguard said as they tried to unlatch the gate. "It's adult swim right now."

Lowen groaned. "It figures that adults would get the hottest time of the day," he grumbled to Sami as they ambled away.

She was quiet for a moment. Then her face brightened. "Want to swim in the river?" she asked.

Lowen wasn't sure . . . but he was hotter than Hades, and he didn't want to return to the shop. He nodded.

As they approached the mill, Sami told him that the company that owned the buildings planned to tear them down. "That will be sad for the people who still think it's going to make paper again."

He thought of asking her why she was so sure that it wouldn't make paper again, but it was too hot even for talking.

After finding a hole in the chain-link fence that surrounded the mill buildings and crossing the rusty train tracks that had once led trains to Millville twice a day (according to the video they'd seen), they found a spot where a tiny trail led them through tall grass down to the water.

There was a bit of foam floating on the river's surface.

"Do you think it's polluted?" asked Sami.

Lowen watched the flowing water. Perhaps it was just the small waves that caused the foam. He took a tentative step forward.

"I wouldn't if I were you."

Lowen jumped a mile.

It was Dylan, standing on the incline, a few feet behind them.

"Dylan! You scared us!" cried Sami. "What are you doing here?"

"Did you follow us here?" Lowen didn't even bother to keep the irritation out of his voice.

"I didn't know the two of you wanted to be alone."

Lowen rolled his eyes. "Do you even have your swim-suit on?"

"No, but—"

"Well, I'm going in," Lowen said. "I can't stand this heat any longer."

"There are eddies," said Dylan.

What was an eddy? A fish? An eel? "Are they close to the shore?" Lowen asked.

"Probably not," said Dylan.

"Then it should be fine." Lowen peeled off his T-shirt, kicked off his flip-flops, and waded into the swollen river. The water was cold, but refreshing, and he tried not to think of all the chemicals the mill might have poured into it in days past. Or eddies, whatever the heck they were.

Waist high in the water, Lowen called out to Sami, "It feels good! Come on in." And then he wished he hadn't said that. For all he knew, he was coaxing her into a dangerous situation. What was it about him, anyway?

Before Sami could respond, a deep voice shouted, "Get out of the river right now!"

They looked back up the hill.

Mr. Avery was hobbling down the path.

Mr. Avery's command frightened Lowen, but he struggled to get back to shore as the river's currents worked against him.

"What in tarnation do you three think you're doing down there?" Mr. Avery asked when he reached the shore.

"It's so hot, and we . . . I thought it would be OK," said Lowen as he crawled up onto the bank.

"Oh, you did, did you? Do you happen to know that Millville taxpayers support a swimming pool just so you kids can cool off on a hot day?"

"It's adult swim," Lowen said.

Mr. Avery shook his head. "Have you taken the time to learn anything about this town? Have you gone on the website? Learned a little history? Checked out the pool hours to find out the best time for you to swim?"

He turned to Dylan. "And what about you? You know the risks of swimming in this river. The eddies. The sunken logs." He shook his head. "You're more like your father every day. I should have guessed you'd follow these two no-goods."

Lowen waited for Dylan to defend himself, to say that he tried to warn them, but he didn't. Instead he looked down, held in his visible anger.

Both Lowen and Sami started to come to his defense. "He wasn't—" But Dylan didn't wait to be defended. He was already racing back up the hill.

"Go on," Mr. Avery said, using his whole arm to signal them back up the hill. "You two get out of here as well."

While trudging home—still hot, but now with thighs chafing from his wet bathing suit—Lowen could've sworn that someone was following him. Twice he snapped around quickly, but there was no one there. *Abe,* he thought, which, despite the heat, gave him the shivers.

Maybe that's why when he saw Ms. Duffey, the town councillor and librarian, digging a hole in her backyard, he thought, *Something died.* He didn't think she had murdered anyone or anything, but he did think perhaps she was digging a grave for a pet. He stopped by a tree to watch her, assuming he was being inconspicuous.

"If you're going to stand there and watch, Lowen Grover, you might as well come over here and help me," she said, startling him.

He obeyed and climbed over her split-rail fence into her small backyard. "What are you burying?" he asked.

"Now, what makes you think I'm burying something?"

Lowen shrugged. "I guess I can't think of another reason for digging a hole."

"Around here we also dig holes for planting, but it's not planting season."

Ms. Duffey handed Lowen the shovel. "Now, if you don't mind," she said, "I could use some help burying some regrets."

Lowen took the shovel and tried to drive it into the packed ground to make the hole deeper. What kind of regrets can you bury? A torn library book? An unanswered letter?

He was about to ask, *How big are these regrets?* when he saw two tanned boys meandering down the road wearing T-shirts, shorts, and flip-flops. One was bouncing an empty Coke bottle—the liter size—on the back of his neck and shoulders. *Whump, whump, whump.* The other said something, and the first playfully bopped him until he accidently dropped the bottle, and the two immediately moved into a kicking game that resembled soccer.

The bottle flew into Ms. Duffey's yard, nearly hitting the tomatoes growing in a nearby vegetable patch.

"Hello, Joey Larsen," said Ms. Duffey as the boy bounded after it.

"Hi," he said shyly, but the whole time he was staring at Lowen standing there in his wet swim trunks, digging a hole in the librarian's back lawn.

"Have you two met?" asked Ms. Duffey, and when both Lowen and Joey shook their heads, she called the other kid over and introduced the three of them. The second boy's name was Kyle Jacques.

"You'll all be in the same class," she explained to Lowen. "In fact," she said, "the three of you and Dylan Firebrand will make up *all* the boys in your class. Did you ever think you'd be in a class of eight students, Lowen?"

Lowen tried to keep the shock from showing on his face. *Eight students?* Suddenly his dreams of disappearing into the crowd went up in smoke.

Before Lowen could say anything, Joey spouted, "Nice to meet you," and he and Kyle raced off.

So there it was. Lowen had met other Millville boys his own age, and they hadn't seemed interested in him at all. Nor, Lowen guessed, did they care much for Dylan Firebrand. Seeing the boys jog off together gave Lowen a peculiar pang of loneliness. It was one thing to decide when to hang out with others, another to be ignored.

He finished digging the hole, said good-bye to Ms. Duffey, and was nearly home before he realized that he'd never found out what she was burying.

13.

THAT EVENING . . .

The loneliness he felt after seeing the boys continued right through dinner. Dad had already boarded the bus to return to Flintlock. Clem was full of talk about the high-school soccer preseason that would begin the next day (middle-school practices didn't happen until September), and Anneth was blabbing on about her new friends and her idea of starting her own YouTube channel, where she would talk about fashion. Apparently, she had wanted to start one in Flintlock but Megan had discouraged her. *First of all, you have to be someone who sets trends,* Megan had said, *not follows them. Secondly, all the best teen fashionistas are connected with fashion designers who send them free stuff.*

"Didn't you point out that the fashion designers find the girls because they have YouTube channels?" asked Mum.

"I was going to, but I didn't think I had a unique perspective," said Anneth. "But I do now. I'm going to talk about making fashion in a town where there are no department stores—and not even any fabric stores. I'm going to talk about making fashion from nothing."

"That's ambitious!" said Mum. "You might see if there's an old sewing machine at the antique store. I'm not sure if sewing machines qualify as antiques yet, but that store seems to carry a little bit of everything."

"Everything that doesn't land on our lawn," Clem said with a glint in his eye.

"Mum." Anneth hesitated. "What about our allowance? We haven't gotten one since we moved here. I'm not sure I have enough money saved for a machine."

Though she hardly stirred, anxiety crept around Mum's eyes. Sure Mum and Dad had savings—that's what allowed the shop to get up and running. But they had counted on the shop getting off to a good start. The opening days of a restaurant are supposed to be the busiest, but she had had no customers other than the other Dollar Families and Dylan.

"It's OK, Mum. I can wait for my birthday money. Or I could get a job," Anneth said.

"Me too," Clem said.

"Me three," Lowen said.

"You kids make me proud," Mum said. "But we'll figure something out. I was counting on small-town curiosity to get the eatery off the ground, but perhaps I need a marketing plan." Her smile was reassuring.

After Clem had excused himself to hang out with his buds, and after Anneth had excused herself to Skype with Megan (who hadn't shown up for their last scheduled call), Lowen announced that he was going to practice his soccer skills.

"Where will you practice?" Mum asked.

"In the parking lot out back."

"Be careful." She never used to say that pre-shooting.

Lowen retrieved Clem's soccer ball from the crowded garage. He hoped that Clem wouldn't be mad at him for using it without permission.

In the empty parking lot, he placed the ball down and practiced dribbling. He had watched enough videos to know that he had to concentrate on far more than his feet. His arms needed to be pumping, his back needed to be straight (though leaning forward slightly), and his knees were to come up in the air. He found that it was much harder than it looked. The first time he tried it, he felt like an uncoordinated marching-band leader. And he hardly moved the ball any distance at all. In fact, he tripped over it twice. He looked around to make sure no one had seen him. There was no one on the streets, but he didn't doubt that people were looking out their windows wondering what in the world he was trying to do. It seemed as if Millvillians were always investigating.

He decided to concentrate on the feet alone for a few minutes, focusing on moving the ball with his laces (as advised) except when turning. This took a little bit of coordination, and the laces on his skate shoes were long. It occurred to him that he would need cleats if he were to play properly, and he wondered how to broach the subject with his mother.

Surprisingly, when he took his thoughts off his feet for a moment, he actually did a little better, gained a little momentum. He dribbled, dribbled, tried a turn (that didn't work so well), dribbled, and kicked!

Yes! The contact was good. The ball flew into the air, bounced on the edge of the parking lot, and popped into the open garage of Field's Funeral Home . . . where a large black car, the hearse, was parked.

Lowen waited a moment, hoping that Mr. Field was in the garage, that he was just about to shut the door when the ball came bouncing inside. Perhaps he would be angry with Lowen, telling him to be more careful, to have some respect for the dead. But Lowen wouldn't care. He'd say that he was sorry, thank Mr. Field for handing him back his ball, and hightail it out of there.

But no one came out. No one but Lowen appeared to know that the ball was inside.

Clem's ball.

The snake's mouth was open. If snakes could laugh, that's what the one inside was doing right now, rising up with its beady eyes to emit an evil cackle, as if Lowen didn't stand a chance.

Lowen edged closer. In the front of the garage was an enormous, gleaming box that appeared to be a refrigerator. It probably *was* a refrigerator. It had to be the place where the bodies were stored.

Lowen crouched and then got down on his belly to see if he could spot the ball inside the garage. There it was! Under the hearse, up against the left front tire. Lowen was going to have to get awfully close to the car. He worried about the door of the refrigerator (freezer?) suddenly opening, or the garage door suddenly closing. He didn't know which would be worse.

What he did know was that if he didn't get Clem's ball, his family would be looking at his dead body at Field's. *Just pretend it's any old garage,* he told himself. *Just pretend it's any old car with any old tire.*

He walked forward, leaned over, picked up the ball, and turned to run out. But his feet felt frozen to the ground.

Unable to stop himself, he peeked into the curtained window of the hearse.

Withholding a scream, he raced out, back through the parking lot, and into his own backyard.

He'd looked into the hearse, all right.

And his own reflection had stared back at him.

Lowen was too upset to go back into the house. He tucked Clem's ball back into the garage and headed up the street. He walked past Millville Central School to the town pool, where the lifeguard had just blown his whistle: end of family swim. Lowen could see Sami, her sisters, and Rena getting out of the water at the deep end. Sami must have looked up the hours online after all.

He walked farther down the road to the soccer field. Clem was just arriving with some buds for a pickup game.

"Do you want to play?" asked the kid carrying the soccer ball, who seemed about Clem's age.

Lowen glanced at Clem.

Clem's thought bubble: *NO. Absolutely not.*

Lowen shook his head and said he just wanted to watch, and it was true. He knew he wasn't ready.

"He hasn't played much," said Clem, confirming Lowen's decision.

"Well, let us know if you change your mind," the boy said, and ran onto the field with the others.

Lowen imagined himself running up and down the field, pumping his arms in quick spurts the way the video had demonstrated. He wasn't a bad runner. He and Abe often raced home from school. He liked the feeling of movement, the feeling of eating up the sidewalk. He liked how racing allowed him a chance to be with Abe, but not be with Abe. Running allowed him time in his own world.

Abe was smaller, and younger, but he was fast. Every day he came closer and closer to legitimately beating Lowen.

Now he never would.

"Pick up your feet!" a man yelled.

A group of adults had congregated on the side of the field, diagonally across from him. They were hanging out in their sunglasses. Some had dogs at their feet. Some were holding drinks in cans.

"Looking good!" a woman called.

"Turn it. Now! Turn it!" yelled a familiar voice. Mr. Avery's. Dylan was in the game. He had control of the ball and was moving down the field. He paused, looked around, searched for a teammate.

"Fire! Don't pass again. Fire!" shouted Mr. Avery, but Dylan turned the ball—with a lot more finesse than

Lowen had come close to achieving—and backed it up a bit.

"What are you doing, Firebrand? Get up there!" shouted Mr. Avery.

Dylan stopped searching. He turned away from the goal and kicked the ball as hard as he could out of bounds. Then he jogged away. Just like that.

Mr. Avery shook his head. Lowen couldn't be sure what he said, but it was loud and sounded like "just like his mother."

A woman in the crowd gave Dylan's grandfather a sympathetic pat on the back.

Lowen didn't know what to feel. Just like the river, this town had unseen currents. A lot was happening beneath its still surface. Lowen walked off in the opposite direction from Dylan.

The sun was setting when he passed the school on his way home. And there it was: the sound of Luna's cello. There was no doubt in his mind that it was her playing.

The windows were too high to peek in, but he had to get a glimpse. He climbed the wall behind the school, hoping it would give him a view into the lit classroom. It did.

Luna.

There she was, with her teacher, both of them playing, no doubt lost in the passion of the music. Lowen was too far away to see her face, but he could imagine it: eyes closed, chin jutted. Intensely focused, while at the same time lost in a rippling stream of feeling.

Lowen came back down from the wall and sat under the lit window, his back against the building. The music rose and fell, capturing everything he'd felt that day: the empty space at the restaurant, the cool river flowing over his toes, the punch of Mr. Avery's anger, Ms. Duffey's buried regrets, the lack of interest from the other boys in his class, losing Clem's ball, fleeting thoughts of Abe . . . He thought of a snake charmer playing music to hypnotize a snake. But Luna's music didn't just mesmerize the snake inside him; it lulled it to sleep. He breathed deeply.

The piece ended. Lowen pulled himself up and headed for home.

14.

LATE AUGUST

Before the month was over, Mrs. Grey dropped by the Albatross to ask if Anneth and Lowen would be willing to babysit. Dr. Grey had scheduled a visit to another rural vet clinic, and she was going to drive her father to the airport. (Apparently he had been staying with them only temporarily, to help out as they settled in.) The day would be long, which is why she thought it might be better if the two of them did it together. Anneth wanted the sewing machine, and if Coach was really serious about Lowen needing to be on the soccer team, then Lowen needed cleats. Both said yes.

The first few hours went quickly. The day was sunny but pleasantly cool, and there was no end to the games that Lagi, Lily, and Wanda wanted to play in the park across the street: Hide-and-Go-Seek; Mother, May I?; Freeze Tag; Duck, Duck, Goose (Lagi's favorite); and Red Light, Green Light. By noon, the three Greys were still raring to go, but Lowen was worn out. He collapsed onto the newly cut grass, where Lagi proceeded to turn him into a pillow.

"What do you see in the clouds?" Lowen asked.

"A cheeseburger," Lagi said. "And French fries."

Lowen laughed. Clearly, it was time for lunch.

He dutifully pulled himself up and held Lagi's hand as they crossed Maple Street, Anneth and the girls behind them. As they entered the living room, Lily ran over and turned on the TV. She and Lagi plunked themselves down on the rug on the newly varnished wooden floor. "This room looks great," Anneth said to Wanda, who was following them into the kitchen.

Lowen agreed. He remembered the filthy green carpet that had been there the day of the lottery. Recalling other unpleasant aspects of this house, he held his breath as they entered the kitchen.

"Whoa," Anneth said as she turned the corner. "You have a new kitchen, Wanda!" The once pink cabinets were now gleaming white. The countertops, appliances, faucet, and flooring were all brand-new.

"Yeah. What a pain!" Wanda said. "The workers have been banging like crazy! My grandfather couldn't wait to go back to Honolulu for the peace and quiet."

Lowen ran his hand along the smooth, stony kitchen counter. There wasn't a trace of the pink lady and her cupcakes. It was as if she had never existed.

After helping Anneth and Lowen find the peanut

butter and jelly, Wanda drifted back into the living room.

"Do you think the Greys are rich?" Lowen asked in a low voice.

"Richer than we are," said Anneth. "But maybe they *had* to repair their kitchen to meet the requirements."

Lowen sighed. "It makes me feel way behind on our house."

Anneth agreed. "But we'll do work on the house when Mum and Dad aren't so busy with Mum's shop."

After Lagi's nap, they decided to head to the playground. But they weren't the only ones who had decided to hang out there. Clem and his buds were goofing around on the rec equipment. Mason and a group of boys and girls were camped out on the merry-go-round. (And Lowen had thought *he* was too old.) They were seated between the animals and using their feet to twirl themselves around, though their movement was more of a jolt, jolt, jolt than a whirl.

"Don't get too dirty," Anneth said to the Grey kids in a too-loud voice that annoyed Lowen. He knew she was trying to make it clear that she wasn't just hanging out with little kids—that she was working. But at the same time, it sounded as though she were babysitting him, too. He tried to think of some order he could give the Greys, but since they were just standing there, watching the older kids, he had nothing.

144

Clem stood at the base of the slide with two Millville kids — a guy and a girl. All three kids held cans of soda.

"Catch me, Clem!"

Lowen looked up. There, at the top of the slide, sat Luna. She was wearing shorts and some sort of top that looked floaty. He imagined himself at the base of the slide with outstretched arms.

"Aren't you worried about hurting your bow hand?" the other boy asked.

"What? And never do anything?" she snapped back.

Clem smiled. "I've got a better idea," he said. He ran up the ladder and sat down behind Luna. "Ready?" he asked.

They pushed forward — but didn't go very far. The slide had lost all its luster. Instead of providing a slick surface, the weathered sheet of tin offered only friction.

They laughed as they inched their way down.

Anneth laughed, too.

That's when Clem glanced up and saw them. With a small, almost undetectable look he suggested to his buds that they move on.

Lowen went from feeling totally self-conscious to feeling shunned. He could tell that Anneth was feeling disappointed, too. Ever since she was a little kid she'd wanted to tag along with Clem and his friends.

With Luna at his side, Clem walked right by Lowen and didn't say a word. Not one.

But he did slip him his can of soda.

Cool!

Lowen hid the can behind his thigh, then walked toward the picnic table. The Grey kids raced toward the equipment and called out for Lowen to join them.

"In a minute!" he shouted. He snuck sips of soda. What was it about the bubbles, the caramel-y sweetness, that made it taste so welcome on a hot day?

The kids came running over, begging him to join in their swing game.

Knowing he was caught, he tilted the can to his lips and gulped the final drops.

"Where did you get that?" Lily asked.

There had been something in the can, something solid. Now it was in his mouth. Something vibrating. Something alive.

Lowen jumped up and spat, projecting whatever it was onto the picnic table.

"A bee!" cried Wanda. "You almost swallowed a bee."

"Did it sting you?" Lily cried.

Lowen opened and closed his mouth a few times as if to try it out. He hadn't been stung. He'd had a bee inside his mouth and he hadn't been stung.

He looked down at the wet insect on the table.

Lagi leaned over, too.

"Stay away from it, Lagi!" cried Wanda. "It will hurt you."

The bee was pinned on its back, its wet wings stuck to the surface of the table. Tiny, spindly legs pedaled the air, trying to gain traction.

"Kill it!" Lily said. "Quick, kill it!"

"No, don't!" Lowen cried. The legs started to slow down, but still the bee hadn't turned over. Feeling a rising panic, Lowen looked for some scrap of paper, a bit of foil. His eyes landed on a twig. A twig would do it.

He hovered the stick just above the bee's legs. The bee grabbed on to it and Lowen slowly lifted it off the table.

The kids screamed and backed away.

The bee flew.

As Mrs. Grey had warned, the day had been long. By the time she returned, both Anneth and Lowen had run out of ideas for entertaining the kids. But she paid them in cash, and when Anneth suggested they go to Dollar Mart before heading back to the Albatross, Lowen agreed. It would be fun to buy a small treat with the money. He chose Doritos.

He was already munching on them when they turned the corner to head up Maple. Three older boys that Lowen didn't recognize called out loudly:

"Hey, got a dollar?"

"Yeah, I could really use a dollar."

Lowen's heart beat faster. He put his hand in his pocket and wrapped it around the bills Mrs. Grey had just given him.

"If I had a dollar, I could buy a house."

He exhaled. The boys weren't out to mug him.

"Then I could spend the rest of my money on Doritos," said one of the kids, cracking them all up.

"Dipheads," Anneth mumbled as they climbed the hill, pretending to be deaf.

Lowen didn't know what else to say. They'd just been ambushed. Back in Flintlock, when they told other kids they were buying a house for a dollar, everyone thought that was so cool—that Lowen had been so smart to see the announcement in the magazine. But here in Millville, lots of folks seemed to think that the Dollar Families were so poor that they could only afford to pay one dollar for a house. Even though Lowen's family had never been super well-off—Mum had always encouraged them to economize and be smart with money—they'd been comfortable enough, and it felt weird to be treated like a moocher.

When they passed the garbage can at the park, he dropped the rest of the Doritos bag in.

15.

SEPTEMBER

School hardly felt like school. It felt more like the arts day camp Lowen attended at the Flintlock elementary school the summer he was nine. Like then, the Millville Central School halls were mostly empty and echoey. All of the old wooden desks had been washed over the summer, and since most were not in use, the school never lost that wet-wood and disinfectant smell. There was only one classroom for each grade, but since the teachers could pick the classroom they wanted, kids were spread out all over the building. Lowen's classroom was the farthest from the entry to the middle-school wing—his teacher, Mrs. Kachanowski, explained that she wanted a room that received sunlight in the early morning only.

Ms. Duffey had been correct: there were eight kids in his class—four boys and four girls—whose desks formed a semicircle at the front of the room. He and Sami were the only newcomers. And here was the weird thing:

whenever one of their teachers told them to choose a partner, or to pair-share, he ended up with Sami.

"Again?" Lowen said when they buddied up for a brain break on the second day of school. They stood side by side, waiting for instructions. "Don't get me wrong," he said quickly. "I just figured I'd be paired with Dylan."

Sami nodded. "I'd predicted the same thing. And I figured I'd be with whichever girl was on the outs with Taylor, who is clearly the alpha girl. But Amber nabbed Dylan instead." She shrugged. "Tribal impulse, I suppose."

Lowen raised his eyebrows. "You and I are from a different tribe from the others?"

Sami nodded. She had a resigned look on her face. "There are the *Millvillians* and then there are the *Dollar Kids*."

The same segregation happened at lunch. Because the school was so small, elementary and middle school ate together, but the Millville kids sat with the kids they'd known all their lives. They joked about Fourth of July parties, and snow days, and the time that practically the whole town had come down with the flu together.

That left one table for the Dollar Kids. While Diego Muñoz and Lily Grey entertained the table with silly stories, Lowen and Sami ate the food the younger kids refused to eat. Sometimes Dylan would pop over to their table for a moment and grab one of Meera's discarded sandwiches. "Hey!" Meera yelled every time, but they could tell she loved it. She probably left food just so Dylan would steal from her. Other than Dylan's sandwich stealing, though, no one crossed the Millville / Dollar Kid line—except Anneth. She sat between Corrine and Ruby, the two Millville girls who had befriended her after she'd been rescued from her room.

Sami was jealous of Anneth's ability to join in. She spent half the time glancing over at the Millville kids.

"Did you have lots of friends in your old school?" Lily asked Sami.

Sami sighed. "Not really. I didn't fit in very well. I guess I thought Millville would be different." And then, under her breath to Lowen, she said, "At least here, though, they think we're *all* bizarro."

Lowen nodded, surprised by his own longing to be on the other side of the room. He wasn't sure that he wanted to be friends with Joey and Kyle—and certainly not with Dylan—but he didn't like being excluded, either. He realized that in the past, his drawing had been his superpower, his ticket to acceptance. Kids admired it. Without it, he didn't have anything to offer. No cool juice at all.

Not only that, but the longer he and Sami were pushed aside, the more she counted on his friendship. And the more she looked to him for support, the more he felt like a poser. *Again.*

The same week school started, Lowen had his first soccer practice. It was one of those strikingly beautiful fall days; the sky was somewhere between cornflower and cobalt blue, and a light breeze carried the scent of sun-dried grass. Lowen, in a pair of Clem's hand-me-down shorts, congregated with the other boys on the soccer sidelines.

The middle-school team included kids in sixth, seventh, and eighth grades. A few of the eighth-graders seemed to be pointing Lowen out. One of them he recognized from that day he and Anneth were taunted coming home from Dollar Mart. He couldn't tell if they were making fun of him now or if they were just remarking on his height. Either way, it made him wish he were anywhere but there.

He tried to remember everything he learned by watching *How to Become Great at Soccer* fourteen times and practicing that one time in the parking lot, and hoped that his brain and muscles would cooperate. Perhaps he'd discover that he wasn't half bad after all.

Coach divided all of the kids into two teams, and Lowen put on a blue pinny as directed. It didn't take long on the field before he realized that it's one thing to dribble and kick a ball by yourself, and another thing entirely to race up and down a field for forty minutes with twelve other kids who are showing off their stopping, tapping, dribbling, juggling, passing, and power-shooting skills.

At one point the ball came at him with the speed of a bullet. By the time he registered its approach and got himself in position to kick it, it was stolen by an opposing player.

"Pass it to Grover again," Coach called.

The kid gave the ball one bounce, and then, after a couple of taps, dutifully kicked it in Lowen's direction.

As Lowen dashed toward the ball, a memory flashed: he and Abe racing home from the elm tree. As usual, he'd given Abe a twenty-count head start and then bolted. But when he turned the corner onto the street where they lived, Abe was nowhere in sight. Had he fallen? Hurt himself? How had he missed him? Lowen had turned and started to jog back toward school when he heard a gleeful "Ha! Ha!" Turning back around, he saw Abe sprinting, way ahead. He must have hidden behind a tree. *Cheeky kid,* as his mother would say.

"Grover!" Coach yelled.

An eighth-grader with red cleats had stolen the ball.

Coach blew his whistle. "Pass it to Grover. Again."

The eighth-grader rolled his eyes and passed the ball in Lowen's direction.

Lowen shook his head. *Concentrate!* This time, he ran at the ball, turned his foot in, and kicked with as much force as he could muster. As Lowen's foot flew up, slicing the sky, the rest of him followed: a rapid ascent, and a faster landing.

He had only one thought before he hit the ground: he had completely missed the ball.

Lowen opened his eyes to clouds, his ears ringing. Unfortunately, the clouds were quickly replaced by concerned faces that wanted to know if he was OK.

Hands were held out to help him up, but Lowen didn't take them. Instead, he rolled over and pulled himself to standing. As was typical in this town, adults who didn't work all the time had begun to gather on the sidelines. They applauded when he stood.

Which made him feel doubly ridiculous.

Coach motioned for him to take a seat on the bench.

That's when he noticed Clem, on the sidelines, surrounded by his buds. His friends were laughing. Clem was not.

When practice ended and the other kids gathered around Coach for a post-practice pep talk, Lowen jogged off the field and planned to keep right on going toward home. No way Coach would make him play now.

"Hey, Grover!" Coach yelled. "Where do you think you're going? Get back here!"

Lowen hesitated. The last thing he wanted to do was go back.

Everyone turned his way, watching, wondering what he was going to do.

The air was still.

Lowen took a breath and jogged back onto the field. He could feel all his frustration and embarrassment pressing against the backs of his eyeballs. Determined not to lose it, and thereby shame his brother further, he closed his ears to Coach. He did what he used to do in boring classes in Flintlock: he imagined the next scenes of his comic book. The limbo sequence with Abe and his killer immediately came to mind.

Limbo.

What would Abe do if he were face-to-face with the kid who shot him?

He'd say something. That's what Abe would do. He wouldn't be able to stop himself. He always had something to say.

But what? *What* would Abe say?

Lowen's lip curled at Abe's wisecracking remark. He couldn't help it. It was exactly the sort of thing Abe would say.

Unfortunately, Lowen's brain wasn't able to come up with anything after that, and so Coach's words started to penetrate.

"You know that I can't make any of you play. It's your choice. But we're counting on everyone. Without you, we don't have a team." Lowen could swear Coach was looking right at him.

"And we need to appreciate anyone who shows up to be part of this team," Coach continued. "If you've played on this team before—or on any team, for that matter—I expect you to help those that are new to the sport."

Lowen didn't need to look around to know that eyes were rolling. And it was the same message: he couldn't quit. If he did, he would jeopardize the program for everyone.

He was completely miserable.

As Lowen dragged himself off the field, Sami, who was as good as any eighth-grader on the team, caught up to him.

"I can help you, you know."

"Huh?"

"We could practice together."

"Thanks, but my brother's offered to teach me," he said.

A total lie, but he was saying it for her own good.

16.

Lowen went directly from the soccer field to the Cornish Eatery. To his dismay, Sami had planned to meet her mother there, so she followed him, all the while telling him about the consignment store her mother was going to open. "We've done the business plan," she said, "and it seems that given the distance of other clothing stores, the price of gas, and the need for folks around here to earn a little extra money—they get money for the clothes they bring in that we sell—it should be a sure bet. My mom wants me to study the psychology of store displays. You know, what kinds of things to put in the front of the store to lure people in, what types of things to put near the cash register to get people to buy more."

Lowen didn't say anything. He didn't need to. Sami carried the conversation all the way to the shop.

"How did it go, love?" Mum asked when he walked through the door. The shop was closed, but Mum always stayed until the end of the workday. She and Rena were sitting at the table, an assortment of pasties spread out in front of them. Sami's sisters were sitting in the front window playing some sort of clapping game.

"Terrible." Lowen chose a juice from the cooler. He grabbed a second drink for Sami.

Mum got up and went over to him, ruffled his hair, and then recited the usual mother stuff about being proud of him and how he'd get better with practice. She led him back to her chair. "You must be famished. Try one of these."

Lowen took a bite of "chicken pot pasty." "It's good . . . really good," he said with a full mouth, and it was true.

"I've noticed," Mum said, "that people around here like things that are, well, *familiar* and fear they won't fancy foreign pasties. So I've decided to make pies that Millvillians have probably tasted before. Here, try this one."

The one Mum handed him was similar to the beef pasty she usually made, but it was made with hamburger rather than chunks of steak. And there was something soft. . . .

"I used ground beef, mashed the potatoes, and added corn."

"Shepherd's pie pasty," Lowen said, smiling.

"Try this one, Sami," said Mum.

Sami took a bite of her individual pie. "Yum!" she said. "It tastes like a sweet potato burrito!"

"Exactly," said Mum.

"But how are you going to get the word out?" Lowen asked. "If no one comes into the shop, how will they know about the new flavors?"

Mum smiled. Even though her shop had only had a few customers each day since it opened, and even though most of her customers were out-of-towners passing through on Highway 27, she still looked happier after a day in her own restaurant than she ever did after a long day of working as an assistant chef at Sonny's.

"You and Sami can take menus door to door," she said.

Sami shot Lowen an *Is she kidding?* look.

Lowen sure hoped so. Enduring soccer practice was humiliation enough.

Suddenly the door of the eatery opened and a man in a flannel shirt and a baseball cap came in. He was carrying a stack of papers.

"I'm sorry," Mum said. "We're closed. I've already turned the oven off for the day."

"That's OK ma'am," he said. "I was just wondering if I could post a community notice on your bulletin board."

He was referring to an old board that was adhered to the outside of the building.

"Sure," Mum said. "What's the event?"

He held out the paper and she glanced down.

Mum went white in the face.

"No. No," she said, flustered. "I'm sorry, but I just can't allow it."

The man looked taken aback. "You can't allow a notice about an upcoming class?"

"Not if it involves guns," she said.

"But this is a gun *safety* class."

"I know," she said. "You don't understand—"

The man turned. "You're right, I don't. Believe me, I won't bother you again." As he opened the door to leave, he muttered, "I doubt that many in this town will bother you at the"—he looked up at the sign—"at the Cornish Eatery." The last three words were said in a snobby English accent.

In every class Lowen had ever been in, one kid was treated as the mark. Maybe the kid did something to be singled out. But maybe he didn't. Ganging up on one kid made everyone else feel normal, secure in the group. It was like Sami said: tribal impulse.

Up until his arrival, Lowen figured, Dylan had been the outsider. He'd been the one who others jibed—either to his face or behind his back. But even though Dylan sometimes acted as if he were out to lunch, or followed others around like a puppy, he was darn good at soccer.

And Lowen was not. Not by a long shot.

He had already overhead Kyle saying to Joey, "Why does that kid talk so formal?"

And Joey had responded with a toity accent: "His mother is British."

Now that Lowen had made a total fool of himself, in a place where probably every kid was born with ball-handling talent, he'd basically given his classmates a pass to ridicule him. He was the mark, and he had no one else to blame.

Trudging to school the day after practice, he kicked a bottle cap and tried to predict the type of teasing that would come his way.

The closer he got to school, the slower he walked, hoping to arrive just as the bell rang. Then he wouldn't have to join the other kids waiting outside the door of the middle-school wing.

No such luck.

"Hey, Grover, don't they have soccer where you come from?" Joey called out the moment Lowen set foot onto school property.

162

Lowen took a deep breath, determined not to show weakness. "What's it to you?" It was a retort often used by Globber Dog.

"Just wondering," said Joey, undeterred.

"Those were some moves," piggybacked Kyle, who was usually pretty quiet. Things were definitely bad if the quiet kid was joining in.

Lowen shifted his backpack and feigned a look of surprise. "Don't tell me you guys have never heard of distraction moves."

"Distraction moves?" asked Kyle, who turned to Joey as if to ask, *Is there such a thing?*

"Oh, come on!" said Lowen with a slight smile. "The point was to surprise the other team, giving you a chance to run with the ball, Kyle."

"You meant to wipe out?" Kyle asked.

Lowen rolled his eyes. "Duh! But you missed your chance. You could have gone all the way. Scored a goal." He glanced at Joey.

Joey smiled. *Shazam!*

Lowen smiled back.

"It was good of you to take one for the team, Grover," said Joey.

Lowen knew that Joey saw through his lies but appreciated his wit. It was probably the best possible outcome.

An outcome that he couldn't take full credit for, he thought while he was tossing his backpack into his locker. Because it hadn't been *his* voice in his head that had come up with the "distraction technique" comeback. It had been Abe's. Abe was quick like that, always taking the challenge, knocking others off guard.

And at that moment, Lowen turned away from his classmates, his eyes stinging.

17.

THAT AFTERNOON . . .

Lowen couldn't wait to get home from school. He was really looking forward to seeing Dad, who was coming for the weekend. Mum had borrowed Rena's car and was picking him up at the bus station in Ranger.

So the weird, clumsy feeling that came over him when he and his brother and sister came through the door and saw their father sitting at the kitchen table, a mess of papers—likely bills—spread out before him, surprised him.

Maybe it was because he wasn't used to seeing his dad in the Albatross. Or maybe it was because Dad looked so uncomfortable, leaning back in his chair, his smile a moment too late. Or maybe it was because Mum had jumped up from the table and darted to the dining room. Had she been crying? But whatever it was, it caused Lowen to stand back and wait for Clem and Anneth to say hello first.

Clem, suddenly shy, held back, too. Only Anneth raced over to hug their father and then slid into the chair beside him. "Look what I've been doing," she said, taking out her laptop and bringing up her new YouTube channel.

"Fashion tips, huh?" Dad said, but not with his full attention.

"Well, not just fashion, Daddy. It's about creating your own style by choosing clothes and repurposing clothes—very inexpensively—to become your own person."

"Play the video," said Mum, moving back into the kitchen and sliding into a seat opposite Anneth.

Anneth's voice on the video sounded confident, authoritative: "Don't think of your clothes as matching sets. Just because you bought the blue flowered top to go with your dark jeans, it doesn't mean that you have to pair them every time. Instead, approach your closet with an open mind. What's calling you? Your blue flowered top and your polka-dot skirt? Try them on! You'll be amazed how many patterns look great together. Wear *exactly* what you feel like on any given day, and you'll always be expressing who you truly are!"

Dad leaned back. "Clever girl. It's fine advice, Annie. You've got a talent for this sort of thing."

He looked up at Lowen. "What about you, Lowen? Have you drawn anything lately?"

Lowen shook his head.

"Not even your comics?"

For a moment Lowen thought Dad was referring to the Abe comics, but he realized that he simply meant his Globber Dog series. "Nope," he said, and moved out of the way so Clem could pull some leftover pasties and juice out of the refrigerator. "Too busy."

"But Lowen's made the soccer team!" said Mum, with way too much enthusiasm. "He's a proper sportsman."

"Everyone made the middle-school soccer team," said Anneth.

Dad still looked surprised—and maybe a little dubious, too.

"It will be good for him," said Mum. "He'll be out in the fresh air, part of a team, learning new skills."

"I suppose," Dad said. "What about the skills he already has?"

"Yeah, because anyone can play soccer," said Clem, banging his cup down. "Right, Dad?"

"Oh, Clem, no one is saying that," said Mum.

"Aren't you?" Clem said to Dad. "Isn't that what you're thinking? 'Cause guess what! Someone else made a soccer team, too. The high-school team—where there were actual *tryouts.* Only no one's asked how my practices have been going, or whether I'm ready for my first game next week."

"Oh, love, of course you made the team," said Mum. "We never questioned it!"

"Well, you should have," said Clem. "Turns out kids in Millville are really good at soccer. And I mean *really* good."

Dad nodded. "Makes sense. There's nothing else to do here. Kids aren't distracted by other pursuits. . . ."

"You mean more *worthwhile* pursuits, right?" asked Clem.

"Clem, I didn't say—"

Clem blurted, "I made varsity."

"As a sophomore!" Mum said.

Again, Dad nodded. "Makes sense—low enrollment . . ."

Clem placed his cup in the sink and walked out of the kitchen.

"Honestly, Weaver," she said. "Must you steal his thunder?"

"I don't get it," Dad said. "I wasn't trying to be negative. . . ."

The air between Mum and Dad started to crackle. Both Lowen and Anneth left the room.

The following morning, after Clem was pulled from bed, the Grovers had a family meeting around the dining room table.

"As you know," Mum began, "my shop is not doing as well as anticipated."

Clem sat up tall.

Lowen quickly looked at Dad, trying to gauge the seriousness of this conversation. He knew that the slow start to the restaurant meant that his family was far from meeting the second requirement: repairing the dollar house. But how could they afford to make repairs if the restaurant wasn't making any money—was in fact *losing* money each day it was open?

"But it's only September, Mum," Anneth said, and Lowen realized that sometime between the end of June and now, his sister had gotten fully on board.

"We're not ready to throw in the towel yet," Mum continued, "but we're going to have to adjust our schedule—"

"—and our budget," Dad added.

"Dad is going to stay in Flintlock longer than we had hoped," said Mum.

Anneth reached for their father's arm.

Sadness draped over Lowen. He wished for a moment that they could all go back in time—before Millville, before the shooting. Life seemed so predictable then.

"Since I won't be able to devote as much time to the repairs," Dad said, "we'll need to hire out the bigger jobs. That'll cost money, of course."

"What jobs?" asked Clem.

"Replacing the rotted porch, steps, and siding, for starters."

Clem jumped up from the table. "You can still do those, Dad. On the weekends. What happened to 'It will be good to have creative projects—to do things with your hands'?"

"It's my fault," said Mum. "I foolishly thought that the shop would take right off. That we'd have money, that your father could leave his job and—"

Dad put his hand on Mum's. "We all had a little magical thinking."

Anneth looked panicked. "I didn't want to come, but now I don't want to leave."

"Me either," said Clem with urgency. "I'll take on more of the house projects."

"That's sweet, Clem," Mum said. "But you've got school, and soccer, and you've signed up for driver's ed."

"Not to mention that these jobs require some expertise," Dad said.

"I can learn. Lots of high-school kids in this area have building experience," Clem said, and then added, "I don't have to get my license this year. I won't be able to afford a car anyway."

"Well, let's take this one step at a time," Dad said.

"I'll borrow the Fields' lawn mower," offered Anneth. "Our yard is beginning to look like a meadow next to theirs. I know it's not much, but at least it'll show people that we're trying."

"And I'll rebuild the porch," Clem said.

Lowen stood. "I can help you, Clem—"

"No, dude—"

"You can help me today, Lowen," Dad said as if he hadn't heard his declaration. "We'll work on getting the mold out of the upstairs bathroom. It's a big health hazard."

He had heard that line, *You can help me,* all his life—whenever his parents wanted to give his brother and sister some space. But at least today he'd be the one getting to spend time with Dad.

They walked down to Handy Hardware to buy supplies: a tape measure, hammer, drywall, screws, an X-Acto knife, a putty knife, and building mud. They also rented an electric drill. Lowen didn't know whether Mr. Corbeau had sold his mother the blue kill-your-appetite paint on purpose, so he was wary when the clerk gave them something other than what they had asked for.

"Is wallboard the same thing as drywall?" asked Lowen. Drywall had been on their list, but Mr. Corbeau had pointed them toward wallboard.

"Yes, sir," said Mr. Corbeau, "same product."

"Is joint compound the same as mud?"

Dad looked at Lowen as if he were being disrespectful.

"That's right," said Mr. Corbeau, smiling.

On the way back, Dad carried the drill case in one hand and one end of the eight-foot drywall in the other. Lowen carried the other end of the drywall, and everything else in two bags. He felt a little like a cartoon character walking at one end of a long but very light board.

So, of course, that was the exact moment that he should almost bump into Luna Muñoz. She was wearing a yellow dress and a bouncy ponytail, her cello case strapped to her back.

"Lowen!" shouted his dad when Lowen stumbled out of the way to avoid knocking her over. "This board is fragile! You almost broke it in half!"

Lowen's face flamed. But Luna smiled at him—it was a kind smile, a smile that told him that she recognized him from that afternoon in the gym.

It was pure sunshine.

His mortification melted.

And then he stumbled to keep up with Dad—almost clown-like—and Luna was gone.

18.

LATER THAT DAY . . .

When they got back to the house, Dylan was sitting in the corduroy recliner.

"Come on, Dylan," Dad said as they entered the house. "If you're going to be here, you might as well make yourself useful."

Lowen groaned internally. So much for one-on-one time with Dad.

Dylan joined them in the small bathroom without any complaint.

Dad handed Lowen the hammer. "See this black speckled stuff on the wall?"

Lowen nodded. How could he not?

"That's mold," Dad said. "We've got to remove all the infected drywall." He handed Lowen the sledgehammer. "You can make the first hole."

"Really?" asked Lowen.

"Sure," said his father. "It's likely that most of this wall will be infected, so if your blow goes beyond this patch, it will be OK."

Dylan spoke up, something he rarely did unless addressed. "But, what about the—"

"It's OK," said Dad, anticipating Dylan's concern. "I've turned the electrical current off. If you hit wiring, Lowen, it won't hurt you. Just strike the wall this way." Dad pantomimed hitting the wall sideways with two hands. "That way you won't pull on anything."

Dylan croaked. "There's—"

"Stand back!" said Lowen. He was doing his best to ignore Dylan and just have fun. He held the sledgehammer with two hands like Dad showed him. Then he wound his arms back and smashed the wall with as much force as he could muster. The wallboard was as flimsy as the one he'd been carrying. His sledgehammer created a satisfying hole: *THWAP!* And an instantaneous *GUNG!*—the clang of hammer on metal. Water sprayed in all directions. He'd hit a pipe!

"Augh!" Water squirted at Lowen's face.

"Plug the hole!" yelled Dad. "I'll go try to shut off the water!" He ran out of the room.

Dylan handed Lowen a towel, which Lowen tried to wrap around the strip of pipe that was leaking. But holding his hands over one spot created a second leak.

"Dylan!" yelled Dad from somewhere below. "Where is the turn-off valve?"

Dylan looked at Lowen and shrugged as if he didn't have a clue what Dad was referring to . . . but then some glimmer of recognition registered on his face and he went racing out of the bathroom.

Meanwhile, Lowen's soaked towel began dripping. He reached over to get a dry towel from the rack and . . .

Whoops!

. . . slipped on the wet floor. He fell back and hit the wall, nearly bashing his head on the toilet. The pipe he was meant to be plugging was now partially in his hand.

Water gushed everywhere.

"Dad!" Lowen yelled. "Come quick! Dad!"

Suddenly the water stopped. Lowen stood slowly, his jeans soaking wet. He guessed that he would have been standing in a foot of water if it hadn't spread into the hall and soaked the carpet. He headed down the stairs to find Dad and Dylan.

And whom should he meet while coming down the stairs?

Mr. Field, of course. He probably had a funeral that afternoon and had come to ask the Grovers to stop screaming.

"We had a pipe burst, Mr. Field," Lowen said, intersecting his path. "In the upstairs bathroom."

Mr. Field stopped short. "Oh." He seemed to be satisfied with this explanation. "I'm sorry to hear that," he said, likely with the same tone of voice he used when responding to the bereaved. He started to descend the stairs, but stopped and asked, "Do you know Carl, the plumber?"

Lowen nodded. He hoped they wouldn't have to wait as long for him to repair their plumbing as they had had to wait for him to fix the plumbing at the restaurant. That could mean going without water for days or even weeks.

"Do you have another bathroom?" asked Mr. Field. He seemed to be having the same thought regarding Carl.

"My parents' room has a toilet," said Lowen, "but it doesn't have a tub or shower."

"Does your mother or father know how to shut off the water in one bathroom but keep it on in the others?"

Lowen shook his head with one hundred percent certainty.

"OK, then," said Mr. Field. "Let me show you."

Mr. Field had just finished explaining how when Clem arrived home, covered in sweat and dirt. Mum, who had recently returned herself, filled him in on the situation. "No shower?" he asked, incredulous.

176

"You'll have to take a sponge bath," she said.

Clem looked down at his legs. They were caked with dirt and grass stains.

Mr. Field shook his head. "You can take a shower next door. We have two full bathrooms."

Clem's eyes grew wide.

"There you go!" said Dad. He was holding the sledge-hammer that Lowen had dropped. "Problem solved."

Thought bubble over Clem's head: *Really? You want me to shower in a* funeral home?

"That's OK," said Clem. "A sponge bath doesn't sound so bad, actually—"

"No, no, I insist," Mr. Field said.

Clem looked to both Mum and Dad, but neither came to his rescue. "Lowen should come, too. Look—he's covered in gunk from the pipe breaking."

Mum started to speak up, to suggest an alternative (or so Lowen guessed), but he didn't want to be treated differently from his brother. They'd all lived next door to Abe, not just him. "I'll go with Clem," he said bravely.

"Good," said Mr. Field. "Come now. My service starts at four."

Lowen expected Clem to look grateful, maybe even drape his arm around him and say, "Come on, runt." Instead he just sighed loudly and went to get his stuff.

Mr. Field led them and their armloads of clothes and towels across the parking lot and through his back door. Straight ahead was a stairway leading to the second floor. "There is a bathroom down here," Mr. Field said, pointing down a hall, "and another upstairs."

"I'm upstairs," called Clem. He bounded up several steps and waited. Mr. Field glanced at Lowen, then shrugged and followed Clem. He called out to his wife to announce Clem's arrival.

Lowen stood still, taking note of a room to his right that looked like a kitchen but wasn't a true kitchen. There was a little refrigerator, a microwave, and a coffee urn. In the center of the room was a table, and on the table was a silver tea set and silver serving trays.

Lowen could hear Mr. Field chatting with his wife upstairs. The talk was slow, casual. That's when Lowen got it: the Fields must live on the second floor, above the funeral home. No wonder Clem had called the upstairs shower so quickly.

The hall leading out of the kitchen was lined with dark wood paneling, but there was light coming from the rooms at the front of the house. He ventured down the hall and tapped open a door to his left, fairly certain that this was the bathroom that Mr. Field had pointed out.

Sure enough, it was an old-timey one with a deep claw-foot bathtub. Lowen put his clothes on the toilet lid and then turned to shut the door.

But wait. What did a funeral home look like? He wished now that he'd been brave enough to attend Abe's funeral. Other kids in the neighborhood and even kids from Abe's third-grade class had gone. If Lowen's imaginings were true, Abe had looked straight into the barrel of a gun, and here he hadn't even been brave enough to say good-bye.

He left the bathroom and headed to the end of the hall. There was a room on his right about the size of the Grovers' living room, but it was set up with folding chairs all facing in the same direction. Like church.

Feeling downright courageous, Lowen turned and walked across the hall. Here was a larger room with clustered armchairs and small tables. At one end, in front of a dark paneled wall, was a partially opened casket with bouquets of flowers all around.

Lowen froze. The snake wrapped around his lungs.

He turned to bolt but bumped into someone.

"Haven't you ever seen a dead body before?"

It was Dylan. His pant cuffs were still wet and he was carrying a bouquet of flowers wrapped in cellophane.

"What are you doing here?" Lowen asked.

"I work here," Dylan said. "What are *you* doing here?"

"You work here?" asked Lowen, ignoring his question. "Why didn't you tell me?"

"You didn't ask," Dylan said. "Want to look in the casket? She doesn't look too bad."

"Who is she?"

"Mrs. Doucette. She used to teach kindergarten. You can tell she's wearing a wig."

Lowen tried to imagine the corpse of a woman. He shook his head no.

"Come on," said Dylan. "It's not that scary."

Lowen shook his head emphatically.

Dylan peeled the cellophane off the bouquet, made sure the gift card was prominently displayed, placed the flowers in a vase, and placed the vase on a table near the casket.

"How come you work *here*?" Lowen hadn't meant to emphasize that last word, but come on, what kind of kid voluntarily worked at a funeral home?

"I'm not supposed to be working yet. It's against the child labor laws. But Mrs. Field has arthritis and can't do the stuff I do, like unwrap flowers, fold the programs, spread out the little cakes. So they pay me under the table to help out from time to time." Then, almost as an afterthought, Dylan added, "Don't tell anyone, OK?"

"What about your parents?" It was the first time he'd asked Dylan about his family, and the minute he saw Dylan's face, he regretted it.

"What about them?" Dylan asked, sounding defensive.

"Where do they work?"

"My dad works at a mill in Buchanan. My mom doesn't work—not anymore." Dylan pulled out a couple of the flowers and put them back in different spots.

"What are you doing?"

Dylan shrugged. "Flowers show up better when there's space between them. Hey," he said, pulling something from his pocket, "you don't think your parents would mind if I kept this, do you?"

It was a piece of broken tile from the bathroom.

Lowen was about to ask him what he wanted with a fragment of tile when they were interrupted.

"Dylan, you're here," said Mr. Field, coming into the viewing room. "I didn't hear you come in." He turned to Lowen. "Haven't you taken your bath? Your brother has already gone."

Lowen couldn't believe that Clem had not only grabbed the upstairs shower, but had left without even waiting. He decided to take his time soaking in the tub. Heck, he still had a half hour before mourners arrived. And when he returned home he would tell Clem that not only was he not afraid to take a bath downstairs, he had stood in the same room as a dead person.

Unfortunately, Clem wasn't home when he returned.

Mum and Dad were in the dining room surveying the water damage. Water was leaking through the upstairs flooring and had formed a substantial stain on the dining room ceiling. Lowen thought it looked like a giant hamster.

Dad sighed. "If the leaking continues, I'm afraid the ceiling is going to come down."

"If it doesn't come crashing down on our heads, we'll probably have to take it down," said Mum. She had none of her usual patience. Lowen guessed that, like most days, she'd used it up watching streams of Millvillians walk into the Busy Bee for lunch. "And we'll need to pull up the floor under the carpet. And who knows where all that water inside the wall is going!"

"I thought of turning off the wiring," Dad said. "But it never occurred to me that the pipes might run horizontally."

"It's probably not your fault," Mum said. "Coach said that Dylan's father was the kind of do-it-yourselfer that was apt to use milk jugs and bubble gum for building materials."

"Maybe we should cry uncle before we lose everything," Dad said.

But Mum shook her head firmly. She wasn't the quitting kind.

19.

OCTOBER

The best thing about playing soccer was the bus rides to games. Lowen had never been on a school bus before. In Flintlock, if his class went on a field trip, they walked or took vans. But in Millville, buses had to travel great distances so the kids could play other schools. Dylan, Sami, Amber, Joey, Kyle, and Lowen were dismissed from class a half hour early to board, which made Lowen feel kind of important—even though most of his class went with him.

It was always the same. The eighth-graders sat in the back of the bus. The seventh-graders sat as close as they could to the eighth-graders. The sixth-graders spread out over the front seats. Though Lowen could have sat with Sami, he chose to sit alone. Coach passed out snacks.

There were sixteen kids on their team: eleven first-string and five second-string. Unless their team was way ahead, he and a seventh-grader nicknamed Rats got to sit out most of each game. That wasn't so bad.

Practices were much harder. Coach barked at them while they ran or performed repetitive drills, and there was always an audience, which made Lowen feel especially uncoordinated.

One of the worst days was "left foot day." Coach explained that soccer players who could kick using both their feet were far more successful, and since most of the team had a stronger right foot, he wouldn't allow them to use it that day. They had to remove their right cleat. Lowen caught his socked toe in a chipmunk hole and went flying tail over teakettle.

Of course, that was the same day that Luna happened to be standing on the sidelines watching.

And the same day that Sami offered again to give him a tip.

"Thanks, but—"

She stepped in front of him. "People aren't born knowing how to play soccer, you know."

"I didn't say they were," Lowen said. He could feel his annoyance rising. "But why does everyone feel the need to give me advice?"

She hesitated. "Because . . . you need it?"

"Ugh. I can't be the only one on the team who needs help."

"I know. But I thought we were friends."

He scrambled for an answer. *We're not friends*—too mean. *I'm not friend material*—that would only lead Sami to ask why. "All right. Show me," he said, with a bit more annoyance in his voice than he meant.

Sami went silent.

"No. Sorry. I mean it. What's your tip?"

She stopped and placed the ball on the ground. "Don't take this the wrong way," she said, "but you often treat the ball like it's a bomb rolling toward you. You kick it away as quickly as possible."

"I'm defense," he said, knowing that he was taking a similarly defensive position now.

"Yes, but the ball often goes off in a direction that gives the other team an advantage."

Truthfully, he had no idea where the ball would go when he kicked it. He just wanted it to be someone else's responsibility. But Sami was right: often it landed at the feet of an opposing player.

"This will probably sound ridiculous," she said, "but try to imagine the ball as, well, your loyal pet."

She demonstrated some footwork. "You don't want it to be so close to your feet that you step on it," she said as she tapped it along. "But you don't want it to get too far away, either—not while you're trying to control it. Then look up and spot the exact place you want it to go, and then, as if it were an extension of your own foot, send it there."

She ceased tapping. "Wow. Sorry. I never realized how stupid this sounds."

But he knew exactly what she meant. He could imagine interacting with the ball this way. "It's like drawing," he said. "It's easier to imagine that your pencil is part of your arm, and that your arm knows exactly how to make the form; you just have to relax, stop thinking so much—"

"I didn't know that you drew."

Lowen nodded, but then corrected himself. "Used to draw."

"Will you show me sometime?"

"Maybe," he said.

Sami smiled.

He turned away. This lie felt an awful lot like the lies he used to tell Abe.

20.

MID-OCTOBER

The shower was out of commission for three weeks. Lowen got increasingly comfortable taking baths next door at Field's Funeral Home. Invited to come and go as he pleased, he challenged himself to explore a little more of the funeral home on each visit. In the paneled basement, he discovered a large carpeted display room filled with caskets. There was a dark mahogany casket lined with red velvet pillows. Something about it made him want to crawl inside, lay his head on the cushion. What would it feel like? But then he imagined the top slamming down and latching, trapping him inside. He'd bang on the cover repeatedly, hoping to be heard. It reminded him of something his teacher, Mrs. K., had told them.

Apparently, during the Victorian era, corpses had ropes tied to their fingers, head, and toes. These ropes led to a bell on the tombstone. If the body somehow revived, the not-really-deceased person could pull on the ropes and ring the bell. Hopefully a night watchman would hear the bell and the coffin would be dug up. "Had anyone actually been rescued by one of these safety coffins?" Sami had asked, but their teacher didn't know.

Next to the fancy mahogany casket was a tiny white casket lined with pink satin pillows. No doubt that one was for a baby. *What had Abe's family chosen?*

Clem never took another shower at Field's. He showered at school after soccer practice or at one of his buds' houses on Sunday mornings. Anneth, like Lowen, had no problem using the downstairs bath at Field's. On her second visit she met Melinda, the makeup artist whose true calling was helping the deceased look their best. Melinda complimented Anneth on her lip gloss color, and Anneth, in turn, asked Melinda a million questions about foundations, eyeliners, and bronzing powders. Later, with permission, Anneth shared Melinda's "Makeup Tips for the Living" on her channel. It was, so far, the posting that had received the most views.

At one point, Lowen was tempted to share his explorations at Field's with his classmates, thinking that they might see him as braver, more capable. But when Lowen told Dylan that he had explored the caskets in the basement, Dylan had said, "I don't think it's very respectful what you're doing. All of us here in Millville have been to Field's . . . you know . . . to say good-bye."

Lowen supposed that might be true in a place like Millville. Abe was the first person he knew who had died. All his grandparents were still alive. In fact, he'd never even had a pet that died (mostly because he'd never had a pet, period). But in Millville, everybody knew everybody. Chances are, every kid in Millville had attended a wake or a funeral next door. In fact, from the number of cars parked in front of their home every time there was a service, he suspected that everyone in town attended funerals.

He recalled the deceased woman who was at Field's that day Dylan surprised him, the one he wouldn't look at. He tried to imagine her now. Was she wearing the clothes she died in? Probably not. Someone must have picked out her clothes. Someone else (he didn't like thinking about who) dressed her.

It was weird thinking about dressing the dead. Did you wear clothes in heaven? Did you wear the ones you died in? Or did you wear the clothes you were buried in? Maybe that was why people always pictured people in heaven wearing gowns, like angels. Anything else was just confusing.

Lowen laughed at the thought of Abe wearing a gown. He thought of the teenage killer, whose name he suddenly remembered—Oliver, Oliver Jenson—wearing a gown. His mind entered back into his comic strip:

190

Abe's reaction, the imagined one in his head, reminded Lowen of his siblings' comments when they first arrived in Millville: *There's nothing here!* Eventually Clem and Anneth had ceased complaining about the lack of a movie theater, a Trader Joe's, or a pizza place in town.

That did not stop them, however, from putting up a huge fuss when, due to a lack of hair stylist or barber in town, Mum asked Rena (who had assured them that she'd had plenty of experience cutting hair) to come to the Albatross to cut the family's hair.

Clem wasn't home from practice yet, so Mum made Anneth go first. She sat up on a barstool that Rena brought. Rena wrapped an old sheet over her shoulders and, with a comb in one hand and a pair of pointy scissors in the other, proceeded to give her a trim.

"Don't leave it too long here," Anneth said, pointing to hair resting on her shoulders in back, "or my hair will flip up!"

Lowen stood nearby, waiting to see if Rena really knew what she was doing. Sami, who was used to watching her mother cut her sisters' hair, was hanging out at the table with Mum, who was, as usual, looking for interesting recipes online.

"So," Mum began, "I've finished designing the new menus and they should be arriving early next week.

I figured you kids could also collect clothing donations for Restored Riches while you're handing out menus." Rena was due to open her used-clothing store in just three days, but so far very few people had brought in clothes to sell on consignment. "Two birds with one stone! What do you say?"

Was Mum for real? He shot Sami a look of horror.

"I hope you're not including me as one of the kids," said Clem, who had slipped in the door and was pausing to read his texts. "I have two papers due, and I still haven't cut the boards for the porch, but I did get permission to use the workshop at school and I found a couple of kids who are willing to help me."

"There's no way I can go around, either!" said Anneth, keeping her chin down as Rena directed. "I can hardly get both my vlog and my homework done on time as it is. Besides, we have none of the cute factor of the younger ones."

Sami's sisters, who had been playing with Barbies on the couch, perked up. They knew they were cute, and going door-to-door probably sounded like fun to them.

"Sorry, kiddos," Rena said to the youngsters. "You are too little."

"Looks like it will be up to Lowen and Sami," said Mum.

"But we have soccer, too!" said Lowen. "And home-work, and . . . and I'm supposed to be painting my room!" (He'd gone back and bought a gallon of the cheap Ambrosia Blue. He figured it would work in a bedroom.)

"Besides, who wants kids knocking on their door?" Sami asked.

Rena held the scissors in the air, as if she were about to stab someone. "Don't you want to live here?" she said. She looked at Sami and then at Lowen. "I'm serious. Don't you want to stay in Millville?"

The room went quiet.

Clem stopped guzzling orange juice from the carton. "I do."

"Me too," Anneth mumbled.

"If we want to stay in Millville," said Mum, "Rena and I *have* to make a living. We *have* to fix up our homes. If our businesses don't succeed, we Grovers will be heading back to Flintlock, and—"

"We'll be heading back to who-knows-where," Sami said softly. She'd already told Lowen that her mom would never move back to the Bronx, so if Millville didn't work out, there was no saying where the Doshis would end up.

Lowen looked at Mum, saw the plea in her eyes.

The Cornish Eatery had to succeed. It was the only way that Dad could give up the apartment, the only way they could have a house of their own, the only way Mum could have her dream. The only way they could stay where Clem and Anneth were so happy.

"OK," he said. "I'll do it."

21.

LATE OCTOBER

It was a drizzly Saturday morning when Lowen and Sami trudged around Millville. Sami pushed a rusty wheelbarrow, one she'd found in the Doshis' garage. Inside her raincoat pocket, she carried a receipt pad. "Remind me to record every single item that someone gives me," she said, "so my mother can pay them later."

Lowen had Mum's messenger bag flung over his shoulder. Inside the bag were take-out menus from the Cornish Eatery, featuring descriptions of her pasties. He felt ridiculous.

They decided to start on the north end of town, where they'd run into fewer people (and would be least likely to run into Luna Muñoz, though Lowen didn't share this fact with Sami), and work their way back to the center. The first house they came to, a double-wide trailer, looked deserted. The empty driveway was covered in wet leaves, and the curtains were pulled shut. Sami stepped onto the little front porch and knocked several times anyway. Just as they were about to give up and head to the next house, the door opened a crack.

"Are you trick-or-treating for UNICEF?" came a frail voice. Lowen and Sami exchanged a look. Halloween was still a week away.

"No," said Sami. "We want to talk to you about *making* money, not donating it."

The door opened wider, revealing an old woman with blurry eyes. "Now, see here! I don't want any part in a get-rich-quick scam! Our town may be down, but we Millvillians have never been stupid!"

Lowen prepared to retreat.

"No, no," said Sami quickly. "My mom, Rena Doshi, is opening a consignment store on Main Street. She would like to help you sell clothes you no longer wear."

"Why would I stop wearing perfectly fine clothes at my age? I don't care about trends!"

"Let's go," whispered Lowen.

Sami gave him a stern look. One that said, *Come on. You're in this, too.*

Lowen reached into his bag and pulled out a menu. "Have you ever had a Cornish pasty?"

"What?"

Lowen drifted closer. "A meat pie. Have you ever had one?"

"My mama used to make tourtière pie." The woman smiled for the first time. "It had pork, potatoes, and onions. Goodness, I hadn't thought of that in ages!"

Lowen had never heard of tourtière pies, but he said, "It sounds just like my mother's pasties, though they have steak instead of pork."

The woman nodded. "English instead of French."

Sami stepped in. "I bet Mrs. Grover could make one of your tor−tor−"

"Tourtière," the woman said to Sami, and then looked back at Lowen. "If your mother makes one of those, bring it to me. I'll pay her for it."

Lowen nodded, even though the restaurant didn't have an official delivery service. But he'd bring the woman the pasty himself if it meant more business for Mum.

The lines on the woman's face softened. "You're Dollar Kids, aren't you?"

So even the grown-ups called them that. Lowen nodded again, still holding out the menu. The wind nearly blew it out of his hand.

"Oh, come in. Come in. I shouldn't have made you stand outside in this damp weather."

Lowen looked at Sami, who shrugged. The rain was picking up.

"I'll make tea," said the woman as the kids stepped inside, "and I just made cake."

He and Sami stepped inside a cozy living room and handed their coats to the woman, who introduced herself as Mrs. Lavasseur. Then they sat together on a mildly sagging couch that was covered in colorful afghans.

"Does your mother accept men's clothing?" Mrs. Lavasseur asked Sami, peering into her front closet.

"Oh, yes!" said Sami. "Men's, women's, and children's."

"Well, then, I do have some clothing for you to take along. You see, my husband died. . . ."

A half hour later, Sami and Lowen were on the road with a wheelbarrow half full of men's clothing and some women's purses. All were stuffed into garbage bags to keep them dry.

At the next house, they agreed that Lowen would talk about the pasties first, but the thin man who answered the door said he was gluten intolerant and couldn't eat crust. Before he could shut the door, Sami called out, "Your neighbor decided to make money by selling clothes she no longer needed."

The man paused. "Come again?"

Sami pointed out the bags of clothing they had collected so far and gave a brief pitch for Restored Riches.

That's when the man's wife, a short woman with dark bangs, peeked out from around the door. "You're that talented young soccer player!" she said to Sami. "I have some dresses I no longer have the opportunity to wear." While she went to retrieve the dresses, Lowen handed the man a menu. "Look," he said. "The Cornish Eatery has gluten-free crust. You just have to call ahead."

The man glanced at it for a moment and was about to give it back when he pointed to the classic Cornish pasty that not only had beef and onion and potato, but had rutabaga as well. "Rutabaga! I haven't had rutabaga since—"

"Since Janelle," his wife interjected, handing Sami the dresses zipped into a garment bag. They smelled like vinegar.

"Janelle used to live on the other side of us." She pointed to the empty house next door. "But she moved away when the mill closed . . . she and her husband and their three extremely athletic kids—two of them were All-State, weren't they, Dave? Their yard was always immaculate, wasn't it, Dave?"

Water dripped off the roof and down Lowen's face.

The man sighed. "As I was saying, I haven't had a rutabaga since Janelle used to drive to a co-op in Ranger and bring us back fresh produce."

"Oh, I miss that produce," said the woman. "Don't you, Dave? Janelle—"

"My mother gets a shipment of rutabagas from Canada every week," said Lowen. He didn't add that since the Cornish Eatery had so few customers, he and his brother and sister usually ended up eating most of those rutabagas in soups. In fact, all of the leftover meat and produce went into soups. He was really, really tired of soup.

"Oh . . . your mother opened the new lunch place," the woman said. "We always eat at the Busy Bee, don't we, Dave? We're predictable that way. Plus, we do like to give our business to Virginia Corbeau. Virginia and I go all the way back to—when did we meet the Corbeaus, Dave? Was it 1973?"

The man looked up at the sky. "Looks like we're going to have another shower," he said. "You probably want to get going."

"Thanks," said Sami, handing him a receipt.

The man nodded, folded the menu and receipt, and tucked them into the back pocket of his trousers.

At the next house, they secured a bag of high-heeled shoes, and at the one after that, they received two whole bags of baby clothes. They made their way back to Restored Riches to empty the wheelbarrow, then headed out again.

"We make a good team," said Lowen as he took a turn pushing the wheelbarrow.

Sami smiled and nodded in agreement. "We do. Don't we, Dave? Dave?"

Lowen laughed.

"Yup," said Sami. "A good team. You, me, and the bandwagon effect."

Lowen thought for a moment. "OK, I think I know what that is."

Sami shifted Lowen's messenger bag on her shoulder. "So what is it?"

"First, you make sure to tell people that their neighbors have already donated clothes."

"Why?"

"Well, if their neighbors are doing it, it's probably an OK thing to do. And that probably makes them want to do it, too. They don't want to miss out on an opportunity." He looked at Sami, waiting for her response. "It's like a big parade float that everyone suddenly wants to hop on."

She smiled.

"I'm right, aren't I? See, I'm not that stupid." Lowen

tried to steer the wheelbarrow straight up the next hilly street, but it was hard to keep it going in the right direction when it was empty.

"I never said—"

"Do you want to skip this house?" Lowen asked. They had arrived at Mr. Avery's perfectly manicured home. There wasn't a single leaf anywhere on his lawn.

"Why?" asked Sami.

"Don't you remember the last time we ran into Mr. Avery? At the river?

"Keep pushing," said Sami. "He's old. He probably won't even remember that it was us. Besides, this is where Dylan lives, right? Let's say hi."

Lowen sighed. "You go first."

Sami confidently rang the doorbell and waited. They could hear the volume on the TV being lowered, someone's footsteps approaching.

"My grandson isn't here," Mr. Avery said when he opened the door.

"That's OK, Mr. Avery. We'd like to talk with you. I'm Sami Doshi."

"I know who you are."

Sami smiled, undaunted. "Then you may know that my mother is opening a consignment shop in town."

"I had heard that, yes."

"Well, many of your neighbors have decided to sell their clothes at Restored Riches."

"Have they, now?" He looked at Lowen. "And are you simply helping this young lady, or do you have something you'd like to talk me into as well?"

Lowen didn't know if Mr. Avery was being harsh, or encouraging him to give his sales pitch—he hoped it was the latter. He pulled out a menu. "I'd like to convince you to try the pasties at the Cornish Eatery. Many of your neighbors—"

Mr. Avery held his hand up. "And have any of my neighbors told you that you're breaking the law? That the fine folks of Millville don't wish to be annoyed by door-to-door salesmen, or saleswomen, or saleskids for that matter, telling them what their neighbors have or have not done. That's why they passed a no soliciting ordinance."

Harsh. Definitely harsh.

Sami shifted her weight. "But we're just trying to—"

"I suggest," Mr. Avery continued, "that the two of you take your wheelbarrow and your menus back to your mothers' places of business before I have them—and you—fined for disobeying town law."

And with that, he shut the door.

Lowen and Sami couldn't push the wheelbarrow fast enough to the Cornish Eatery, where they were quite certain to find both their mothers at this time of day.

"You won't believe—" Lowen started as they burst into the shop, but he stopped short.

For once the Cornish Eatery wasn't empty. Ms. Duffey was at the counter talking with Rena and Mum. "We've done a fine job of mixing things up here a bit. But we've got to do more than just fill houses," she was saying. "Towns that make a comeback invite small local businesses: coffee shops, bookstores, restaurants—like this one—and spaces for the arts! Believe it or not, music and storytelling and art can bring back a town."

Additionally, Dave, of *Isn't that right, Dave?* was sitting at the table eating a classic Cornish pasty—presumably with gluten-free crust. He must have called right after they left his house. And a young couple whom Lowen and Sami had met on their second trip was studying the menu.

While Sami moved to the back of the counter to tell their moms what had happened at Mr. Avery's, Lowen headed to the cooler to get them some drinks.

Just then, the bell above the door jangled and Coach walked in.

"What can I get you, Coach?" Mum asked, looking distracted. No doubt she was fretting over their encounter with Mr. Avery.

"Actually, I'm here to recruit Lowen," he said, and motioned for Lowen to sit down with him at the table, which Dave was in the process of vacating.

"Great pie!" Dave said, and waved on his way out.

Coach leaned toward Lowen. "I'd like to give you some private lessons in basketball. The season's coming up and I could really use someone on the team with your height."

Lowen didn't know what to say. Being on the soccer team hadn't been as bad as he'd feared, but that was because he mostly got to sit on the bench. It sounded like Coach expected him to actually *play* on the basketball team, though.

No doubt reading Lowen's expression, Coach continued. "I'll be honest—unlike with soccer, we have enough kids without you to qualify as a team. But we could really use someone with your height, and if we can make you a strong player in middle school, you'll be a real asset to our high-school team. Have you ever played basketball before?"

"Well, I—" He was about to tell Coach that he'd played a little in gym class when he was in the second grade, but Mum interrupted.

"Are you sure I can't get you a pasty?" she asked.

"No, really," said Coach. "I thought you were closed by four—that's why I came in at this time."

"We usually do close by four, but today, thanks to Lowen and Sami, we had a bunch of customers who all poured in during the last hour." She ruffled Lowen's hair. "I'll get you something."

Of course! Customers had arrived as soon as the Busy Bee closed. It was the opposite of the bandwagon theory—instead of everyone in town talking about how they were giving the Cornish Eatery a try, they were visiting in secret, when Virginia Corbeau was least likely to find out about it. Rutabaga-loving Dave probably wasn't even going to tell his wife that he had come. How could his mother fight that?

And then Lowen knew—he knew exactly how he could help break this pattern. He waited until after Coach told him all about the importance of basketball to the town of Millville: the need for restored faith in their teams, the likelihood that he'd play center, his chances of being a hometown hero. But mostly, Lowen waited until Coach took his first bite of Mum's chicken pot pasty and said, "Wow."

"I'll tell you what," said Lowen, leaning forward in his chair so only Coach could hear him. "I'll learn how to play basketball under one condition."

Coach finished chewing before speaking. "Sounds like extortion, but I'm intrigued. What's your condition?"

Lowen took a breath. "You have to promise to eat lunch here at least two times a week until basketball season is over."

Coach nearly spewed a mouthful of pasty across the room. "Seriously? That's your condition?"

Lowen nodded.

Coach finished his pasty in silence, clearly mulling things over. "Do you know that the Corbeaus, the ones who own the Busy Bee, are the biggest donors to the sports teams in town?"

Lowen chose his words carefully. "Will there still be sports teams if the Dollar Kids can't stay?"

"Good point. But, the Corbeaus supported the Dollar Program until . . ."

"Until my mother opened a take-out restaurant."

Coach nodded. "It was an unfortunate choice of business."

"But—"

"I know," said Coach. "The Busy Bee didn't offer lunch then."

Mum and Dad were right. Running a successful business in a small town was a lot trickier than it looked.

Unless something changed, it seemed unlikely that his mother's shop would ever take off.

And it was equally unlikely that Lowen would play basketball, but that, he thought, was probably a blessing.

"OK," said Coach.

"Huh?"

"If you'll play basketball, I'll eat here two days a week."

"You will?"

"I wanted to bring you kids here to Millville. It wouldn't be right if I didn't support you."

Lowen smiled.

"Actually," said Coach, "I'm doing it because your mom's pasties are so darn good."

22.

NOVEMBER

Lowen didn't want to get out of bed. It was the first morning he was supposed to meet Coach at the gym for a basketball lesson. Beneath his covers was warmth—warmth and the figments of pleasant dreams, though the specifics of those dreams were already drifting away. Outside his covers, cold loomed like scattered pins.

Each new day here in Millville got colder than the last, but with Mum's shop still not turning a profit, the Grovers couldn't afford to turn the heat up high enough to make the house comfortable—especially at night. So Lowen curled under several old quilts that Mum had bought from Rena's store.

Despite Mum's patronage, Restored Riches wasn't doing any better than the Cornish Eatery. It wasn't that Millvillians stayed away—they didn't feel that Rena was competing with any other store in town—but they never *bought* anything when they did visit. Lowen had seen this firsthand. He was delivering a pasty Mum had made for Rena when he overheard two women gabbing by a dress rack.

WOMAN 1: "Look! This is the dress that Deborah wore to our twentieth reunion!"

WOMAN 2: "And this is the one you wore!"

WOMAN 1: "I remember this white dress, too! Gracie wore it to her baby's christening."

WOMAN 2: "Which baby was that? Which reminds me, have you checked out the kids' clothes here?"

WOMAN 1: "Absolutely not. Times are hard, but I still won't let my kids wear hand-me-downs."

Rena had been listening to the women, too. "Their kids wear hand-me-downs," she said after they left empty-handed. "Only they travel to Ranger and buy from the thrift store there."

"Maybe families in Ranger will travel here to buy from *your* store," Lowen had offered.

Rena just shook her head.

Even the Dollar Families who wanted to help Rena didn't want to buy the secondhand clothing that every-one else in town would easily recognize. So they bought a few household items (household items that would otherwise have mysteriously appeared on the front lawns of dollar homes) and tucked them away.

Lowen crawled out from under his mound of quilts and got dressed as quickly as possible, then walked up to the high-school gym for his first basketball lesson. Frost crackled beneath his sneakers and his breath lingered in the air.

Coach was shooting baskets when Lowen arrived. He moved in for a layup and scored. "You're a man of your word," he called out to Lowen.

Lowen smiled. Coach had kept his promise, too, regularly eating lunch at Mum's shop and even sitting at the table by the window to be sure folks passing by would see him in there enjoying one of Mum's "mean pies," as he called them.

"So, we'll wait a couple more minutes," said Coach, moving in for another layup. Lowen didn't know what they were waiting for, but he was happy to put off the inevitable embarrassment as long as possible.

Turns out they were waiting for Dylan, who came in wearing basketball shorts and basketball shoes—unlike Lowen, who had shown up in jeans and a long-sleeved shirt.

For once, the sight of Dylan didn't annoy Lowen. The more he got to know Mr. Avery, the more Lowen felt sorry for him. Was Dylan's grandfather always that angry—and mean?

"I thought it might be useful to have Dylan join us," Coach explained.

And it was.

For a while.

Coach asked Dylan to model some ball skills: finger grabs, slaps, and finger tipping, that sort of thing. It was soon clear that Dylan was as good at basketball as he was at soccer—maybe even better.

Tipping was not as easy as Dylan made it look. "Keep your elbows straight," he counseled when Lowen tried it for the first time.

After a half hour of working with the ball, Coach suggested that Lowen and Dylan play a little one-on-one while he went down the hall to his office to work on scheduling.

Dylan shrugged and tossed the ball to Lowen, who did his best to dribble it toward the basket.

It wasn't a real match, of course. Dylan easily stole the ball from Lowen and rarely missed an open shot, whereas most of Lowen's shots ricocheted off the rim. Lowen's height helped, though, and he got better at blocking Dylan's attempts.

"So," said Lowen, when he got tired of chasing Dylan around the court, "you live in that white house with the windmill."

"Yup," said Dylan, taking an unobstructed shot.

"Do your parents live there, too?" Lowen asked, catching the ball on the rebound.

"Don't you think you would have met my parents by now if they did?"

Lowen let the tone roll off him. "So where do they live?"

Dylan stole the ball.

"I already told you my dad lives in Buchanan." Dylan maneuvered his body away from Lowen and shot. This time the ball bounced off the backboard.

"How 'bout your mother?" He sounded like Abe, asking any old question that came to mind no matter how rude or intrusive.

"Gone," said Dylan as he shot again. It hit the rim but didn't bounce in.

Lowen was quiet, hoping Dylan would explain.

Instead, Dylan stopped shooting and pounded the ball against the gym floor—each bounce causing a *thump,* followed by an echoing *ping.* "Heard your friend was killed in a random shooting," he said.

Lowen lunged for the ball, but Dylan rolled it to his other hand. "Who told you that?" He was pretty sure that Mr. Avery wasn't supposed to share confidential details from their application—but maybe Dylan had overheard something?

Ping. Ping. Ping. "Anneth," Dylan said.

Of course. He avoided talking to Dylan while he was hanging out at the Albatross, but his siblings didn't.

"What'd Anneth tell you, exactly?"

"She said you guys were always together. That he was always around the house. That sometimes he'd take things."

Anneth had a big mouth. Lowen reached out and grabbed the ball from Dylan's hands. He tried to dribble but kicked it away on the first bounce.

"Said he stole money from her, and he took her Valentine's candy," Dylan called out.

"So what?" said Lowen, scooping up the ball. Really. So he took some of Anneth's candy. He was nine years old, for Pete's sake. Nine years old and *dead,* by the way.

Dylan swooped in and stole the ball. *Ping. Ping. Ping.* "So do you think something like that keeps you out of heaven? Stealing, I mean?"

"He was a kid," Lowen snapped as he grabbed the ball away from Dylan. Again he tried to control his dribble, but the ball bobbed away.

"Yeah, but the guy who shot him was a kid, too, right? Just 'cause you're a kid doesn't mean you automatically get a free pass to heaven."

It wasn't like Lowen hadn't thought of these things. He'd already drawn the cartoon. . . .

Lowen dribbled the ball in place a couple times and then whipped it at the backboard.

The ball hit the glass and banked in.

"Ha! Lucky shot," said Dylan, catching it on the rebound. He dribbled it back to the foul line.

Lowen threw himself down on the floor. He was tired and sweaty from running around the court in jeans. "Anyway, there's no such thing as heaven."

Really, how could there be? He'd looked up the requirements for heaven online, and what he'd found were all these conflicting laws. (Is it OK for a soldier to murder? How about the death penalty?) There were even stages of sins that looked like a rubric his teacher might use: might be pardonable, sometimes pardonable, occasionally pardonable, unlikely to be pardonable. Who decided? God? If so, how did He (or She) ever have time to do anything but judge the lives of the newly dead? It boggled the mind.

"Why would you say that?" Dylan's voice had a razor's edge. *Ping. Ping. Ping.* He dribbled aggressively, moving closer to Lowen's head with each bounce.

Lowen flinched. "Think about it," he said. "Heaven's supposed to be this place where everything is perfect. But what if you love harp playing and I hate harp playing? Then how can it be heaven for both of us?"

Dylan stopped dribbling and shook his head. "There's a heaven," he said firmly.

"Says who?" asked Lowen.

Dylan shook his head. "If you weren't so pathetic, you'd know that." He dropped the ball and walked out of the gym.

"Sure, walk away!" Lowen shouted. "You always do."

He lay back on the floor and stared up at the ceiling. The roof was a long way up. Metal beams, with crisscross latticework, looked like ladders to nowhere.

23.

As he stood to leave the gym, Lowen noticed Coach standing by the locker room doors, watching him.

"Believe it or not, Grover, you've improved already," he said.

Lowen shrugged. "I've got to get to the shop. Mum's expecting me." Another bold-faced lie. Looks like he wouldn't be getting into Dylan's heaven either.

"I'll walk with you," Coach said. "There's something I want to talk to your mother about."

The restaurant was empty when they walked in, but a lack of customers early in the day no longer worried Mum. Ever since Coach had started eating there, she'd had an increase in customers—customers who showed up after the Busy Bee was closed.

"What a pleasant surprise!" said Mum. "How were the lessons?"

Lowen hoped that Coach would just assume that *he* was the surprise, and not Lowen, too.

Coach poured himself a cup of coffee and leaned over the counter where Mum was kneading piecrust.

"Lowen's got some real potential," he said.

She smiled at Lowen. "You must have worked up quite an appetite. Would you like a saffron bun? I'm adding them to the menu."

"Yes, please."

Mum placed two golden rolls on a plate—one for him and one for Coach.

"We don't open for another hour," Mum said, "but I'm happy to fix you a chicken pot pasty, Coach."

Coach chuckled. "I've eaten so many of those you're going to have to name one after me."

Lowen laughed. He finished his bun and started for home, leaving Coach and his mother to discuss . . . Well, he never did learn what it was Coach wanted to talk to her about. But seeing his mum and Coach scheming about something made him miss his dad.

Dad hadn't been able to come to Millville for the past three Saturdays. One of the doctors in his practice had a sick baby, and they asked his father to fill in. The good news was that his father was being paid overtime; the bad news was that he was working weekends. Lowen wondered if his dad had gone into the hospital yet and decided to Skype him as soon as he got home.

But the closer he got to 11 Beech, the slower he walked. Dad would ask lots of questions—questions that Lowen wasn't sure he wanted to answer. He imagined his part of the conversation:

Yes, more of the kitchen ceiling has come down . . . and another kitchen cupboard door . . . and the doorknob on the upstairs bathroom.

I'm not sure how Clem did on his social studies test (even though he was fairly certain that Clem had not done well).

Yup, I got the graphic novel you sent. Yeah, I read it in fifth grade, but they're fun to read again.

No, I haven't had a chance to get back to my comics yet.

More importantly, he knew that he wouldn't like Dad's part of the conversation, the answer to Lowen's most pressing question:

I don't know when I can give up my job and move to Millville. I'm still looking for a medical doctor in the area who can supervise my work, and Mum's shop isn't ready to support all of us.

. . .

Lowen decided not to go home after all. Instead he walked aimlessly. Well, all right. If he ran into Luna, that wouldn't have ruined his day.

He meandered past the First Baptist Church, whose marquee read *A day stitched in prayer is unlikely to unravel*.

Prayer. Before the store shoot-out, prayer seemed so easy. His prayers had all been the same: *Dear God, please [insert request here]*. Now prayer seemed all wrapped up in what he believed and what he didn't believe. If he prayed for Abe to get into heaven, would that mean that he believed in the existence of hell?

Lowen strode past the now defunct filling station, past the cemetery with the enormous spire that read AVERY (a relation of Mr. Avery's?), past the veterans' memorial, and then turned onto a side road: one without sidewalks or even a yellow line down the middle. He walked until the road ended and the woods began.

He'd never come down to the forest before, but he knew Clem and his buds had gone four-wheeling there, and many of his classmates were already talking about snowmobiling in these woods when the snow arrived, which apparently might happen any day now.

Lowen felt kind of like an explorer as he hiked the wide path.

Above, bare branches inked across a steel-gray sky. He heard, and then saw, a flock of geese flying in the typical V formation.

Below, his feet crunched over partially frozen mounds of leaves, and he made a game of finding places where water had pooled and then crystallized. One jump burst the skim of ice each time.

He wandered off the path for a few yards to relieve himself, and felt all the more the outdoorsman for watering a wide evergreen in the brisk air.

And that's when he heard a rustle from behind the tree.

His stomach tightened.

Something was on the other side. Maybe a wild turkey. Lowen had seen plenty of those since they'd moved. But it could also be a deer, a moose, or even a bobcat. From the way kids talked, these animals were as common as mosquitoes in the Millville woods.

More rustling. Lowen zipped his fly and backed up, hoping the tree would continue to hide him from whatever it was that was on the other side.

It didn't.

A large man stood thirty yards away; a shotgun pulled up to his eye, the barrel pointed straight at Lowen.

How many hours had Lowen imagined what Abe had gone through, looking into the barrel of a gun? Imagined what he'd been thinking (or not thinking), imagined what he'd said.

When he'd first learned of Abe's death, Lowen had shook uncontrollably. His mother gave him a Tylenol and put him to bed. He had slept for a while, but then he woke and remembered. He had tried not to think of Abe and instead concentrated on his own body. In his mind, his skin was melting away; his muscles were melting away. He imagined himself as a skeleton. He repositioned his arms and his legs and then pictured what the drawing of his skeleton-self would look like.

Later when his therapist suggested he draw what he'd felt when he heard the news of Abe's death, he refused. She'd want to talk about the drawing, and he didn't want to tell her that it was easier to picture himself as bones than to let the full knowledge of what he had done enter his mind. And later, when it did enter his mind—the fact that Abe was dead and it was because of him—he pictured himself breaking every one of his skeleton bones in half. *Crack . . . crack . . . crack.*

Now standing here, in front of this hunter, Lowen suddenly became bones again. Perfectly still bones held in place by tendons and muscles and skin. Bones that would, in a moment, fall to the ground. Later, his skin and his muscles and his tendons would really disappear. He'd decay. He'd be bones in the ground, like Abe.

Perhaps meeting this hunter was only right.

Raise your hands!

Abe's voice.

Lowen raised his arms into the air. Only a second or two had passed.

"Jeesum!" the man said, lowering his gun. "Jeesum!" He paced in a circle. "What the—? Jeesum! What are you doing, kid?"

Lowen exhaled.

"Don't you know it's hunting season?" The man, dressed in dark green except for an orange cap and an orange vest, was clearly distressed. "Jeesum!"

Lowen tried to speak, but no words came out.

The man continued pacing. "You could have been killed. I could have killed you!"

"I'm sorry," said Lowen at last, but he wasn't, at that moment, thinking *sorry*. Instead, he was noticing that his body no longer felt like bones. Instead, a river of energy was surging through his veins. His tendons were tingling, his muscles were tingling, his skin was tingling.

He was alive.

"Get over here," the hunter said to Lowen.

Fear returned. Lowen thought of turning and running. He was fairly confident that this hunter wouldn't shoot now. But he was more used to obeying adults than disobeying. He did what he was told and approached the man.

The hunter put the safety on his shotgun and leaned it against a tree. Then he took his orange vest off. "Come here. Come here. Put this on, kid. You have got to wear orange if you're going to be in these woods during hunting season."

"I don't want to take—"

"I've got plenty of orange," the hunter said. "More than I need. Look, I've still got my hat, and I have lots of orange back home. We all do."

Lowen let the man put the vest over his shoulders and zip him up, even though no one had zipped him into clothing for years.

"You're tall for a kid your age, aren't you?"

Lowen nodded.

Then the man hugged him. Hugged him like he was his grandfather or something. Held him for fear that time could move backward, that this moment could have been different.

"Who . . . What's your name?" Lowen asked the hunter.

The man made eye contact, and Lowen could see fear dart into his eyes. Lowen realized then that almost killing a kid felt awfully close to actually doing it.

"So I can return your vest," Lowen said quickly.

Lines across the man's face softened, his eyes relaxed. "Carter. Carter Hobbs. But I don't want to see you at my house with this vest until after deer hunting season. OK? It ends on Thanksgiving Day."

"You got it," said Lowen. "I'm going right home now."

"Good idea." Mr. Hobbs nodded. "Be careful."

Lowen turned and walked out the way he came. His legs felt weak, wobbly. He whispered, *Thank you,* with each step down the path.

Thank you, around each bend of the winding country road.

Thank you, over small and large cracks in the sidewalks.

Thank you.

It was his most sincere prayer.

24.

THANKSGIVING

Unfortunately, the national holiday especially intended for thanks began with much despair at the Grover house. The first blizzard of the winter had blasted through Millville a day before, taking down power lines and covering everything in a foot of heavy, wet snow. (Clem and his buds had just begun to tear down the old porch when the storm picked up. Lowen had asked if he could help, and for once, Clem didn't rebuff him. He was given the job of carrying the old rusted chairs and discarded nail-ridden boards to the side of the garage, which clearly wasn't as much fun as demolition, and the swirling snow made the job pretty miserable, but it felt good to be making progress—*any* progress—on the home repairs.) Dad's bus was canceled due to the lack of visibility and icy road conditions. Celebrating Thanksgiving without him seemed unthinkable to Lowen. He worried that if they could get through one holiday without Dad, it could happen again—and again—and each time with less concern.

Lowen, Anneth, and Clem woke not only to the news that their celebration wouldn't include Dad, but to the quick-following announcement from Mum that there was no electricity in the Albatross and therefore no heat. Lowen wrapped himself in one of his quilts while the family huddled in the dimly lit kitchen and contemplated the rest of their losses.

"For the first time in thirteen years, I won't get to see the Macy's parade," Anneth lamented.

"Forget the parade," said Clem. "Without TV, there's no football. It's not Thanksgiving without football!"

"Are you guys serious?" said Lowen. "Without electricity, there will be no Thanksgiving dinner!"

"We might have power at the shop," said Mum. "Maybe we'll have to go into town, have Thanksgiving there."

Just then, someone rapped on the door. It was Mr. Field inviting them for Thanksgiving dinner. The Fields had a generator and would therefore be able to use the ovens upstairs and down.

"The reason they have a generator," Lowen whispered to Clem and Anneth as they stood in the background, waiting to hear how Mum would answer, "is so they can keep the bodies frozen."

"The bodies aren't frozen," said Anneth, shooting him a *Don't be ridiculous* look.

"They are if they can't be buried until spring when the ground thaws," said Lowen.

"Who told you that?" Clem asked.

"Dylan." He wondered if his siblings knew that Dylan worked next door. Probably. They actually talked to Dylan, after all.

"Thank you, Mr. Field—um, Larry," Mum said. "We'd love to have Thanksgiving with you."

Clem stood behind Anneth and shook his head no. He had fear in his eyes. He would rather sacrifice football than eat dinner at Field's Funeral Home.

Lowen couldn't believe that when it came to Field's, he was actually braver than his brother. Could it be that Clem might be more affected by Abe's death than anyone realized? It wasn't as though Clem had actually been friends with Abe, either. In fact, he usually dismissed him with some half-kidding put-down, calling him Ape instead of Abe—that sort of thing. Did this make Clem more afraid? Did he think the dead had the power to exact payback?

Lowen recalled the Christmas movie in which Clarence (who was dead but not an angel yet) showed the main character—what was his name? George. George Bailey. He showed George Bailey what life would be like if he were never born. Those were pretty strong powers for someone who wasn't even a first-class angel. A cartoon popped into Lowen's head:

Mum's voice interrupted his thoughts: "Tell Lorrette I can contribute the stuffing and an apple pie—I made both yesterday."

The Grovers weren't the only guests invited to Thanksgiving at Field's Funeral Home. The Doshis were there as well. And so was Coach. The crowd was too large to fit in the Fields' upstairs apartment, so Mr. Field had removed the folding chairs from the chapel room and joined two long tables there instead. The tables were covered in lace linen cloths and had large bouquets of red, yellow, and orange flowers (left over, Mrs. Field said, from the funeral they held on Tuesday) for centerpieces.

Clem had brutally complained while getting ready to come to Field's. He'd showed Lowen the group text he'd sent—Thanksgiving at a funeral home? You gotta be kidding me!—hoping that one of his buds would come to his rescue and invite him over, but it didn't happen.

No sooner had the Grovers caught a glimpse of the table than Mr. Field herded the Grover and Doshi kids into the sitting room across the hall where the dearly departed were viewed one last time.

"The parade!" cried Anneth.

There, in the spot typically occupied by a coffin, was a large-screen TV. On-screen, a life-size Paddington Bear balloon was floating over the streets of New York.

"It's not Thanksgiving without the parade and football, now, is it?" Mr. Field leaned in to Clem and said, "I used to play, you know."

Clem couldn't hide his incredulousness.

"Yup," said Mr. Field, smiling. "I was a Mount Ida Mustang. Not that great a linebacker, mind you—my real game was basketball. Was MVP my senior year. Would you like some dip?" He and Clem left the room talking about some player Lowen had never heard of.

Anneth squeezed onto a love seat with Meera and Hema.

Lowen was about to join them, but Sami said she had to put an eggplant casserole in the oven.

"Eggplant on Thanksgiving?" asked Lowen, following her.

"Vegetarian, remember?" replied Sami. "What did you guys bring?"

"A pie and stuffing to go with the turkey."

"There isn't going to be a turkey," said Sami.

"No turkey?"

Sami rolled her eyes. "Not everyone eats turkey on Thanksgiving, you know. It's bizarro. Thanksgiving is an immigrant celebration, but here in this nation of immigrants, everyone is expected to eat the same thing."

"Never thought about it that way," said Lowen.

"You carnivores are having venison and partridge."

"Venison?"

"Deer meat," said Sami, pouting. "Mr. Field says it's a hunter's Thanksgiving."

A hunter's Thanksgiving. Lowen made sure they were alone, then he told Sami about his encounter with the hunter in the woods. It was the first time he'd spoken of the event; he hadn't even told his mum about it.

"Scary," Sami acknowledged. "Why won't you tell your mother?"

"I don't want her to freak out. She's . . . very sensitive about guns."

Sami looked at him strangely, probably sensing there was more to the story than that, but she didn't pry, which he appreciated. "Well, at least now you know better than to hang out in the woods, without orange, during hunting season."

For a moment, Lowen thought of defending himself. He was a city kid—what had he known about hunting season or wearing orange? But the relief of having shared the story overtook his need to convince Sami that his actions were defensible.

As he shrugged in a good-natured way, it occurred to him that maybe, without his consent or even trying, he and Sami were becoming friends. For a moment he imagined himself telling her the story of Abe, of what it might feel like to have the truth out in the open, to share his burden with someone. But he knew instantly and without a doubt that he couldn't. Unlike the hunting story, there was no defending his actions that day.

They headed back into the chapel, where Mrs. Field was gingerly placing a sweet-potato-and-marshmallow casserole on the table. "I hope you don't mind that we're eating early," she said. She was wearing jeans and a silver-and-blue Lions jersey. "This way we get to see all three games." Lowen realized two things: 1) Mrs. Field was nothing like he imagined; and 2) he didn't really know most of his neighbors yet.

"We don't mind in the least," Mum said to Mrs. Field. She glanced around the table and smiled. "Who would've thought we'd spend our first Millville Thanksgiving in a funeral home!"

"You should have seen Clem when I brought him over here to take a shower!" Mr. Field said to everyone. "He bolted upstairs as fast as his legs could carry him, leaving poor Lowen downstairs."

"Can you blame me?" said Clem, laughing. "I mean, I was taking a shower in the same house where dead people were lying around!"

That was one of the things that Lowen had always admired about his big brother: not only was he good at making other people laugh, he could laugh at himself.

"But people don't die in funeral homes," said Sami. "Most people die in hospitals. But no one thinks, *Wow, this place is full of dead people.* Or *I wonder if the spirits of the dead are hanging around here?* But say 'funeral home' and everyone gets freaked out."

"Exactly," said Mr. Field, leaning back in his chair. "My high-school friends, especially the kids on the football team, couldn't believe that I was going to mortuary college."

"Sounds to me like a smart move," said Rena.

For some reason, Coach couldn't stop smiling at Rena. He nodded in agreement.

"It was!" said Mrs. Field. "Businesses come and go, but a town is always in need of a funeral director."

Rena sighed. "But not, it seems, a used-clothing store. I'm afraid that I have to find a part-time job just to stay afloat."

"I'd hire you if I could," Mum said. "But I'm still in the hole."

"Things are getting better, though!" Anneth said.

Mum nodded. "Now that Millvillians are willing to stop in once the Busy Bee is closed." She looked at Coach. "You know, I think we have you to thank for that. It's a pretty big deal to have one of the town pillars sitting front and center in our window where anyone can see him!"

Lowen studiously avoided Coach's eyes and hoped that Coach wouldn't out him.

But Coach just laughed. "I don't know that I'm *that* influential. But your pies are delicious! I'm only too happy to help spread the word—officially and otherwise."

"You ever think of staying open later?" Mr. Field said to Mum. "Providing pasties for dinner?"

"The thought has crossed my mind," Mum said. "But then I'd never be home in time to make a decent dinner for my own kids."

"Yeah. I sure would miss all the gourmet meals we're having now," said Clem. "Can't get enough of chicken potpie soup. Or shepherd's pie soup."

"Or rutabaga and steak soup," Anneth added.

"I thought that was called upcycling." Mum laughed, but her laughter quickly turned to tears.

"It's OK, Mum," said Lowen, putting his arm around her. "Clem and Anneth were just teasing. The point is that family dinners don't have to be the be-all and end-all."

"Yeah," said Clem. "We just want you to beat the pants off of Mrs. Corbeau!"

Anneth nodded enthusiastically. "And maybe once the shop is a huge success, you can hire someone to cover the dinner shift."

Mum sought out Rena. "What do you think? Would it be worth it to miss dinner with your kids if it meant Restored Riches could get off the ground?"

"Tough call, to be sure," Rena said, but she seemed distracted. "You know, Julie," she added, "you and Anneth have given me an idea, with your 'upcycled' soups and your 'upstyled' clothes. Folks in town might not want to purchase one another's used clothing, but perhaps they would if they couldn't recognize it."

Lowen's brow furrowed. "Huh?"

But Anneth knew exactly what Rena was thinking. "You could combine different used items to upstyle: make dresses from men's shirts, skirts from jeans, and make fancier sweaters by adding bows or faux fur!"

Rena smiled. "Exactly! I'm no slouch when it comes to sewing, but I'd love your creative input! Will you help me?" she asked Anneth.

Anneth didn't hesitate to say yes. "I can highlight the new fashions on my vlog!"

The talk of later hours and upstyled clothing continued until after dessert. The Grover kids gathered in Mr. Field's office to Skype with their father, who had shared a Thanksgiving meal with Abe's mom. "It was OK," said Dad. "She seemed happy to talk to someone who knew Abe."

After the call, Clem joined Mr. Field and Coach in front of the TV for the first of three football games, and Lowen told his mother that he wanted to go out for a walk.

She nodded, no doubt assuming that he wanted to think about Abe a bit. But he had something else in mind.

Sami asked if she could go with him, and Lowen wouldn't have minded, but Rena reminded her that her father might call as well.

"If I had my own cell phone . . ." Sami was arguing— again—as Lowen headed out.

Lowen crossed the parking lot and retrieved the plastic bag that he'd left in the garage of the Albatross. As the sun set, he walked up the hill to the home he hoped belonged to Mr. Carter Hobbs. (He'd looked him up online.)

Lowen could hear a crowd inside and he rang the doorbell several times before someone answered.

Finally a woman came to the door.

"May I please speak to Mr. Hobbs?" Lowen asked.

The woman squinted, looking none too pleased that someone was bothering them on Thanksgiving Day. But she finally turned. "Carter, one of those Dollar Kids is at the door. Asked for you."

Lowen wondered if he'd ever get used to being called a Dollar Kid.

Soon Mr. Hobbs appeared at the door. "Oh!" he said. "It's you."

"Hunting season is over," said Lowen. "I brought you your vest."

Mr. Hobbs laughed. "You didn't have to come today," he said. "But I'm glad you did." He held up the bag. "This here vest will remind me that I have a lot to be thankful for."

"I do too," said Lowen, hopping down off the steps.

"Do you want to come in?" asked Mr. Hobbs.

"No, thanks," said Lowen. "Gotta get back to my own family." He waved.

"Be safe!" Mr. Hobbs called.

Lowen, whose feet had grown another size since they moved to Millville, tromped home in new boots purchased at Handy Hardware. Though the sun had set, the sky retained some of its blueness. A fingernail clipping of a moon hung low in the sky. A lone bright star—probably a planet—made the night feel calm.

But only for a moment.

The stillness of the night awakened the snake inside of Lowen. It curled around his lungs.

Lowen puffed out a burst of air to make more room. His breath, the thing that kept him alive, hung in the air before him.

His dad had spent the day with Abe's mom—something that probably wouldn't have happened if either of them knew. If they knew what really happened the day Abe died. He felt like he was suffocating.

When he returned home, he went to his room, took out a sheet of paper, and wrote, *Dear Mrs. Siskin* . . .

He had no intention of ever mailing the letter to Abe's mother, but he had to shed some thoughts—the same way he had shed the debt of the orange vest. The same way a snake sheds its skin.

25.

DECEMBER

The snow that started the night before Thanksgiving kept on coming through December. In Flintlock, it took no time at all for the snowfall to be plowed up into icy mud monuments. Here in Millville, snow blanketed the town — hiding the long grass, the dingy roofs and porches, the abandoned junk in the yards of empty homes. Now every house was somewhat restored to an earlier glory. It seemed to lift spirits.

So did basketball season. Most of the middle-school games were scheduled for Wednesday afternoons. Miraculously, the other middle-school boys welcomed Lowen. Sure, they'd seen his lack of coordination on the soccer field, and his legs were just as likely to get tangled up on a basketball court, but having a kid with height did have its advantages. If he were in the right place at the right time, he could swat an opposing shot down. Also, thanks to Coach's lessons, he could shoot the ball with some accuracy — if he was standing in place. Layups were still beyond him. Mostly, they thought of him as a secret weapon, a way to psych out the other team.

Lowen wasn't sure how much psyching out he was doing, since he spent most of his time sitting on the bench. According to Coach, to get more playing time he needed to work on his "burst" — that is, he needed to move more energetically, and he needed to think like a basketball player. He wasn't quite sure how to do either.

That wasn't for lack of advice. Like soccer, middle-school basketball games were well attended, and it seemed that everyone hung around to give the *tall kid* some tips. On the one hand, it made Lowen feel valued, and from time to time he wondered if he might actually have potential. On the other hand, he didn't understand half the tips, and he feared that if he didn't start playing well, folks would write him off. Or worse, turn on him.

He had seen how ardent Millville fans could be. The high-school games were every Tuesday and Friday night, and the attendance at the first game was unlike anything the Grovers had seen in Flintlock. The gym was so packed with teenagers, families, and retired folks that it was impossible to get a seat. So Mum, Anneth, and Lowen had stood between the bleachers and the cement wall for the length of the game, listening to the *boom, boom, clap* of the cheerleaders, the swells of shouting from the crowd (sometimes supportive, sometimes not so supportive), and the jarring blast of the buzzer. The excitement was contagious and Mum couldn't help jumping up and down every time Millville scored (and twice as high when Clem did).

Lowen could understand why folks in Millville loved attending games—they were a fun distraction from daily worries. And the Grovers certainly had their fair share of those. Mum was putting everything she had into making the shop work, and the rest of the family was trying to upgrade the house, but every effort they made seemed to hit a dead end. Replacement tiles for the bathroom? Discontinued. The same was true for the kitchen cabinet doors. Replacing the glass in the living room window? The woodwork around the window was rotted. So was the wood in the kitchen beneath their nonexistent dishwasher. It seemed as if every project began with determination and ended in frustration.

So Lowen was relieved when on the second Saturday in December, he had to duck out on repairs in order to visit the seldom-open library. Mrs. K. had assigned the sixth-graders a report on the history of

Millville and told them they could work in pairs. Once again, Lowen and Sami were paired by default, though he didn't mind. They agreed to meet at the library soon after it opened.

Lowen was the first to arrive. When he told Ms. Duffey that he and Sami had chosen to write about the closing of the mill, she led him to a back room and told him to wait at the table. The room was cold—so cold that Lowen sat on his hands. Finally Ms. Duffey returned with a couple of books (including one that looked to be handmade) and some actual newspapers (the library didn't have a microfiche machine) that were quite old and had to remain in the library. She also directed him to a site online where they could read articles about the mill closing.

"Ms. Duffey," Lowen said as she was leaving him there to do his research, "I never asked you—what was the regret you buried?"

She thought for a moment, and then said, "Why, I don't know. It's buried!" But she winked, and Lowen knew that she had chosen not to tell him.

He couldn't bury the letter he'd written to Mrs. Siskin in the frozen ground, but he had buried it deep in his closet. That hadn't seemed to help.

"A sixth-grader like you hasn't lived long enough to have regrets worthy of burials," Ms. Duffey said, as if reading his mind. She gave him a reassuring smile and returned to the circulation desk.

If only you knew.

Lowen opened his notebook but was too distracted to begin reading. Instead he continued to ponder what Ms. Duffey might regret. As far as he knew, she lived alone. If she had kids, they must be grown by now. Maybe her kids had moved away and she regretted letting them go? Maybe someone she knew had died and she never got to tell them something important?

The snake inside Lowen stirred, and his thoughts drifted. He remembered hearing about a book written by a kid who had supposedly died and come back to life. The kid claimed that when you die, deceased loved ones emerge from a tunnel of light to greet you. But what if there was someone in your life you didn't want to see again? When Abe's grandfather died, Abe told Lowen that his grandfather had always been really mean to him. What if his grandfather was the one who met him at the entrance of the tunnel?

Lowen could see it now:

"I can see you've accomplished a lot." It was Sami.

"I knew better than to start without you," Lowen said. "You'd just go ahead and redo any work I'd done."

Sami punched him in the shoulder. "I don't know about that," she said. "You organize your thoughts well. That's why I like working with you."

Ha! If Sami knew all of the confusing thoughts he'd had of late, she'd know that he could use some real help with brain housekeeping. But he was determined to focus this morning.

One of the first things they discovered is that paper mills are not all the same. Some make wrapping paper; some, paper for books; others make paper for checks or envelopes. The mill in their town had made wax paper.

"What's wax paper?" asked Sami.

"It's paper that's been coated in wax. My mum used to use it sometimes to wrap stuff like her pasties so they wouldn't stick together. But you can't recycle it, so she uses parchment paper now, which can be reused."

"I've never even heard of it," said Sami. "And according to this article, that's one of the reasons the mill closed: people stopped using wax paper regularly."

"Why didn't the mill make another type of paper?"

"Like what?"

"Well, like parchment paper. Or newspaper or books or something?"

"Given how specialized paper mills are, my guess is that it would have taken a huge investment to convert to a different type of mill," Sami pointed out. "Besides, it's not just wax paper that's on the decline. Newspapers and even books are being replaced by devices. People aren't using as many paper bags. Even stationery and envelopes have probably taken a hit, now that most people have e-mail."

No wonder the mill had been abandoned. And it wasn't just the mill workers who lost their jobs. Landowners who grew the trees for paper, loggers who cut the trees, and truckers who transported them were all down on their luck as well.

Lowen had heard kids in his class grumble about jobs going overseas, where people worked for less money. And maybe that was part of the problem. But it seemed like the bigger part was that computers were making things like paper unnecessary. He couldn't help wondering what other jobs would disappear. Would a machine replace his father in diagnosing people? Could a robot make better pasties? And what about comics? Could a machine draw better?

It was a depressing thought.

26.

LATER THAT DAY . . .

Lowen and Sami worked together until the library closed. From there they headed through the falling snow to the Cornish Eatery.

They had no sooner walked through the door than Lowen's heart splintered.

There, at the table, was Clem.

And Luna. Together.

Together, together.

Clem and Luna leaning over the table, sharing one of Mum's sweet potato pasties. Clem gazing at Luna. Luna taking little bites of the pie and laughing.

Lowen could feel heat rising from his neck to his cheekbones.

When he looked away, he caught Sami staring at him. He knew by the expression on her face that his feelings had been discovered. *Great.* As if things weren't bad enough!

"Hello, you two," Mum called from behind the counter.

Luna looked up and gave Lowen a smile just for him.

"Do you want some help, Mum?" he asked, already hurrying toward the back.

"That would be great," she said.

He went behind the counter and popped a saffron roll into his mouth — whole.

"Go easy," said Mum.

The place was pretty packed for an early Saturday afternoon. It seemed as if people in town were getting braver about visiting the Cornish Eatery — even when the Busy Bee was open. Sami entered into a conversation with two teen girls who were talking about Restored Riches while waiting for pasties. Sami pulled out her phone (a recent gift from her father, who was probably just as sick of going through Rena as Sami was) and appeared to be showing them a picture of an upstyled shirt.

And that's when Mr. Avery walked in.

His presence surprised them all. Maybe it was a sign that Mum really would be able to make a living here in Millville.

"May I speak to you, Mrs. Grover?" he asked.

"If you don't mind talking to me while I finish making this batch of buns," said Mum.

"If you wish, but I'm afraid I have some bad news." The tone of his voice sounded more like he'd just discovered a cure for cancer.

Mum raised her eyebrows.

"Coach tells me that you plan to stay open through the dinner hour several nights a week."

"That's right," said Mum. "Until eight."

"Well, I double-checked," he said, waving a paperbound book in the air, "and I'm afraid there's an ordinance that will prevent that. You see, any Millville restaurant that provides food after the hour of four must have at least four tables for dining, and fifty percent of the menu must require a knife and fork for eating."

Mum laughed cheerfully. "That's rubbish."

"It's right here in these pages," said Mr. Avery, holding the book up again. "The people of Millville had foresight. They have always known that families who eat dinner together are happier and healthier. This ordinance was intended to squelch the very thing you're trying to do, Mrs. Grover, and that's encourage families to eat on the run rather than sit down at a table with one another."

"That doesn't make sense. We're a take-out establishment. Most people order their pasties to go, and presumably they eat them at the family table."

"I don't make the laws, Mrs. Grover. It's simply my job as a town selectman and code enforcer to remind people that a lot of careful consideration went into creating these laws and they shouldn't be dismissed simply because newcomers think they should."

"But surely there's some—"

Mom stopped short as Mr. Avery grabbed his knees and bent at the waist as if he were about to throw up.

"Mr. Avery?" Mum moved out from behind the counter. She reached for his arm, but he pulled away.

"Mr. Avery? Are you all right?"

Mr. Avery straightened, looking pale. He teetered for a moment and then put his hands on the counter to steady himself. "I'm fine," he gritted out. "Would it be possible . . . for me to have . . . some juice?"

Mum nodded to Lowen, who retrieved a bottle of juice from the cooler.

Mr. Avery drank the juice down in one long gulp. "Thank you," he said gruffly, placing the empty bottle on the counter. "I'll let you get back to work." With that, he headed out the door.

Lowen walked to his mother's side. "What was that about?"

"If I had to guess," said Mum quietly, "I would say that Mr. Avery suffers from low blood sugar."

"What's with him trying to close us down?" called Clem from the table. "That's the dumbest law I have ever heard of!"

"There must be some way to change it," said Luna, her voice as rich as her cello playing.

"Changing laws takes time," Mum said. And then she muttered, so that only Lowen could hear her, "More bloody time than I have to make this shop succeed." She wrapped four pasties in foil and slid them toward the girls Sami had been talking to.

Sitting down that night to a Dad-cooked meal of chicken piccata and risotto, the Grover kids took to brainstorming Cornish meals that would require a knife and fork to eat. Under roast? Pease pudding?

The kids shook their heads. Way too strange for Millville tastes.

"What do you think we should serve, Mum?"

Mum put her fork down, took a sip of her water, and then rubbed her forehead. "I'm thinking that even if we can think of dishes that require a knife and fork—a law that demonstrates the sometimes ludicrous thinking of this little town—I still can't fit four tables in the front of the shop. Trust me, if I do, Mr. Avery will be back citing me for fire safety violations."

He didn't know if it was the tension from the dinner conversation, but Lowen lay awake that night for hours. The full moon was a headlamp beaming into his room. He reminded himself for the millionth time to ask his mother for window shades.

On the other hand, Clem, whose snores traveled down the stairs to Lowen's room, apparently had no trouble sleeping.

Clem, who was so clearly in love. He'd been giddy at dinner. . . . Every comment, every random thought expressed led straight back to Luna.

It goaded him. It wasn't that he believed that a girl who was three years older would actually choose him over Clem; it's just that he hated the thought of her choosing anyone. Her smile, the way she moved her hands when she talked, the texture of her voice, her music . . . She was just . . . just . . .

Definitely too good for Clem.

27.

MID-DECEMBER

Dad kept a promise to stay in Millville through Sunday night to attend the Winter Concert. Lowen sat next to him during the first half when the kids in first through fourth grades sang "jolly songs" — that's what Mum called them anyway.

During intermission, Lowen led his father into the hall to see the poster he and Sami had constructed when doing their research on the history of Millville.

"This was the Wood Room," Lowen said, pointing to the first in a series of sepia pictures that he and Sami had photocopied. "Men had to feed the logs into this machine here that cut them into four-foot lengths. Then the smaller logs were fed into another machine to remove the bark. If a log came out with its bark still on, men used this tool — this long pick — to lift the logs off the belt and load them onto another."

Mr. Avery was suddenly behind them. He pointed to the photo of the men wielding the picks and said, "See here, we Millvillians have had a long history of working hard. We're not afraid to roll up our sleeves."

"It does look hard," said Lowen.

"That's right, young man. We don't expect anyone to give *us* handouts."

Lowen's eyes snapped from the poster to his father's face. Was Mr. Avery implying that he and his father were not hardworking? Why? Because they hadn't started the big house repairs? Did he have a problem with Mum making a go of the restaurant without Dad's help? (Not likely, since Mr. Avery was trying to stop her progress.) Or was he somehow saying that buying a house for one dollar was charity? (And when had charity become such a bad thing?)

Lowen shifted from one foot to the other. Dad was always super friendly, until he decided that you didn't deserve his friendliness.

"Yes, sir," said Dad.

Lowen's body tightened. Dad was whittling his words, which only served to sharpen their point.

Dad nodded. "You and I are a lot alike, Mr. Avery," he said. "I see that now."

Mr. Avery pulled his shoulders back and tugged on the waistband of his pants.

"Oh?"

"We tend to oversimplify."

"Well, I don't know where you think I'm coming from—"

"And," said Dad, interrupting Mr. Avery, all friendliness gone, "we tend to underestimate the opposing forces."

Mr. Avery scowled, but Dad was done. He put his arm around Lowen's shoulders and led him back into the gym, where Lowen headed up onstage to lip-sync all six verses of "Winter Wonderland" (due to the fact that Sami had told him that he had a voice like a fish—and you can't tuna fish) and then to sit back down, only to have his heart busted wide open.

Luna came out onstage in a long gold dress. She sat in the chair in front of the pianist (another high-school kid) and stilled herself, lifted her head, and began to play her cello. While her right hand slid the bow up and down over the strings, her left hand danced over the fingerboard. Lowen's stare moved away from her hands to her face—her face that dove and lifted, dove and lifted, following the trail of each note. The room was full of people, but Luna was in her own world of sound and sensation.

It wasn't Luna's beauty—though he would admit that she was the most beautiful girl he'd ever seen—but the quivering of her bow that affected him most. It was as if

258

she were playing strings in the center of his body, in his chest, under his ribs. It made him feel open, vulnerable, raw. There was no other way for him to describe it: the music peeled his skin off.

Dad turned to him, his face filled with curiosity, and Lowen wondered if he'd been moving—matching Luna's swaying. He didn't feel embarrassment. Instead he felt that all-too-familiar sting in the back of his eyes, and staying in his seat suddenly became impossible.

He excused himself and went to wait in the hall, where the music could still be heard, but remotely. Like a memory.

When he arrived at school the next day, Kyle and Joey were waiting for him, Joey with a basketball in hand. Coach had given the boys permission to play a little ball in the gym before the first bell rang.

"Dylan quit the team," Kyle said as Lowen placed his backpack by the bleachers and peeled off his coat.

"No way! How come?"

"Who knows?" said Joey. "He used to be fun. Not anymore."

"It's like he's always proving something now," Kyle said.

"What does he have to prove?" Lowen asked.

Kyle shrugged. "That he's not a screwup like his old man . . . or too starry-eyed like his mom was."

"How does quitting the team prove either of those things?" asked Lowen, accepting the ball and moving up the court. "I mean, quitting seems like the opposite."

"Like Joey said, who knows? He sure isn't thinking of the team."

Lowen's head was full of Dylan: *Where was his mother and–?*

"Traveling, Grover!" Joey yelled. "We won't have a team if we can't get your head in the game."

"What do you mean? I scored on Wednesday."

"Yeah, but you always look like you have no idea how the ball landed in your palms," said Kyle, not unkindly.

Joey laughed. "Or what to do with it when it does get there."

Lowen couldn't dispute their accusations. Even though he had made some improvements, his mind still wandered.

And his mind was still wandering, thinking about Dylan's quitting, when he walked to Mum's shop that afternoon.

"Hey, shrimp," said Clem when Lowen came through the door of the Eatery.

He and Dad were sitting at the table . . . no, make that *four* tables. All were fairly small. One had a wooden top with years of scratches. Another had a brightly colored tile top and had probably been used on a patio or porch. Two were square and two were rectangular, but pushed together they fit like a puzzle, making one large table.

Lowen laughed. "Where did these tables come from? And what are you doing here, Dad?"

"Two of the tables came from Rena's shop," Mum said, coming out from behind the counter. "And the third one, the tile one, Dad found at the dump."

"The dump?" Lowen said, wrinkling his nose.

"Yup," said Mum. "And your father stayed here in Millville yet another whole day to repair the wobbly legs on it."

"It's amazing what you can find out on YouTube," Dad said.

"So now . . . ?"

"So now your mother is in compliance," said Dad. "She has four tables and food that must be consumed with a knife and fork."

Lowen looked up at the menu on the wall. She still offered all the same flavors: classic, chicken potpie, sweet potato, veggie, shepherd's, but next to each flavor were two options: pasty or full pie. And the pie had to be eaten with a fork.

"But what about the knife?" Lowen asked.

Dad's eyes sparkled. "Mum sets the pies out on the cutting board. You have to use a knife here or at home to cut your pie."

Lowen laughed at his parents' cleverness in outwitting the Millville ordinance.

"I hope I'm here when Mr. Avery comes back to see if Mum is in compliance," said Clem.

"Now, now," said Dad, but Lowen could tell that his father was not really reprimanding his brother. In fact, his father probably wished he could be there, too.

When the door to the shop opened, everyone in the family half expected it to be Mr. Avery. But it wasn't. It was the entire Grey family. Mum jumped up to take their order.

"I'm afraid this is our last order from the Cornish Eatery," Mrs. Grey said.

"Why?" asked Mum, somewhat alarmed. "Has Mr. Avery found another way to shut us down?"

"Oh, no!" Mrs. Grey said. "It's that—"

"We've decided to throw in the towel on this experiment," Dr. Grey said.

Mrs. Grey pulled her kids away from the chair where Lowen was sitting, afraid that they were being intrusive. "We're heading back to Hawaii."

"The cold?" asked Dad.

"Not that," said Dr. Grey. "There just aren't enough people left here in Millville to support a veterinary practice. I knew that. I knew that I would have to open one office here and another in a nearby town. I just hadn't realized how difficult it would be to travel one hundred twenty miles in a day to get to that other office. And neither office has many clients. People in this part of the country can't afford to bring their pets to the vet unless it's a dire emergency."

Lowen couldn't believe what he was hearing. "But you've done all that work to your house!"

"Our kitchen is lovely, but the additional renovations—the ones required for inspection by the town—are just too costly," said Mrs. Grey.

"We're going to cut our losses while we can," Dr. Grey added.

Lagi slipped away from his mother and climbed up onto Lowen's lap.

"And well, we thought we better go back before the kids get too attached to life here." Mrs. Grey pulled a sad Wanda close.

"I never should have quit my practice back home," said Dr. Grey. "It was foolhardy."

Lowen lowered his chin onto Lagi's shoulder.

"I'm genuinely sorry to hear that," Mum said.

Dad nodded in understanding.

Lowen didn't know if the news was making him really sad, or really scared—scared that they wouldn't be able to make this move work, either.

Either way, he knew that he didn't want to say good-bye to this little guy who made him laugh.

28.

JANUARY

The Grover kids already knew what the Millville kids had had to learn in the past few years: Christmas can be just as much fun with a few small but well-chosen gifts. Instead of spending the morning unwrapping, the Grovers played games, recited all in their favorite lines the Santa Claus movie on TV before the actors did, and retold their favorite family stories.

"Remember when Clem put Lowen into the clothes dryer?" Anneth had asked as she was folding her new sweater. "Mum nearly freaked!"

Lowen was too young to remember the incident—he'd been a toddler at the time—but he'd always enjoyed hearing the story. After all, it was pretty funny . . . or was it? Up until their move to Millville, he'd assumed that Clem had liked having a younger brother around. Now, though, he wasn't so sure.

The middle-school team didn't have basketball practice over break, so Lowen helped Dad (who had taken the week off as well) move some of the boxes they had been storing in the garage, which, due to the wide cracks in the siding, got covered in snow whenever there was a storm.

It was early in the morning, before his brother and sister were scooped up in their plans, when he opened a box of papers, and right there on top was a faded newspaper article about the shooting at Georgio's Grocery. With the article was a picture of a poster that had hung on Georgio's wall with photographs of all four of the children who had been shot. Above their faces were the words *You will always be in our hearts.*

Lowen froze. Stared at the picture.

Curious, the others came up behind him.

Dad placed his hand on Lowen's shoulder. If there was any warmth coming from Dad's fingers, Lowen couldn't feel it.

"I sometimes forget there were kids other than Abe," Anneth said when the quiet no longer seemed bearable.

"You didn't know them like you knew him," Dad offered.

"Remember how Abe used to snort when he laughed?" Clem asked.

"Or ask the same questions over and over and over?" Anneth added, wrapping her arms around her body.

266

Lowen looked up at Dad. Surely he would reprimand them for being disrespectful. But he was just smiling, seemingly lost in his own memories of Abe.

"He was so young," Dad said finally. "They all were. Way too young."

"Do you ever think of how often we went into Georgio's?" Anneth asked. "I mean, all it takes is one decision, one moment, and your life is entirely different."

The snake hissed. He'd thought that many, many times. Only he didn't just think it. He wished a thousand million times that he could have changed the one decision he made on the day Abe was murdered.

"Did they ever find out why the Jensen kid did it?" asked Clem. They'd stopped asking these types of questions after they moved to Millville. Perhaps they were afraid that talking about Oliver Jensen would mean bringing Abe's murder with them — as if keeping quiet about it meant they could forget it.

"From what Georgio could recall," Dad said, "he thinks some kids had been teasing Oliver earlier in the day. It's not certain whether it was these kids here." Dad tapped the article. "But Georgio believes Oliver brought his father's gun to the store to scare the kids — get them to stop. Unfortunately, his rage took over."

"I know Abe wasn't one of the kids that teased him," Lowen said. And then added, "Because he was with me earlier that morning." He turned away from Abe's face, the face that seemed to see everything.

It was weird. While alive, Abe seemed pretty clueless when it came to Lowen's feelings. Lowen would be drawing Globber Dog, and trying to figure out whether his slobbering was actually acidic or just plain gross, when Abe would pepper him with questions. It didn't matter if Lowen answered him with short, cursory responses, or sighed heavily each time a new question was asked, or ignored him altogether — the questions kept coming.

Once, Lowen had barked at Abe, "No more questions! Let me draw in peace!"

Abe had gone quiet, but the last thing Lowen experienced was peace. Instead his mind had been trapped in a continuous loop of self-reprimands: *he's only a little kid; he's only curious; his questions help you to come up with good ideas.* And justifications: *I can't concentrate; he asks the most random stuff; he doesn't even listen to my answers.*

Lowen felt as if Abe had *forced* him to snap back, and that the snapping had made him less kind, less accepting, less the sensitive person his father claimed he was. He felt like Abe had changed him.

And here was the kicker: the moment Lowen had lifted his head from the work, the moment he glanced at Abe, the questions had started all over again.

Now, in the garage, the others wandered off.

Lowen put the clipping back in the box and headed up to his room. He had a new idea for a comic:

Now that Abe was dead, Lowen no longer thought of him as clueless. Instead, he feared that he had attained some sort of superpower: the power to read minds, to be all-knowing.

Last week the marquee at the First Baptist Church had read *You can run from God, but you cannot hide.* That was sort of how Lowen pictured Abe: as someone who could see everything he did, know all of his thoughts—even thoughts he'd had in the past. The Unseen Force.

If that were true, did he know that Lowen had often wished Abe didn't live across the hall? That he had wished he could walk past the big elm after school and that Abe wouldn't be standing there? Did Abe know that while he had been asking Lowen questions, Lowen's internal voice was usually screaming, *Shut up!*

What would it be like to die, only to find out that the person you considered your best friend had never really wanted you around?

Right then and there, Lowen decided that when his mother asked him whether he'd like a birthday party for his thirteenth birthday in ten days, he'd say no. It would be his way of honoring the fact that Abe never got the chance to grow older.

♪ ♪ ♪

Later that morning, Lowen returned to the boxes and opened one full of children's books. Because they didn't have any bookshelves in the living room of the Albatross, Lowen was supposed to determine which books belonged to which kid and place them in the appropriate bedroom. Of course this job was nearly impossible, because many of the best books had been read by Clem and then later read by Anneth and then passed on to Lowen. Mum had read a few of the books aloud to all three. How could he possibly decide ownership?

"Just divide them in three piles," Dad said, "and then you can do some swapping."

Easier said than done. The first books he pulled out of the box were part of a trilogy. Should he give all three to one of them, or divide them up? Would book three be considered the best or the worst of the series?

Lowen heard Clem come home and head up to his room.

"Clem," Lowen shouted from the bottom of the stairs, "do you want the first book or the last in the Winsome trilogy?"

He could hear Clem's voice, but he couldn't discern the answer, so he climbed the stairs to Clem's room to ask again.

"I didn't hear. Do you want—"

"Get out of here!" said Clem. He was sprawled out on his bed, FaceTiming with Luna.

Luna's voice flowed through the speaker. "Is that Lowen?"

"Uh, yeah," said Clem, clearly surprised that Luna knew his little brother's name. "He's invading my space."

"Let me talk to him," said Luna.

"Talk to Lowen?" asked Clem. He started to object, but then he leaned over and held out the phone.

Lowen didn't know whether to be pleased or mortified, but he did manage to squeak out a "Hey."

"So, Lowen," said Luna. "Clem says you're an artist."

"Used to be!" Clem shouted.

Lowen nodded, but then realized that Luna might not be able to detect a nod on the small screen and said, "I like to draw, or at least I used to."

"Will you draw me a picture?"

His first reaction was a shrug, but again he figured Luna would just think he'd gone silent. "I wouldn't know what to draw," he said, and for the most part it was an honest answer. He hadn't drawn anything but the Abe comics for nearly ten months; who knew if he even *could* draw something else, assuming he wanted to?

"You said my cello was beautiful. Draw that."

Lowen hadn't said that her cello was beautiful, he'd said that her *playing* was beautiful, but he wasn't about to correct her—especially not in front of Clem. In fact, at that moment, Clem was holding out his hand, gesturing for Lowen to fork over the phone.

"I gotta go," Lowen said. "Here's Clem." He placed the phone in Clem's hand and left the room.

29.

THE NEXT DAY . . .

Lowen woke determined to work on the house. He'd over-heard Sami telling Taylor all about the changes Rena was making to their home. They had put down new floors and updated all the lighting. It made Lowen nervous about the Albatross. So far they had accomplished little more than eradicating the mold and painting the interior rooms, and the requirements for fixing up the house had to be met by June.

"When's the porch going to be done?" Lowen asked Clem at breakfast.

Clem looked at his brother as if to say, *Who's asking?* But he answered him nevertheless. "I've got all of the wood cut, except for the railings—I don't have the right machine for that."

"Can you build the floor this week?" Lowen asked. It would be great to cross this project off their list.

"Are you the new building supervisor?"

"I'm just wondering. I can help you."

"Unfortunately we can't do anything until the ground thaws. The porch is built on posts that have to go into the ground."

"Can we paint the pieces you cut?"

"Too cold for the paint to dry outside, and Mum doesn't want us to do that in the house. So unless you can make me railings for a fifteen-foot porch, we're out of luck. Anyway, Mum may have to settle for boards."

Lots of the porches in town, like their own collapsing porch, were enclosed by wooden panels, but Mum had wanted a porch with railings like the home she grew up in.

Lowen couldn't even imagine how railings were cut, but picturing them in his mind gave him an idea. Many homeowners had removed their rotted front porches. (Some folks just left them off and used their back doors. Those houses had front doors that floated above the ground.) Other folks, perhaps inspired by the Dollar Families, had begun to do some repairs on their homes. Those that could replaced their old porches with composite material that didn't rot. (The Grovers couldn't afford the composites.) Chances were, not all of those discarded railings were rotten. Maybe they could be salvaged—with the homeowners' permission, of course? The houses in Millville were so similar in architecture;

surely a lot of the porch railings were roughly the same shape and size, too? It was worth a try, at least. Clem would be so surprised.

But Lowen had another motive for wanting to stay busy. It was the anniversary of Abe's death. According to Mum, anniversaries often stirred up old grief. Anyway, he was tired of just sitting around, thinking about Abe.

He threw on his coat and headed out the door to see if he could find old railings. He walked slowly, scanning yards as he walked up Beech and across Church. A couple of front yards still held the detached front steps he'd seen the day they arrived. Stairways leading nowhere.

Heading down Cedar, he practically crashed into Sami.

"What's up?" she asked.

He shrugged. He wasn't eager to share his idea, which was starting to feel not only improbable but also rather silly.

"Why are you walking around town?"

Sami could be so direct. He didn't want to lie. "I'm looking for discarded porch railings. No one asked me to. I'm just exploring."

"I'll help," she volunteered.

Something about the way she said it annoyed Lowen. Like she thought he wouldn't do a good job without her help. She wasn't older than he was, and even though she was smarter about some things, it didn't mean he was stupid.

"That's OK," he said. "I've got this."

"No, seriously," Sami said.

"Thanks anyway!" he said, and walked on.

Around the corner, covered in snow, was a pile of lumber next to a porchless house. Lowen walked back and forth on the sidewalk, trying to determine whether the pile had railings. He didn't want to trespass, and he certainly didn't want to look like he was stealing anything. He'd have to ask. He went up the walkway and knocked on the door. No one was home.

As he walked by the lumber, he got a little braver and lifted a large board to see what was underneath.

"What is it you're looking for?" asked a man coming out of the home next door.

What could he say? "I thought folks in town might have wood—porch railings, actually—that they're no longer using."

Thankfully, the guy nodded, and didn't act like Lowen was being stupid or acting inappropriately at all.

"Have you been to the Board Barn?"

Lowen shook his head. "What's that?"

"Well, some people, like my neighbors, leave their wood in their yard knowing that eventually someone will come along and take what they need. But those that don't want it lying around take it to the old barn up on Forest Street. There's all kinds of discarded building materials there. You can help yourself to what you need. It's all free."

"Seriously?"

The guy laughed.

"Seriously. I'm surprised you Dollar Families weren't told about the barn when you arrived in town."

Lowen thanked the man and headed up to the Board Barn. It was a large, somewhat dilapidated building that looked more like a warehouse than a barn, but it had lots of random kitchen appliances in the front, so he guessed he was in the right place. It's funny, he must have passed this building before, but he'd paid no attention.

"Hello?" he called, but the building seemed to be unattended. There was some light coming in from the windows, but he took the liberty of turning on the lights.

Like the man said, the building was full of random wood that someone had taken the time to sort according to type and size. In one aisle he passed sheets of paneling, wallboard, two-by-fours, and boards that looked as if they'd been used for flooring. At the back of the building, he found discarded clapboards, shingles, and some trellises. When he turned the corner, he saw what he'd come for — railings.

As he had predicted, there was a predominant type of railing: square, around two feet long, painted white. The paint was chipped or faded on most, but if there were enough, they'd probably work.

"Find what you're looking for?"

Lowen nearly jumped out of his skin. It was Sami. She was sitting on a pile of wood, her empty wheelbarrow beside her.

"You knew about this place?"

She smiled. "Coach showed us."

"Are you gathering supplies, too?"

She shook her head and slid off the wood, then headed toward the door, leaving the wheelbarrow behind. "Just make sure it gets back to our garage." And with that, she was gone.

30.

THREE DAYS LATER . . .

It was near the end of vacation when Lowen finally opened one of the boxes that had come from his old room. At the top were some worn and ragged stuffed animals. He didn't know what to do with them. He was too old to play with them, but they'd been his companions for so long there was still a part of his brain that believed that they would feel sad and rejected if he threw them out. Maybe he'd give them to Rena to sell, though he couldn't imagine who would want to buy a rabbit with only one ear.

Below the stuffed animals were his sketchbooks. His breath caught for a moment as he lifted them out. His first inclination was to throw them all away. Why be constantly reminded of a prior life—a time when instead of being so wrapped up in drawing superheroes, he could have been acting like one? He could have been a superhero to one particular kid.

The snake inside glided upward, wrapped itself around his heart. Tighter, tighter, tighter. Lowen slid to the floor and made himself open the book lying on top, made himself look inside. He thought, *I deserve this pain.*

He found his most recent book, the one he'd been working on the day Abe had died. It was the story, as always, of Phenom (his version of Wonder Boy) and his trusty dog, Globber. In this episode, Phenom was tackling poverty. He was pulling up large mansions and tumbling them into areas where folks needed housing. Since Phenom could turn himself into any natural disaster, folks just assumed that tornadoes were lifting the houses and depositing them in other areas of the city, where several families could live together. (Of course, The Wave was trying to block his progress.)

Lowen had to laugh at his own naïveté. It wasn't the drawing that was simple but his thinking. Now that he'd moved to Millville, he knew that transferring a house from one owner to another and expecting life to go on as normal was silly. Sure, the owners of the mansions might collect insurance and build bigger, better homes. They might be fine. But the people who had lived in the poorer neighborhoods would no doubt be fighting over who got to live in the mansions. Even the people who already had homes would probably feel entitled to better digs—just as many of the homeowners in Millville were clearly envious of the fact that the Dollar Families could buy their houses so cheaply, when they themselves were struggling to pay their mortgages.

Dad stood over Lowen's shoulder. When he saw that Lowen had his sketchbooks spread out on the floor, he sat down beside him. "Ready to get back to these?"

"Nope."

Dad inhaled. "You're a sensitive kid, Lowen. . . . I'm worried that you think it should have been you on that day instead of Abe."

Lowen had heard all about survivor's guilt in therapy—when someone feels bad because they survived a trauma when others didn't. But it didn't make sense. "I wasn't even there!" said Lowen.

"But perhaps you might have been," said Dad.

Lowen shook his head. Dad had it all wrong, wrong, wrong, and he didn't want to talk about it any longer. But his father rarely let a subject drop unless he felt that he'd arrived at a satisfactory conclusion. So Lowen tried to say something helpful, something truthful. "It's hard to draw now because it reminds me of Abe. It makes me too sad."

Dad nodded. "I get that. But you're sacrificing who you are. I hate to see you bury that part of yourself along with Abe."

For a moment Lowen was tempted to tell Dad everything; everything that had happened on that awful day. He was tempted to say that he didn't have survivor's guilt but just plain guilt: that because of him, Abe had lost his whole life. It seemed only fair that he lose at least part of his.

He closed his journal and went to put it back in the box. Below it was another journal, but this one wasn't his. "Where did this come from?"

"Oh, yeah." Dad said. "Mrs. Siskin gave me this journal at Thanksgiving. She thought you'd like to have it. I forgot that I put it in the stack with yours."

"I gave this to Abe so he could draw comics, too."

"That was nice of you," said Dad.

Not really. It was annoyance that had prompted the gift-giving. Abe had been criticizing Lowen's drawing, trying to get him to make corrections: Globber Dog's nose was too square; Phenom should have longer arms. Finally, Lowen had gone into his room and brought out this sketchbook.

"If you're so clever," Lowen had said to Abe, "draw your own!"

Abe had created characters similar to Lowen's. There was a dog, and a boy, and a villain. Only the names were different. A speech bubble over the boy's head read,

I'm Super Aberacadabra! The name was not a misspelling of abracadabra, but a play on Abe's name: Abe-racadabra. Abe had been so pleased when he'd come up with it.

"He wasn't half bad." Dad pointed to a dog as Lowen leafed through the sketchbook.

Lowen didn't have the heart to say that *he'd* drawn the dog. Abe was a beginning artist and he couldn't make his characters come out the way he wanted them to. So he'd ask Lowen to draw an arm, or the angle of a tall building, or the nose of the dog. By the time he'd asked for the dog's nose, Lowen had been so frustrated by the interruptions that he'd simply drawn the whole thing. He had to admit that "Abe's" dog looked a lot like Globber Dog.

"I wonder if Abe would have kept drawing if he had lived," Dad said.

Lowen shrugged, but doubted that Abe could have continued. He was too impatient. To become good at something, you had to be willing to live through the maddening time when you don't have the skills, when you don't come anywhere close to what you can picture in your head. You try, you struggle, your performance stinks. You fail. A lot. Drawing had taught him that. So had soccer and basketball. (Though he still mostly failed at both of those.)

There were only a few pages of cartoons. Lowen studied the last one: a picture of another dog, a smiling dog, sleeping in the branch of a tree. The caption read, *His bark was worse than his height.* He chuckled.

Abe *was* funny. And he didn't care if you made fun of him, either. He laughed right along with you.

"You know, Lowen," Dad said, "drawing your comics might be one way of honoring Abe."

Ugh. Dad would never understand. But hopefully he'd give up.

31.

LATE JANUARY

By all accounts, the Cornish Eatery was doing better. Staying open longer seemed to help. People stopped in after the Busy Bee closed and ordered food for take-out, or they sat around the big table in the middle, catching up on one another's lives.

In fact, the four tables pushed together, the thing Dad had done to outwit Mr. Avery and his codes, actually made Mum's shop more popular. Unlike any of the tables at the Busy Bee, the entire garden club could fit around this large table and hear one another clearly. So could the birders and the folks who had begun to help Rena refashion clothes for the fun of it (and for a discount at her store).

So it surprised them all when during the last week of January, an entire afternoon went by and only two customers had come into the shop.

The next day there was only one.

And the day after that? No one. Nada. Zilch.

That Saturday, in the half hour time block between Lowen's and Clem's basketball practices, Dad called a family meeting at the shop.

Mum set a platter of pasties on the table and sat down with the family. There wasn't a customer in the eatery.

Dad cleared his throat. "I called a meeting," he said, "because, well, something's changed."

Lowen put down the second half of his pasty.

"Your mom has barely had a customer all week."

Mum looked down, fiddled with the strings on the front of her apron.

"We thought one of you might've heard something . . . something that might shed some light on this sudden change in business," Dad said. "A rumor, perhaps?"

Mum raised her eyes to look at them. "You guys are out and about more than we are. Did someone get food poisoning? Have I offended anyone in town?"

"Mum, no!" Clem said as the other two Grover kids shook their heads. "You haven't done anything!"

"Well, there must be some reason for the change," Dad said.

"It's only been one quiet week," Anneth said. "Every business has some weeks that are less busy than others."

"True," Mum said. "But there's usually a reason."

287

Both Clem and Lowen reached for their phones (Lowen's being a new birthday present from his parents).

"Leave them alone," Dad said. "We're having a family discussion."

"I was going to text Coach," Clem said. Lowen nodded. He'd had the same plan.

"I said—"

"Dad," said Anneth. "If anyone can tell us what's going on, it's Coach."

His father waited a moment and then gave Clem a nod.

Clem read a return text from Coach: Busy Bee is selling tailgate boxes.

Tailgate boxes?

Dad raised his eyebrows. "Ask him what the heck that means."

Rather than keep texting back and forth, Clem decided just to call Coach. Now on speakerphone, Coach explained to the family that once the holidays were over, nearly everyone in Millville attended the high-school basketball games. And they didn't just attend home games; they followed the Cougars to their away games. And on the days of the week when the Cougars weren't playing, they drove to watch teams in other divisions—

to predict which teams might have the best chance of ending up in the state tournament.

"But you would think all that driving would increase business," Dad said. "People like take-out for road trips."

"Yeah," said Coach. "That's why the Busy Bee started offering tailgate boxes. The boxes have a sandwich, macaroni salad, and a basketball-shaped cookie. Plus, ten percent of the proceeds go toward the basketball team. I feel bad. I probably should have let you know this was coming."

Mum heaved a great sigh.

"Thanks, Coach," said Dad. "You've been very helpful."

"Sorry, Mum," said Anneth when Clem had hung up. "I guess I've been too busy this week to notice that things have gotten that bad."

"I realize now that I've been seeing the tailgate boxes at games," Lowen said. "But I didn't even think to ask what they were."

"It's not your fault!" Mum said. "You have your lives to live here in Millville. You shouldn't have to be thinking of the next big roadblock Virginia Corbeau or Mr. Avery is going to put in our way."

"I don't get it. Without the Dollar Kids, there wouldn't even be a high-school basketball team," said Clem.

Dad agreed. "If more Dollar Kids leave, there won't be a Central School. As it is, this town and several others should have merged their schools, made one consolidated school. But folks here want things to stay the way they've always been."

"No kidding," Anneth said.

"I can help," said a quiet voice.

The family erupted out of their huddle to see Dylan standing in the doorway. How long had he been there? Had he been listening to the entire conversation?

There was an awkward silence and then Mum said, "We'll take all the help we can get, Dylan. Come. Join us."

"I'm free after school," said Dylan, coming closer but still standing. "I could make deliveries."

"Deliveries?" asked Mum. "But don't you have after-school activities?"

"I heard you quit basketball," Clem said.

"I had to."

"Forget about deliveries," Lowen said. "You should come back to the basketball team, Dylan. You're good. The team needs you. Heck, *I* could quit the team and start making deliveries."

Dylan looked down. "I know where everyone lives," he said.

"The town's not that big," said Lowen. "I can learn."

"That aside, I'm not sure deliveries could compete with these tailgate boxes," Dad said.

"There're lots of old people who aren't able to go to the games," said Dylan. "Like Mrs. Lavasseur, and Mr. and Mrs. Owens."

Lowen remembered Mrs. Lavasseur—she was the one who liked that French pie: *tour*—, *tour*—? He couldn't pull the name of it.

"Some don't get out a lot," Dylan continued, "especially in the winter. Seems like they might like to have a pasty delivered."

"That's a good point, Dylan," said Mum, her face scrunched with the effort of calculating. "And offering free delivery might help with those holdouts who are afraid that Virginia Woolf will see them stepping foot in here."

"*Virginia Woolf?*" asked Anneth.

Mum laughed. "I meant Virginia Corbeau. But sometimes I do feel as if she's the wolf at the door."

Dad, still pondering the logistics of Dylan's proposal, interrupted: "Do we really want to offer *free* delivery?"

"It seems like the only way to compete," said Clem.

Dylan lifted his head and looked Mum right in the eye. "I need a job, Mrs. Grover, and because I'm only twelve, delivery is the only real paying job that I'm allowed to do. By law, that is."

"By law?" asked Dad.

"Yeah, kids my age have always been allowed to make deliveries so they could get jobs as paperboys—or girls. Only not that many people get the paper anymore."

"I think you have an idea worth considering," Mum said. "Mr. Grover and I will talk about it—see if we can pay to have food delivered—and I'll get in touch with you either way."

As if he were releasing a heavy load, Dylan's shoulders dropped and his face lit up. Lowen wondered again about Dylan's family situation. He couldn't imagine that he needed money living with Mr. Avery. From the looks of his house, Mr. Avery seemed to be the only one in town with any money at all. Dylan said his father was working for another mill. . . . Did his dad need extra money? Would he really bother his twelve-year-old son for help with his bills? And what about his mother? He'd said that his mother was gone. Did that mean she was living somewhere else or . . . ? Lowen suddenly recalled the argument he and Dylan had had in the gym, the one in which Dylan defended heaven (and called him pathetic). *Of course,* he thought. *Dylan's mother must have died.*

Mum gave Dylan an encouraging smile.

Lowen was glad.

"Yikes! I got to get to basketball practice!" Clem shouted, and that was the end of the family meeting.

32.

FEBRUARY

Lowen routinely took a shower at home after basketball practice. But on this particular day, he was greeted with a large pool of water on the cold tile floor. His first thought was that Clem had been careless, but that didn't make sense. Clem didn't shower until after his practice. And Anneth, who frequently complained of having to share a bathroom with two slobs, wouldn't have left water on the floor.

Looking up, he spotted water dripping from the ceiling and a large stain similar to the one that had formed over the kitchen after the pipe broke.

"Dad! You better get up here!" he shouted.

After examining the dripping water for a moment, Dad directed Lowen to turn the water valve off the way Dylan had the last time something like this happened.

But when Lowen returned to the bathroom, the water was still dripping. "Did you turn it in the right direction?" his father asked.

"I think so," he said. "Righty tighty."

"Then why is the water still coming?" Dad asked. If anything, it was dripping faster.

"Maybe it's not a leaking pipe," said Anneth, joining them in the bathroom.

Dad thought for a moment and then walked downstairs and outside. He didn't even stop to put on a jacket or boots. The kids followed.

Looking up, they could see the likely problem. Heaps of snow and ice had collected on the roof over the bathroom.

"It must be melting into our bathroom," said Anneth.

"But it's freezing out here." Lowen rubbed his hands over his bare forearms. "Why would it melt?"

"The rising heat from inside the house," said Dad. "I'm guessing that there's not enough insulation to keep the heat inside and prevent the ice from melting."

"What do we do?" Anneth asked.

"We've got to find a way to get the snow and ice off the roof," said Dad, "or we're going to have another ceiling falling down on top of us."

Lowen looked over at Field's Funeral Home. He could tell that they used some tool to remove the snow on their roof's edge. He shared this observation with his father, who sent him over to Field's to find out what it was.

After slipping on his boots and jacket, he walked around to the Fields' back door and rang the bell. No one answered, though Lowen was quite certain he could hear voices downstairs and thought they might be coming from the serving kitchen. He opened the door just a crack and called out, "Hello?"

Still no one answered, but certain now that he could hear someone talking, he let himself in, slipped off his wet boots, and called out once more, hoping he wasn't interrupting a conversation between Mr. Field and the loved one of a newly dead person.

No answer.

He followed the sound down the long hall and into the viewing room on the left. There wasn't a coffin in the room, and Lowen could see, for the first time, that the paneling on the viewing wall hid a cupboard at one end. Inside the cupboard was a sound system and a control panel. Lowen recognized the radio program that was currently being broadcast through the speakers—it was the same news program his father liked to listen to from time to time. He stood there and tried to figure out what all of the buttons on the panel could possibly control.

Without Lowen touching anything, the paneled wall began to move. Lowen jumped back and prepared to run.

"Why, hello there!" said Mr. Field as the wall opened to reveal an elevator. Mr. Field was pushing a closed coffin on a rolling cart. "I didn't expect to see you here, Lowen."

"I didn't expect to see you here, either! I mean, not in a hidden elevator." It felt funny to be talking in such a normal way with a coffin between them.

"Yes, well, we do try to keep the nuts and bolts of the operation out of sight. We need the elevator to get the coffins upstairs."

"I never thought about it," Lowen said, but it was clear now that a coffin couldn't be carried up those narrow basement steps.

"We operate all sorts of things from this paneled wall." Mr. Field walked over to the cupboard, switched off the radio, and turned on soothing organ music. Then he turned a knob that changed the overhead lighting from a bright yellow glare to a soft pink glow.

"Cool!" said Lowen.

Again Mr. Field adjusted the sound system, changing the music to some sort of singing, a deep rhythmic sound that was less familiar to Lowen. "What's that?"

"Greek monks chanting," Mr. Field said as he turned the lighting from a rosy pink to a sea blue.

"Eerie."

"I like this one." Mr. Field switched the chanting to a more familiar type of music, a deep and soulful sound that opened something up in Lowen's belly, lifted his heart, and sent vibrations pulsing through his veins.

"That's a cello!" Lowen whispered as the string sound climbed higher.

"Good for you," Mr. Field said. "Which reminds me, have you heard Luna Muñoz play?"

Lowen nodded, not trusting his voice.

"The family of the deceased—of Mr. Rossi here," he said, tapping the top of the coffin, "have asked her to play at the service. Mr. Rossi was postmaster here in town for many, many years. It should be a packed house. But," he said, shaking his head, "I bet you came over here for reasons other than a friendly chat about Mr. Rossi."

Lowen explained about the roof leak, and Mr. Field told him about the long-handled rake he used specifically for pulling snow and ice off the shingles. "You're welcome to borrow it, but would you mind going out to the garage and getting it on your own?" he asked. "This is a three-coffin week for me."

"No problem," said Lowen. He headed down the stairs to the basement, past the embalming room, and out to the garage. There was the big black hearse and the

298

enormous refrigerator. He recalled Mr. Field saying that it was a three-coffin week and wondered if either of the other two bodies was currently stored in there. He was tempted to open the door and peek. What would he see? The tops of heads? The bottoms of feet? He didn't think Clem could ignore him at dinner if he told the story of opening the funeral home fridge. He wrapped his fingers around the handle and . . .

Stopped.

It wasn't that he was scared. It really wasn't. It was that one minute his brain thought of the dead as something creepy—stiff blue bodies, half-dead zombies, ghosts—and the next minute he was remembering that the dead are someone's loved ones, someone's son or sister or friend.

A new Abe comic came to mind. He imagined Oliver Jensen as having a similar kind of split brain—only he was realizing that the *living* had been someone's loved ones.

The rake worked well. The Grovers kept the snow and ice off the roof of the Albatross, but a week later, when Mum returned home from the shop, she reported that the gutter had fallen off the front of the house and was lying in the front yard.

"Water must have been dripping and freezing inside the gutter," said Dad during a Skype call. Once again, he had to work on the weekend. "And the weight was too much. Though you'd think that everyone would be having this problem."

"It's probably just one more thing that wasn't installed properly," said Mum, who had saved a piece of the gutter for Dylan. Now, in addition to all of the jobs they had put on the to-do list in June, she had added *repair dining room and bathroom ceilings* and *replace all the gutters*. The only thing they had crossed off was *eradicate mold*, though the bathroom tiles had still not been replaced. The way Lowen figured it, they had about three and a half more months to finish everything on their list. Was that even possible?

After dinner, Anneth pulled out her sketches of refashioned clothing and spread them out on the table. Whereas before she had gotten her ideas from the Internet, she was now experimenting with her own designs. She had fashioned a dress from a man's hunting jacket and a scarf from a fisherman's sweater. And her sketches? They weren't half bad. Three faceless girls stood together, one with her toes turned in, another slouching with her hand in her pocket, and the third standing sideways, her chin tilted in such a way that you knew this girl had the most confidence.

"Wow," Clem said, pausing on his way out the back door. "You can tell the girls' personalities just by the way they're standing."

Mum leaned over to look. "We have another artist in the family!" she said.

The comments made Lowen feel strange . . . as if he'd given something away—something precious.

"Thanks," said Anneth, "but I wish I could draw faces. All of my models look the same." She turned to Lowen. "Will you help me? Will you show me how to draw expressions?"

"Wonderful idea!" Mum said, heading into the kitchen to finish the dishes. "Lowen has always been able to capture the essence of a person in their face."

Lowen allowed his own face to distort into a decisive and emphatic *NO*. He hadn't drawn anything but the Abe comics for ten whole months now. In this one small, probably ridiculous, way, he had honored Abe. On top of all of the other hard feelings he had about Abe's death, he didn't want to feel weak, too.

"Please, Lowen?" Anneth asked.

Did Mum or Dad put her up to this?

"I've tried watching videos, but my girls' expressions make them all look like paper dolls. It's the angle of their eyes, right?"

Her question seemed sincere. He'd had the same trouble when he made his first comics. Every character looked the same.

It occurred to him that by refusing to help Anneth, he was being just like Clem. He was withholding. Would she think it was because he didn't want her to become a decent artist? (Was that why Clem didn't want to show him how to play soccer? Was it Sami's scarcity principle again? Was there only enough room in a family for one athlete, one upstylist, one artist?)

"I used to think that all of a person's personality came from the eyes, too," he said, coming closer. "But in cartooning, which may be different from drawing more realistic faces, the feelings are shown more with the mouth."

"The mouth? *Really?* Like in the shape of the lips?"

He paused, started to speak, paused again.

"Here," she said, thrusting the pencil into his hands. "Show me."

The way she insisted reminded him of Abe: *Draw a better ear, draw action lines, make things go flying more.* The snake rose to his throat.

He took the pencil.

He sketched two identical faces with two identical eyes and noses. Then on one face, he drew a mouth that was sort of smirky, with one side higher than the other. He added an eyebrow that lifted up on the same side. On the other face he drew a wide smile, with a couple of laugh lines. Not bad!

"Cool! The eyes almost seem to be twinkling, even though you didn't touch them!" Anneth said.

Lowen straightened and twirled the pencil in his fingers. He wondered if his own eyes were twinkling, too; drawing those two faces for Anneth had been like drinking a tall glass of cool water on a sweltering day.

He returned to his room and, pulling out his unused sketchbook, decided to take one more sip. Sure, drawing his old Phenom comics brought on horrible memories, but maybe he could satisfy his itch by drawing something else. Something entirely unrelated. Recalling a challenge his art teacher used to give him, he drew a random squiggle. What did this look like? How could he incorporate the scribble into a drawing?

The line sort of looked like a man lying down, he decided. Like his dad, the last time he was in Millville. "I'm glad it's impossible to get this chair up to your room, Clem," Dad had said as he stretched out in the brown corduroy recliner and rested his eyes. "I've become accustomed to its comfort."

The truth was, Dad almost never relaxed. Ever since they moved into this house, all Lowen's parents did was try to figure out ways to keep the Eatery running in order to earn the money to make the repairs to the house. So far, not so good.

But Lowen had liked seeing the rare contented look on his father's face and decided now to draw him. While drawing the chair, it occurred to him that it might be more fun to make this picture cartoony rather than realistic. He exaggerated the puffiness of the chair, his father's belly, the droopiness of his eyelids, and his smile.

His pencil darted up and down, in and out, like a puppy rediscovering all its favorite places at a park.

"You've done a caricature!" said Mum when he showed it to her.

Lowen recalled a man at the Flintlock school fair who drew funny drawings of people and remembered that he had called them caricatures. The name reminded him of the word *characters*. He smiled and wrote *Dad Chillin'* at the bottom.

Mum laughed.

"May I have this drawing, Lowen?" asked Mum. "I know just what to do with it."

Later that night, Lowen watched some videos on how to draw caricatures and realized these types of drawings had a lot in common with comics. Both required fewer lines and used exaggerated facial features to demonstrate emotion.

While waiting for basketball practice the next day, he took out his sketchpad (what could it hurt?) and drew a caricature of Coach as he dismissed the bus lines. He gave him a large forehead, big ears, and a wide toothy smile. Then he gave him a disproportionately tiny, but muscular, body, as he'd seen other artists do. Around his neck he added a large whistle, and under one arm a basketball.

"That's Coach!" said Joey, looking over his shoulder. "You are goo-ood, Lowdown! How come you haven't drawn for us before?"

The nickname wasn't lost on Lowen. *Lowdown.* He liked that.

Other members of the team came over to admire his drawings; some asked if he would do one of them, and he might have if Coach hadn't told them to stop dilly-dallying and get changed. They were playing in the middle-school finals that weekend and every minute of practice counted.

"Grover!" Coach yelled as the others hustled to the locker room. "Get over here. Let me see your drawing."

Lowen walked slowly. Clearly someone had ratted him out. Would Coach think he was making fun of him? Being disrespectful? He wished he hadn't made Coach's ears so big, his smile so crazy wide.

Coach snickered. "Not bad, Grover. But next time have me doing something exciting with that ball, you know, like knocking it down."

Maybe it was the relief that came from drawing again, or maybe it was the new nickname — Lowdown — that had quickly caught on and made him feel like part of the team. Whatever the reason, practice went better that afternoon. Coach divided the kids into two groups for drills. While sitting on the bench waiting for his turn to do a shooting drill, Lowen began to notice, for the first time, how the ball bounced off the rim. He started to imagine lines that would demonstrate the ball's course—like the lines he drew to show action. He found that after a few rounds of watching the other group, he could predict, with some accuracy, where the ball would come off—what direction it would take. Later, when they scrimmaged, Lowen positioned himself where he expected the ball to land. Several times he was there for the rebound.

"Whoa, Lowdown! You must have had your Wheaties this morning!"

For once, he'd found his focus.

Lowen couldn't wait for school the next day. He had spent a good deal of time drawing caricatures of famous people the night before and hoped there would be an opportunity to show them to the guys. Maybe Joey or Kyle would ask him to draw them again, and then he could turn the pages of his sketchbook slowly, searching for a blank sheet of paper, giving them a chance to *ooh* and *ahh* over his other pictures.

Unfortunately, by the time he arrived, they were already huddled around Kyle, who had just announced that his family was moving out of Millville. Apparently his parents found good-paying jobs in the southern part of the state, where mills were never part of the economy.

"I can't believe it, man!" Joey cried. "You'll at least wait until after the basketball finals, right?"

"We leave the weekend after finals."

Joey shook his head in disbelief. "But we were in kindergarten together. Kindergarten!"

"Back when there used to be three kindergarten classes," said Taylor. That there was more than one class for each grade here in Millville seemed impossible to Lowen, but he'd seen all the empty classrooms.

"We're really going to miss you, Kyle," Lily said.

The kids all nodded in agreement, even Lowen, who had gotten used to their class being, *well,* their class.

"My mom keeps talking about us moving, too," said Amber.

"I think everybody's family talks about moving," said Taylor.

"Can we not talk about this?" asked Dylan.

No one knew what else to say then. Whereas most kids' families probably lost income from the closing of the mill and had to cut way back, Dylan had somehow lost his house and, as far as Lowen could tell, both his parents.

The bell rang and kids strode to their lockers, seemingly eager to put the conversation behind them. But

Lowen felt lousy. He realized that Dylan might have been asking him about Abe that day in the gym because he'd had someone close to him die, too. That all this time they'd had this thing in common and he'd shut Dylan out. His insides began to grip the same way they did whenever he thought of Abe. How could he be such a jerk without even trying?

He strode over to Dylan's locker and waited for Dylan to acknowledge him, but he seemed to be searching for something. "Hey," Lowen started, figuring Dylan could hear him fine. "Hey, you know that day . . . that day I . . . well, I'm sorry I said there wasn't a heaven. I didn't know."

Dylan lifted his head out of his locker and stared at Lowen. "Didn't know what?"

"About your mom."

"What about my mom?"

"I didn't realize . . . I didn't know that she died."

Dylan slammed his locker shut. "What are you talking about? My mother didn't die. Who told you that?"

"No one. I just . . . Sorry," he said, meaning it, but not sure if it sounded as if he meant it.

"I said she's *gone.* She's gone to North Carolina, where my aunts and uncles live. Not that it's any of your business."

Lowen remained still.

"You know," said Dylan, "if you want to get to know someone, you could just put in a little time. Hang out. Talk about stuff. You might find out that a lot of the things you guessed, a lot of the things you think, are just plain wrong." And with that, Dylan walked off toward homeroom.

Dylan hadn't laid a finger on him, but Lowen felt sucker punched just the same.

33.

END OF FEBRUARY

It was hard to believe that basketball season was winding down. No doubt Lowen would have been nervous during the first finals game between the Millville Cougars and the Jeffer Grizzlies even if his family weren't sitting in the bleachers. *It was the finals!* But the finals were held on weekends and that meant that not only was his mother present, but so was his father, and that made it harder for Lowen to just let go and let his body recall how to dribble, pass, and shoot. Instead, he tried too hard to think about all he had learned, and that made his efforts clumsy and awkward.

Right after Coach's halftime huddle, in which he told the boys to calm down and have more fun, Lowen gave himself a pep talk: *You don't have to think when you draw. Your hand knows what to do. So stop thinking so much. You've been practicing! Trust both hands. Trust your feet. Be the rebound king!*

And it worked! As he dribbled down the court, he repeated these words: *Trust your hands; trust your feet.*

He made a chest pass to Joey, who moved in for a layup. *Swish!*

He leaned in for a rebound and was fouled. He went to the line to take his free throw. *You've been practicing. Trust your hands.*

Whoosh!

"Go, Lowen!" he heard Anneth yell from the stands.

The second shot bounced off the rim. But at least he'd made that first shot!

In the fourth quarter, the Grizzlies were up by one. Joey was called on a foul, and as their center took careful aim in the circle, Lowen stood at the ready in the bucket. He was the closest member of his team to the basket. Feet balanced, knees slightly bent, calves tight, he was a cougar ready to pounce.

A voice in his head: *Get ready to fire.*

The Grizzly sunk it.

Again he positioned. Again he heard, *Get ready to fire.* Abe's voice. *Get ready to fire.*

I got it, Abe, Lowen thought. *I got it.* He tightened again. Waited, waited, waited . . .

Bam! The ball bounced off the rim and into action. Lowen fired. He grabbed the ball, dribbled.

A Grizzly was coming toward him. He swiveled. Kept the ball. Swiveled again.

The guard was all over him.

He passed the ball from one hand to the other, broke free, dribbled to the basket, and shot. Score!

Lowen turned and noticed that all of his teammates were clustered at the other end of the court. They weren't shuffling to get into a defensive position. They were banging themselves on the head.

The Grizzlies, on the other hand, were cheering — bent over laughing.

Lowen had scored, but in his excitement he'd shot the ball into the Grizzlies' net. Jeffer was now up by a solid four points.

Lowen glanced up into the stands. His father held his head in his hands. Mum gave him a weak Mum smile.

Then his glance moved down. Anneth was showing her friends her phone. Had she filmed the moment? Perhaps, but maybe not. She might not have cared enough.

His eyes moved lower still to the spot on the bleachers, now empty, where Clem had been sitting with friends just moments before.

The buzzer sounded. The basketball season for the Millville Cougars was over.

No doubt Abe was laughing.

For the next week, life in Millville was one humiliating encounter after another. Everywhere Lowen went, folks ribbed him about the game. First, they'd tell him (with a big grin) that they'd seen the tournament. Then (after he made some self-effacing remark) they'd jibe him by saying he needed a map, a compass, or a GPS. Finally they'd ask him if he'd seen the video a spectator took (if it was Anneth, she wouldn't say)—a clip of the exact moment when Lowen turned himself around one final time and sunk a shot for the Jeffer Grizzlies.

So on the following Saturday, when Ms. Duffey walked into Mum's shop, he responded to her "Hello, Lowen" with "Yes, I scored for the other team. Yes, I need a compass. And yes, I've seen the video—and so has everyone else in Millville, given how many times it's been viewed."

"Lowen!" said Dad. He was in the front of the shop, washing the big window.

Ms. Duffey made a very sympathetic face and said, "Oh, my. I hadn't heard."

"Well, I think you are the only one in Millville," said Lowen.

She patted him on the shoulder. "It can feel that way in small towns. I often feel like an anomaly since I don't spend my evenings at basketball games."

Mum appeared from behind the back shelves and greeted Ms. Duffey. "What can I get you?"

Ms. Duffey looked up at the wall where the menu was posted on the chalkboard. "What's a Dad Chillin'?" she asked.

"Pardon me?" asked Mum.

"What's in a Dad Chillin' pasty?"

Lowen burst out laughing. His mum had taken the caricature he'd drawn of his father and taped it to the sandwich shop wall, just beneath the menu board.

"It's a steak and cheese," improvised Mum, smiling.

"That's my favorite!" Dad called from the window. "Don't know where it got that name, though. I sure haven't done any chilling since we moved to Millville."

Mum and Lowen shared a conspiratorial smile. Dad could be so blind sometimes.

Just then Coach walked into the shop.

"Hello, Barb," Coach said to Ms. Duffey. "What are you up to?"

"I'm having myself a Dad Chillin'," she said, pointing to the picture.

Coach turned to Lowen. "Where's my picture? How come it's not on the wall?"

"You drew a picture of Coach?" Mum asked as she cut a pie. "Let's see it."

316

Lowen had been revising a caricature of Mum, but he turned to the picture of Coach, as directed, and held it up.

"Oh, we definitely need to have this picture on the wall, too," Mum said.

"And I want a pie named after me," said Coach.

Dad chuckled.

"Let's see," said Mum. "Coach's favorite is chicken potpie. Can you come up with a caption for this picture that matches that one, Lowen?

He thought for a minute. "How about Kickin' Jump Shot Pie?"

Coach loved it. So did Mum and Dad.

"Would you draw me?" asked Ms. Duffey. "I'd like to have a pie named after me." She sat down at the table across from Lowen and waited.

Well, this was awkward. The tricky thing about drawing a caricature was that you were supposed to take a person's most prominent features and exaggerate them. This didn't exactly create the most flattering picture. What if he hurt Ms. Duffey's feelings?

Nevertheless, Lowen began sketching. He drew the librarian with a long neck, high cheekbones, and a warm (but slightly tired) smile. She was sitting on top of a pile of books.

"What's your favorite pasty?" asked Lowen.

Ms. Duffey took a bite of the Dad Chillin' that Mum put in front of her. "This one is going to be hard to beat," said Ms. Duffey, "but I've been meaning to ask if it would be possible to add lamb and mint to the menu? It's one of my favorite combinations of flavors."

"Lamb and mint pasties are wonderful!" said Mum. "It's one of my favorites, but I just haven't been daring enough to put it on the menu here. You've inspired me. I'll order lamb this week."

Lowen wrote the caption: *Sweet Bleat.*

Dad gave him an approving nod. "Go put it on the wall." Then his father changed the subject. "We still on for that double date tonight, Coach?"

Ms. Duffey raised her eyebrows at Lowen.

Lowen shrugged. This was the first he was hearing of any double date.

"Rena can be ready at six thirty," Mum said. "She just wants a little time after work to clean up."

"Of course," said Ms. Duffey, nodding at Coach. "You and Rena." Like it was the most obvious match in the world.

"Now, don't go getting any ideas," said Coach. "It's taken her months to say yes and it's only dinner in Ranger."

34.

MARCH

The pictures of Dad, Coach, and Ms. Duffey were only the beginning. Rena's *(Upstyled Tomato and Cheese)* went on the wall next, followed by Sami's *(Sporty Artichoke)* and Carter Hobbs's *(Prime Buck)*. From then on, business really picked up. People stopped in to get a peek at the "pasty gallery," and asked Mum to create unique pasties so Lowen would draw them. (To keep the pasties in the realm of the possible, Mum put a list of ingredients she was willing to combine on the blackboard.) And with basketball season over and baseball season not yet begun, the tailgate boxes were no longer an issue. For the first time since they moved to Millville, it looked like the shop would succeed.

Perhaps that's why, one afternoon in March, when Clem was out in the garage with Luna, and Anneth was helping Rena, and Lowen was putting the finishing touches on a caricature of Dave (who loved rutabaga), Lowen looked out the window and saw Mr. Corbeau, husband of Virginia Corbeau, taking pictures of the Albatross, with the peeling paint, the boarded window, and the gutter resting in the melting snow in the front yard.

"I was afraid this was going to happen," Clem said as he popped in the house for two glasses of water and some cookies. "Looks like they've given up on shutting down the Cornish Eatery, and instead they're going to run us out of town for not making the repairs."

Clem called the shop to tell Mum, but Mum was too frantic to talk. Apparently Dylan hadn't come in to make deliveries.

On Saturday, when Dylan hadn't shown up for a third day in a row, Mum called home and asked Lowen to come down to the shop. "Dad's helping me make pasties, I need you to do the deliveries," she said.

So much for working on his drawing. It made him more than annoyed than ever at Dylan. Where was he? And why wasn't he doing his job?

As Lowen helped Mum pack up a rather big order, which included one big chicken potpie and several pasties, Dylan came running into the shop with ratty slippers on his feet.

"Hey," said Lowen, about to make a crack about the footwear. But Dylan ignored him.

"Mr. Grover," said Dylan, "Something's wrong with my grandfather."

320

Dad nodded and jumped into professional mode—rushing to the sink to wash his hands. "Come with us, Lowen," he said. "I may need your help."

The inside of Mr. Avery's house was fussier than Lowen would have predicted. Dainty furniture tiptoed on flowered rugs. Curtains were frilled. Photographs in silver and gold frames covered many of the surfaces. It was nothing like the Grovers' home.

Equally surprising was the kitchen, which was a total mess. Blackened pots and pans, some with crispy chunks of food stuck to the bottoms or sides, littered the sink and the counter. Greasy spatulas and serving spoons pointed to plates of untouched food. Wrappers were scattered over everything. It smelled like days-old garbage.

Dylan led them through the living room and into a nearby bedroom.

"Gramps," said Dylan tentatively.

Mr. Avery rustled. "Leave me alone," he slurred. His voice reminded Lowen of his uncle Morgan, who usually got drunk at family gatherings and began to lash out at everyone.

"Has your grandfather been drinking?" Dad asked Dylan quietly.

"No," said Dylan. "He never touches alcohol."

"And you said that he's been like this for a couple of days? Coming in and out of sleep?"

Dylan nodded.

Mr. Avery finally noticed Lowen and his dad. "What in tarnation are you two—" he started to say.

"Mr. Avery," Dad interrupted, calmly and slowly, "I think you've had a stroke. We need to get you to a hospital."

"I told the boy. No doctors! No hospitals!"

"Lowen, call 911." And then to Mr. Avery: "You need to get better—if not for yourself, then for your grandson," said Dad.

Mr. Avery collapsed back against the pillows. Resigned.

As Dad waited for the ambulance to arrive, he arranged to borrow Rena's car so that he could take Dylan to the hospital, too.

"Can I come?" Lowen asked.

"This isn't a field trip. . . ."

"But Dylan might need a friend," said Lowen, acutely aware that up until now, he hadn't been one.

Dad nodded for Lowen to get into the backseat.

Sure enough, Mr. Avery had had a stroke and was required to stay in the hospital for a few days for observation. Dylan was invited to stay with the Grovers. Mum borrowed a camp cot from the Kellings and set it up next to Lowen's bed.

"Does it feel weird to be back in your old room?" Lowen asked as they got into bed. It was the first time they'd been alone since Lowen and his dad had followed Dylan home.

"Yeah, especially since I'm down here, and you're up there where I used to sleep," Dylan kidded.

"Do you want to swap?" asked Lowen. "It doesn't seem right, somehow."

"Nah, it's right," said Dylan. "It's not the Firebrand house anymore."

"Do you miss it?" Lowen asked, turning off the bedside lamp.

"The Albatross, you mean?"

Lowen wondered how Dylan had learned their name for the house. It made him feel lousy. "We don't mean it as an insult."

"It's OK," said Dylan. "My dad built this house for my mom, but it was always a work in progress. And then, when he was laid off from the mill, he didn't have the heart or the money for repairs."

"Tell me about your dad," Lowen said.

"There's not much to tell," Dylan said. "Dad claims he was never really accepted here; his family moved to town when he was in high school. To the locals, that made him an outsider."

Lowen could certainly relate to that.

"A lot of guys resented him when he married one of the most popular girls in Millville. He says that's why he was one of the first men to be laid off from the mill."

"What is your mom like? Besides popular, I mean."

"Why do you care so much about my mom?"

Lowen shrugged, though Dylan couldn't see it in the dark. "I don't know. It just seems weird that you never talk about her."

"Well, don't you think it's weird that you never talk about that kid who got shot?"

The snake lunged, cut off his air.

"Anyway," Dylan said, giving him a pass, "there's even less to tell about my mom than there is my dad."

Lowen thought for a moment. "There's always something to tell," he said.

Dylan was so silent that Lowen thought he might have fallen to asleep.

"Guess you're right," Dylan finally whispered. "Always something."

And then he was snoring.

Lowen, on the other hand, was awake enough to imagine an Abe comic—something he hadn't done in weeks.

He wondered if he'd ever share his Abe comics with anyone. Would people say he was insensitive? That the comics were inappropriate or offensive? Deranged?

In providing Oliver with a friend (Abe), was Lowen forgiving him? And if so, why? So *he*, Lowen Grover, could be forgiven? After all, he had never held a gun, but he was as much a murderer as Oliver and he knew it.

Enough, he told his overactive brain. He didn't need to show his drawings to anyone if he didn't want to. (Just like the letter he'd written to Mrs. Siskin.)

The comics were a safe place for him to work through his feelings about Abe's death. It didn't matter what other people thought of them—they were for *him*, not for anyone else.

On Sunday, Dylan went to the Cornish Eatery to deliver pasties and Lowen was left alone at home again. He took out his sketchpad, which was mostly empty now. For nearly two months he'd been drawing caricatures, but he was getting really tired of it. For one thing, he was always trying to figure out how much the person wanted a true caricature (which is meant to be funny) versus a portrait (which hopefully makes them look good). It turned out that drawing caricatures with other people's feelings in mind was a lot like trying to draw comics with someone else's voice constantly piping up, telling him what to do.

And somehow his art had become something just for others.

He took out his old Phenom sketchbook. He read through it, smiling at times, remembering ideas that had been Abe's—ideas that he had incorporated. He turned to a clean sheet of paper, and without analyzing, drew the next strip.

Instead of refraining from drawing as a way to honor Abe, he'd use his art to honor him.

Lowen drew—both a Phenom strip and a new Abe strip—until the rest of the family and Dylan were home. And then, while Dylan was on the phone with his mother, he tried to draw some more but got caught up in the listening:

"He's really sick, Mom."

"No, really. I think he'd like to see you."

"Just the opposite. I think missing you is one of the things wearing him down."

"People aren't thinking anything. Besides, you could stay at *his* house. In your old room."

"Never mind. I have to go. Forget I even called."

35.

THE NEXT DAY . . .

When Lowen was walking home from school, Ms. Duffey spotted him and waved him into her yard. For the second time, she was holding a shovel.

"How are things? Are you still drawing caricatures?" she asked.

"Continually!" said Lowen.

"Well, that must be good for the Cornish Eatery."

"It is, but now I'm worried about not getting the house repairs done on time. The Kellings and the Muñozes could afford to hire people to fix up their houses, and Rena has Coach to help, but we seem to be moving backward."

"Have you asked anyone for help?"

Lowen shook his head. "Sometimes it seems as if people in this town don't really want us to succeed."

"I'm sure it's not that," said Ms. Duffey. "But there are people who are skeptical of this program. They're watching all of you closely to determine whether it's a help or a drain on the town."

The Dollar Families were lab rats, just like Sami had pointed out on the very first day, and it looked like his family was one that wouldn't make it.

"Here," she said, handing Lowen the shovel. "Take your mind off your troubles and help me dig a hole."

"Burying more regrets?"

She laughed. "No, silly, planting a tree."

Lowen gave her a sideways glance. "Are you ever going to tell me what you buried last summer?"

"Nope. But, I'll tell you this: burying them did me no good. No good at all. So I'm following another book's advice on letting things go. I'm going to embrace my regrets, accept them, love them. Maybe then they won't have such a grip on me."

Lowen stepped onto the shovel and drove it into the crusty earth. He thought of *his* mammoth regret, of how much it haunted him — how he had no right to be happy. How could he embrace that?

Again, he pushed the shovel into the earth and tossed the dirt to the side.

Pushed. Tossed.

Pushed.

Tossed.

The Abe comic he drew last night came to mind. It wasn't a new comic, exactly, but a revision of an earlier one:

WHERE TO NOW?

YOU SHOULD VISIT *YOUR* MOM.

I CAN'T DO THAT!

IT'S PROBABLY REQUIRED. YOU PROBABLY HAVE TO LOOK AT THE PAIN YOU CAUSED BEFORE YOU CAN STOP ROAMING ENDLESSLY.

WHO ARE YOU, ANYWAY? A ZOMBIE? A GHOUL? MY *TORMENTOR*?

I'M ABRAHAM NOAH SISKIN. I'M A NINE-YEAR-OLD BOY.

AND I'M HERE BECAUSE YOU, LOWEN GROVER, KILLED ME!

Lowen drove the shovel into the increasingly hard earth with all the force he could muster.

Ms. Duffey put her hand on his arm. "If it's too hard—"

"It's Lowen!" a girl's voice called.

Lowen stopped and looked to see Clem and Luna walking down the road, holding hands. "Hey, Lowen!" Luna called out.

Lowen could feel the heat rise in his face.

Clem pulled Luna closer to him.

"Hello, Luna," called Ms. Duffey. "Hello, Clem."

"Oh, hi, Ms. Duffey!" Luna said, pulling Clem into Ms. Duffey's yard. "I didn't realize you lived here." She looked up at Clem and added, "Ms. Duffey has asked me to do a recital at the library. She thought it might help to show that there's a lot more to Millville than sports."

Clem nudged her shoulder—a much tamer reaction than he gave Dad whenever Dad downplayed sports.

"Not that there's anything wrong with sports," Ms. Duffey said to Clem, "but if we're going to keep this town alive, we have to start appealing to people interested in jobs that can thrive in a town like Millville. Since Millville has a low cost of living—"

"Houses for one dollar!" Clem sang, as if he were selling popcorn at a baseball game.

Ms. Duffey laughed. "Well, even those sold in the more conventional way are pretty economical. . . . It's the kind of community where artists might be able to make a living."

"Artists like Lowen," cooed Luna. "Are you ever going to draw my cello for me?"

"We've got to keep going," said Clem.

Lowen had been thinking about it. "I might be able to—"

"Luna has an appointment."

And just like that, the two of them were gone.

When Dylan and Mum got back to the Albatross after the shop closed, Dylan announced that his grandfather was coming home on Wednesday. "Is it OK if I skip work tomorrow afternoon, Mrs. Grover?" he asked. "My grandfather's coming home Wednesday and I should clean up the mess."

Mum nodded. "Of course. Anneth or Lowen can do deliveries."

"Anneth, would you do them?" Lowen asked. Then, to Dylan, he said, "I'll go with you, if you want."

Dylan looked at him skeptically.

"I could help—do the dishes or something."

Mum gave him an approving nod, but he wasn't just offering because it was the right thing to do. He wanted to hang with Dylan. But suddenly he wondered if he was acting just like Abe. Was he being a pest? Did Dylan even want him around?

"If you want to come and scrub pots, that's your choice," said Dylan, but his eyes were smiling, and Lowen knew that Dylan was deep-down glad.

The next day, on the way to Mr. Avery's house, Lowen picked up Sami, who wanted to help too. It was rainy, which made the house darker.

"Stop judging," said Dylan as they strolled into the kitchen.

"We're not—"

Dylan stopped and stared at Lowen.

"Well, I suppose I'm thinking that you're not the best housekeeper." Lowen started removing dirty dishes from the sink.

Sami took the dishes from Lowen and placed them in the dishwasher. "So what did your grandfather do in the mill? Before it closed?"

"He was a papermaker," Dylan said. He'd pulled out a trash bag and was collecting discarded food wrappers and boxes.

"Wow," Lowen said. He knew from the research he'd done with Sami that that job title went to men who had moved way up in the ranks. It was one of the best jobs in the mill.

Dylan nodded. "Grandfather Avery always said, 'You put your time in, you work hard, you reap your rewards.' Most of the papermakers had college degrees, but my grandfather got the job without one—he was that good."

"Do you have a stainless steel pad or something?" Lowen asked. There was no other way this burned-on stew was coming off the bottom of the pot he was scrubbing.

"No, but you can try this." Dylan tossed Lowen a sponge that was made for scrubbing, but he didn't look hopeful.

"And what about your dad? What was his job?"

"He was maintenance. He kept everything in working order."

"Oh," Lowen said, failing to keep the surprise out of his voice.

"Yeah," said Dylan. "I know. I think he was better at repairing mill machinery than he was at repairing a home. Mom always accused him of taking shortcuts." He held out his garbage bag. "Throw that pot in here. You're never going to get that crap off the bottom."

Lowen held the pot in his hands. "So the mill closed and your dad and grandfather lost their jobs," he said. "What happened then?"

Dylan frowned. "What do you mean?"

"Well, is that when your mom moved to North Carolina?" It seemed kind of cold, if that was the case—hightail it out of town because your husband and dad are out of work.

Dylan was quiet for a moment, and Lowen wasn't sure he was going to answer. Then he said, "After the mill closed, businessmen in suits kept showing up in their fancy cars, making all sorts of promises about buying the mill. Dad, always Mr. Hopeful, kept thinking they would. But no one ever did."

Lowen wanted to ask what that had to do with anything, but he didn't want to seem rude. Luckily, Dylan continued. "Then my mother, seeing her opportunity to get out of dying Millville, left with one of those suits."

Lowen remained very quiet, not sure what to say.

"She's no longer with the guy, but my grandfather can't forgive her for taking off with him. And my mother can't forgive my grandfather for always thinking that she's doing the wrong thing."

"What about you?" asked Sami.

"What about me?"

"Can you forgive your mother?"

Lowen expected Dylan to get angry, to spout off. But he didn't. He took a deep breath and gave the slightest of nods.

Lowen reached for the garbage bag. He'd throw the pot away if that's what Dylan wanted.

"No, don't," said Dylan. "My grandfather will miss it."

As Lowen walked home from school the next day, he saw Coach walking toward town, carrying a small, square coffee table.

"Cool table, Coach," said Lowen, wondering what Coach was doing walking around with a table.

"Thanks." Coach paused. "I made it."

Lowen ran his hand over the surface. It had a really cool pattern in the wood. "You made this?"

"Yup. From discarded wood. Thought you knew everything about me, did you?"

"Nah." Lowen might only be thirteen, but he'd certainly learned that people were always more complicated than they seemed.

They walked on. "Rena's going to try selling my recycled furniture in her shop."

It was a cool idea—upstyled clothes and furniture—but Coach didn't exactly *have* to walk to Restored Riches by way of the Albatross. Lowen sensed an ulterior motive and braced himself for the pitch Coach was bound to give him about joining baseball.

But he didn't. He didn't say a word about it. Huh?

Coach had come down to Mum's to recruit him for basketball. He'd offered him private lessons. Now baseball was coming up and he hadn't so much as asked if Lowen wanted to try out. Maybe it was just his height that had interested Coach. Maybe Coach thought a tall kid could accomplish anything on the court. Guess Lowen proved him wrong. Coach was probably tired of trying to teach a kid who had no natural talent to play ball.

Lowen walked into the Eatery the same moment as Mrs. Corbeau. *This could only mean trouble.*

"Why, the shop is smaller than I imagined," she said, leaving off any polite greeting, "but, then, there are those offices behind your restaurant."

"Hello!" Mum said. "Is this your first time in here? Beautiful spring evening, isn't it?"

"We could use more rain," clucked Mrs. Corbeau.

"After all that snow?" Mum asked.

"Snow doesn't do a thing for the flowers. They need a good soaking."

"Oh," Mum said, "I didn't realize."

"I came by to tell you to expect a visitor to your home next month."

"Oh?" said Mum again, wiping her hands on her apron.

"As you may have heard, I'm standing in for Mr. Avery on the town council until he's well enough to serve again. The town cannot sign over any of the dollar houses unless they are deemed safe and insurable. An insurance inspector will be coming to Millville to conduct inspections—to basically make sure that you have restored the house per your agreement."

"But we still have more than two months," Lowen said, knowing full well his mother would get on his case for being disrespectful.

"True. Two months to make the repairs" she said. "You might as well know if additional work will be required. A lot can happen to a house in a year. Also, we're trying to gauge the probable success of the program. There are some folks in town—Coach, for one—who would like us to offer more houses next year."

"I take it you don't agree with that plan," said Mum.

"I don't see how giving houses away has helped anyone," said Mrs. Corbeau. "I, for one, believe in people making their own way."

36.

APRIL

The fact that there were only two months left to restore the Albatross put the Grovers into crisis mode. They agreed that the outside of the house had to be tackled immediately. The exterior would provide a first impression; if it still looked run-down, there was no way an inspector was going to accept the rest.

Dad quit his job in Flintlock. Just like that. He decided that the only way this crazy plan would work was if he moved to Millville and worked on the house full-time. He knew that it was risky, but he also knew that if they failed to purchase the house, it would leave them even more battered and sad than when they first arrived. So while Mum kept the shop going (now their only source of income), and Dad repaired the flashing and shingles around the chimney, and Clem and his buds dug holes in the newly thawed ground, placed the porch posts, and began construction on the porch frame, Lowen and Anneth scraped peeling paint off the old clapboards. It was grueling work, but Lowen couldn't help notice, with some satisfaction, that his biceps were growing.

Their house still looked terrible from the outside, but they were clearly on it now. It was great to have Dad in Millville every day, and there was a new energy around the Albatross.

So it was probably no coincidence that one week after they had made significant progress, Virginia Corbeau upped her game and the Busy Bee started serving dinner. And Mrs. Corbeau was offering lots more than pie. She was luring folks in with three-cheese lasagna and baby back ribs. The impact on the Cornish Eatery was immediate and extreme: folks in town were saving their money for dinner out at the Busy Bee. For the first time since they moved to Millville, Mum lost all her fight. She stopped getting up at dawn to make a list of the things she needed to do. She stopped searching for new pie recipes. She even forgot to place an order for flour and shortening and had to close early one day.

To ease their worry about finances, Dad was forced to spend fewer daylight hours working on the house and more time investigating the possibility of opening a clinic in town. He knew he needed the supervision of an actual doctor, and he was trying to convince one of the doctors he'd met when he'd brought Mr. Avery to the hospital to sponsor him. So far he hadn't had much luck. "They all think it's a waste of resources," Dad said. "Millville is too small and too rural—to say nothing of too impoverished—to guarantee steady business. They'd rather have me working out of the hospital. But the commute would kill me; I'd see you guys even less than I saw you when I lived in Flintlock!" But he kept at it, hoping to wear them down; if Mum's shop went under, it would be up to Dad to keep them afloat.

Questions filled Lowen's mind: what would happen if neither Mum nor Dad could find work? Would they move back to Flintlock? Could Mum and Dad get their old jobs back? What about their apartment? Could they get that back, too? Even if the answer to all three questions was yes (which was highly unlikely), he would feel no comfort. He liked his new life—all the Grovers did—and didn't want to give it up. That made him more determined than ever to keep trying. So during spring break, he completed scraping the lower clapboards. (Dad insisted on going up on the ladder himself when the sun was barely rising.) Lowen used wood putty to plug some of the larger holes in the old porch rails, and he stained the porch floor with Anneth.

At noon each day, he'd head down to the Cornish Eatery to have lunch with Mum. While they sat at the table together, Lowen would try to get Mom back to her "there's got to be a way" self. "What if you offered other dinner options?" he asked. "Like deep-dish pizza?"

"Oh, now, that's Cornish," she said, with only half a smile.

Lowen thought harder. "All right, then, how about stargazy pie?"

That got a chuckle out of Mum. Stargazy pie was a whole-fish pie with the fish heads poking out of the top crust, staring skyward. All of the Grover kids refused to eat it.

Lowen knew it wasn't the solution, but it sure did his heart good to see Mum laugh.

Just then the door of the shop opened and in came Sami, with Dylan close behind her. "Hey," she said. "We thought you could use a break from house chores." She held up a bag. "Dylan has to put these flags on grave sites."

"To get ready for Memorial Day," Dylan added.

"But Memorial Day's not for weeks," Lowen said.

"I know. But Field's Funeral has a lot to do to prepare."

"Translation," said Sami, "they have to bury all the people who died over the winter."

"I have to get back to the—"

"No, you don't," Mum said. "You need to go do something else for a while. Dad found a used dishwasher today—you can help him install it when he gets back from Ranger tonight."

Lowen hesitated.

"Go!" she said, with a little more fire than he'd seen in a while. He was glad for it.

On the way to the cemetery, they stopped into Restored Riches so Sami could update her mom on her whereabouts. There were plenty of people poking through the recycled clothing, marveling at the ways Rena (with the help of Anneth) had made the clothing new again. Lowen noticed that a lot of the "junk" that had been left in the house the Doshis purchased—curtains, ribbons, paper clips, lampshades—had found its way into the clothing.

Along the back wall, there were paintings that Lowen had never seen. He wandered closer. They were acrylic paintings of random objects—and they were good. Really good. He was so intent on studying the paintings, noticing the technique and the details, that he almost tripped over the painter!

There was Mrs. Lavasseur sitting in the corner of Restored Riches, painting a picture of a chipped cup that was on the shelf in front of her. Somehow she had made the chip the most beautiful part of the painting.

"I didn't know you were a painter!" he said.

She smiled. "And I didn't know you were a cartoonist!" she said. "That is, until the Firebrand boy brought me the tourtière pie your mom made especially for me. He told me about your caric—"

"Excuse me," said a man Lowen didn't recognize. "I wonder if you could tell me more about that painting over there? The one of the Princess phone on lace?"

Lowen waved good-bye to Mrs. Lavasseur. He hoped she'd sell the man a painting or two; she was really very good.

The winter months may have broken records for the coldest temperatures, but April was no doubt in the running for one of the warmest spring months in Millville history. When they arrived at the cemetery, several people were milling around the graves, cleaning off the winter debris and planting spring annuals.

Dylan led them to a partially underground vault that looked like a little cottage and was built into a hill in the cemetery. The door was shut tight. "The bodies are in there," he said. At first Lowen imagined frozen bodies piled on top of one another, but then he realized that they were most likely in coffins. He wondered how many coffins the vault could hold.

"Did you know that the early Saxons were so afraid of ghosts returning to haunt them that they cut off the feet of the dead?" Sami asked them.

Lowen's mouth dropped open. *"What?"*

Dylan chuckled. "You're making that up!"

"I'm not. And some Aboriginal tribes used to cut off the heads of the dead. They thought that the ghost would be so busy searching for its head that it wouldn't have time to haunt them."

Lowen and Dylan just stared at her.

"I read it in *Psychology Today*."

"Guess I missed that issue," Dylan quipped.

"Har, har," said Sami. She opened up the bag of flags. "We'd better do this systematically or we're bound to miss some."

She divvied up the flags and the cemetery, and then each of them set out.

Lowen tried to keep his eyes searching for veterans' headstones—he could imagine how upset the family of a veteran might feel if they visited their loved one's grave on Memorial Day and there wasn't a flag—but his eye was drawn more readily to the tombstones of children.

They were easy to spot: most had pictures carved into them—things like teddy bears, lambs, babies in blanket hammocks, and starry nights. He wondered if any of the kids buried in this cemetery had died in a terrible accident, the way Abe had.

He'd worked on his Abe comics the night before. He'd decided to start over, trying to draw as realistically as possible.

All right. The truth. Lowen was going back to the beginning because he had no idea how Abe and Oliver's story should end. It was particularly frustrating because he had to admit that when it came to envisioning an afterlife, he was no more imaginative than anyone who'd come before him. There seemed to be only two ways to go: one or both of the boys could go to heaven (and what kind of heavenly setting would be right for both Abe *and* Oliver?), or they were destined to wander around this earth as ghosts. So redrawing the art made him feel as if he were getting somewhere, when quite possibly he was getting nowhere at all.

"Hey, Lowen! Come check this out!" Dylan was calling him over from a distance.

Lowen quickly scanned the area to make sure that he hadn't overlooked any of the veterans' graves and then headed over the small hill to where Dylan was waving.

He and Sami were standing next to an open grave. A large hole had been dug — large enough to bury a cement box (also known as a vault) that would contain and protect the coffin. A few hundred feet away, they could see the vault that would be lowered into this grave; it was secured on the back of a flatbed truck. But none of the graveside workers were in sight.

"The diggers probably went to lunch," said Dylan.

"I thought the hole would be deeper," said Lowen, looking from the vault to the hole and back again.

"Graves used to be six feet or deeper, but now they're only about four," Dylan said.

"How come?" Sami asked.

"Vaults protect the coffins and the body inside. But before people started using vaults, all kinds of stuff could happen: decaying bodies could spread diseases, they could wash away in a rainstorm, and animals could dig them up. So people buried the dead deeper then."

"Makes sense," said Lowen. "But this hole looks a whole lot deeper than four feet, doesn't it? I mean, I'm five foot eight—"

"Try it," said Dylan. "See if it's as deep as you are tall."

Lowen was about to say, *Yeah, right*. But he didn't. Instead, he thought about Abe resting in a grave just like this one, and then he squatted next to the hole and slipped down inside.

The fall took longer than expected. He landed in a crouched position, using his hands to stop himself from toppling over.

"Whoa!" Dylan shouted. "You're in a grave, Grover!"

"Stand up. How tall is it?" Sami asked.

Lowen heard the question, but he couldn't bring himself to stand up. Instead he lay down on the dirt and looked up at the partially cloudy sky.

The next thing he knew, Dylan and Sami had jumped into the grave, too, and were now standing over him.

Lowen spoke softly. "Remember when Mrs. K. told us about tying a string to the toe of a dead person?"

"The string led to a bell," said Dylan as he lay down on one side of Lowen, "in case the person was buried alive."

"Can you imagine that? Being buried alive, I mean?" Lowen said.

"I think that would be the worst thing that could happen to a person," said Sami, lying down on Lowen's other side.

All three quietly looked up.

"Do you think it would be the very worst?" asked Dylan after a few moments. "I mean, would it be worse than standing in front of a firing squad? Or hiding in a room when you know that a killer is looking for you?"

Again they went quiet, until Lowen's voice rose up on the thinnest wisp of a whisper: "How about knowing you're responsible for the death of someone else?"

He hadn't known he was going to say it. The snake rose up, threatening to choke him.

Dylan pulled himself up on one elbow. "That kid?" he said quietly, his words like an arrow. "The one who got shot?"

Lowen felt a wave of revulsion—not just a single snake, but a whole nest.

"You?" asked Dylan. "*You* were responsible?"

Lowen bit his bottom lip and nodded.

"No way!" said Sami. "Unless you plotted with the kid who pulled the trigger, there's no way you had anything to do with your friend's death."

"I'm serious, Sami," he said.

But she shook her head. "Kids always think things are their fault. Like when parents get divorced. But it's not true."

"What happened?" Dylan asked softly.

And so Lowen told them. As the three of them lay side by side, staring up at the cumulus clouds, he told them how Abe had come over to his house that Saturday afternoon. That was unusual. Abe always invited himself over after school, but hardly ever on weekends. Lowen assumed that on weekends Abe did things with his mom, or had piano lessons. And most of the time, Lowen was occupied, too. He was expected to help with the laundry (which was in the basement of their building), or the grocery shopping (which had to be pulled home in a rolling cart), or the light dusting (which was a huge pain because Anneth always had a million things on her bureau). But this particular Saturday he didn't have to do any of those things because he was still getting over a cold. And therefore it doubly annoyed him when Abe showed up during this bonus time.

Anyway, on that Saturday, Lowen was sitting up at the kitchen counter working on a new comic — one about a superhero who could read minds. Abe slid up on the stool next to him, looked over his shoulder, made some comment, and then slid down to wander around the kitchen . . . until he popped up a minute later to give his two cents again: *What's so great about reading people's minds? By the time he reads the villain's mind, the guy will have shut down the city. You should create a superhero who can reverse people's thinking. . . . Or one who can muddle a mind so the villain gets all confused and doesn't even recall the awful thing he's about to do!* "The Unseen Force."

Lowen said these last three words in the same deep voice that Abe would have used.

"Those are cool ideas," said Dylan.

"I know," said Lowen, "but I didn't want to draw Abe's ideas. I wanted to draw my own. I wanted *this* story to be mine alone."

Lowen paused and took a deep breath.

"Keep going, Lowdown. What did you do?"

"Abe loved one thing more than hanging over my shoulder, and that was candy. Especially Twizzlers. Strawberry Twizzlers. So I went to my room, pulled out my birthday money, and sent him to the store to buy one of those gigantic bags of licorice." Lowen waited until he could speak again without crying. "I was actually happy that it was taking him so long to return."

That was all he could say.

It was all any of them could say. But Sami placed her hand on one of his arms, and Dylan placed his hand on his other arm, and they stayed that way until Lowen no longer felt as if the walls of the grave were falling in on him, burying him alive.

37.

LATER . . .

After a time, Dylan hoisted Sami and Lowen out of the grave, then Lowen and Sami pulled Dylan out. They finished putting flags in the holders, and then took off. Dylan headed in the direction of his house, while Lowen and Sami walked toward the Albatross. Rena had texted Sami to say that she had left the younger girls with Anneth, and Sami was to pick them up there.

"Coach talked me into trying out for baseball tomorrow," Sami told Lowen.

Lowen was both surprised and a little hurt. Had Coach really given up on him? "Oh?" he asked, hoping he sounded casual.

"He said that the team needed me."

Then she lowered her voice and added, "He also said that I was too responsible for my own good. That I should relax, take some time to be a kid. Apparently, in his mind, baseball is relaxing."

"And what did you say?"

"I told him that most of my mom's boyfriends don't stay around long enough for me to relax."

"Whoa—what did Coach say to that?"

"He said"—a smile started on the edges of Sami's mouth, though she tried to squelch it—"he said he was up for the challenge."

It was in that moment that Lowen realized that Coach could one day be Sami's stepfather, and even though he himself had a perfectly fine father, his feelings of jealousy increased.

As Lowen and Sami approached the Albatross, they could hear Mr. Field directing, out behind the house. Curious, they wandered out back to check it out.

Clem and Mr. Field were in the parking lot trying to straighten the crooked basketball hoop. Luna was standing to the side.

"Hey, Lowen, Sami," said Mr. Field. "Want to help?"

"Can't," Sami said. "Meera has T-ball, so I have to get her home and into her T-shirt."

"I'm going inside to practice," said Luna. "There's a funeral this afternoon and the family has asked me to play. Lowen, would you like to come hear me warm up? I'll play *Gadfly* for you," she said.

Clem, who was squatting, holding the pole at its base

so Mr. Field could check to make sure it was perfectly straight, looked up and scowled.

Lowen felt his heart leap.

"Sports aren't the be-all and end-all for you." Luna placed her hand on Lowen's forearm, giving him goose bumps. "You have an appreciation for lots of things," she said, "like art and music."

He couldn't help it. He began to sweat.

"Cut it out, Luna," Clem said.

Lowen glanced at his brother. He could see the anger in his taut legs and arms, the redness of his neck. Was it possible that Luna did like him better than Clem?

A twinge of guilt crept in, but he slapped it back down. Why should he care about Clem? What kind of brother had Clem been to him?

"I especially like *your* music," he said. He was surprised at how cool he sounded. He pulled his shoulders back a bit.

"See, Clem. Your brother is sweet," she said, reaching down and giving Lowen's hand a squeeze.

Lowen couldn't believe what was happening. He glanced at Clem, fearing signs of hurt on his face—he didn't think he could take hurt—but Clem didn't seem hurt at all. Just angry.

Clem stood. "Stop messin' with Lowen," he said.

"I'm not messing—"

"It's cruel."

Luna pulled her hand away. "I was just having some fun," she said, pouting. "You've been ignoring me."

And just like that, all the warmth seeped right out of Lowen. The rush of hope was replaced by a tidal wave of embarrassment.

Cruel to *him*.

She was playing *him*. Playing him like a cello. Playing with both of them, really.

He turned and took off for his room, first at a fast pace, then a trot, and then a sprint. He hurled his ridiculously gangly body onto his bed and buried his head in his pillow.

Luna.

She'd been this little patch of light for him, this little bit of magic.

But that was stupid. There was nothing magical about Luna. And now he wouldn't be able to be near her without being reminded of what a dumbass he'd been.

Lowen didn't go downstairs for dinner that night. He said he was too tired to eat. Clem knocked on his door, tried to talk to him, but he couldn't stand the further humiliation, the smugness of his older brother.

Lying there, in the dimness, he thought about lying in the grave with Sami and Dylan. Of how they had listened to what had happened with Abe, but they hadn't judged him. Telling them had helped.

But only for a little bit. All his guilt rose to the surface again. It was as if every bad feeling—in this case, embarrassment over Luna—led him back to the horror of Abe's death, and the part he'd played in it.

He was tired. Tired of keeping his secret.

He thought of getting up, of telling his parents the way he had his friends, but he didn't think he could bear to see the look on their faces. He knew from that moment on he'd no longer be their insightful peacemaker, their sensitive and caring son.

The mass of the secret—not snakes, but the secret itself—seemed to rise in his chest, cut off his air. He couldn't stand it. He might never tell his parents, but he could tell Mrs. Siskin. He could at least be honest with her.

He got out of bed, dug in his closet for the letter. Reread it. Told himself that it wasn't enough to be truthful. He had to be honest.

Giving Mrs. Siskin this information might make things worse. A whole lot worse.

But she deserved to know that Abe had not acted on his own accord. That he'd been put up to going to the store by someone older, someone who should have known better, someone who should have been a better friend.

And that he was deeply, deeply sorry.

He wrote.

As he finished recounting the events that led to Abe's death, he began to remember all the things he loved about Abe: his quick wit, his great sense of humor, his wonderful imagination, and his ability to help (even if it wasn't always needed), and he shared these with Mrs. Siskin, too. He wrote:

> His curiosity, his questioning, it made me question. I didn't always want to stop and take the time to consider his questions. Sometimes it's easier not to think, or to look at things differently, or to come up with answers. But when I did, I was almost always glad. He challenged me. He made me look at things differently. When I took the time to be open to what Abe was saying, I was a better me.

He sealed the letter into an envelope. But then, more worries: Was it right to send it? Was he simply trying to make himself feel better by confessing?

He knew that Abe's mother would never think about that day in the same way again, would never think about Lowen in the same way again. But maybe that was for the best. Because surely, some part of her—however small, however misguided—blamed Abe for going into Georgio's alone, which he wasn't supposed to do. Maybe she was tormented by the thought that if only Abe had followed the rules, if only he'd listened to her, he would still be alive. Maybe by knowing that it was Lowen's fault her son was dead, she could stop blaming her son and finally find some peace.

Maybe by taking the blame, Lowen could finally find peace, too.

He called out that he was going for a walk and in doing so, dropped the letter into the nearest postbox.

38.

MAY

Despite the fact that the house still needed fresh paint, new front steps, and two windows repaired, the Grovers hoped for a fairly good report when the inspector arrived on the second Monday of May.

He hardly introduced himself before he spent what seemed like hours knocking on walls, testing smoke detectors, and looking behind electrical wall outlet covers. He tested the water for lead, the basement for radon, and the roof for structural soundness.

Unfortunately, the final report was anything but good. The Grovers had many infractions that had to be addressed, and most would require a plumber or an electrician. The worst of the news, though, was that the continual freezing and thawing of the past winter had taken a final toll on the roof. It now needed replacing. And that wasn't all. The boards in the eaves (where the ice dam had leaked) were rotten and needed replacing as well.

The blood drained from Dad's face as he read the report aloud. Mum sank into the corduroy chair, and suddenly Lowen noticed how thin she had become, how pale.

He felt cold.

"Maybe the town will give us more time," Anneth suggested, but knowing how hard Mr. Avery and the Corbeaus had worked against this plan, all of the Grovers agreed that an extension was highly unlikely.

Should I even try out for baseball if we can't stay in town? was the question on Lowen's mind when he showed up that same day for baseball tryouts.

"Grover!" Coach said as he passed him, lined up against the backstop with the other kids. "I didn't expect you to be here."

Does Coach know about the house report? Is that why he didn't expect me?

Nah. More likely he was thinking about Lowen's lack of athletic ability. He hadn't exactly been the star athlete in soccer or basketball.

But even though he didn't have an ounce of the skill his brother had, and even though he might not make the team — or if he did, Coach might keep him on the bench the whole season (since girls and boys played on the same baseball team, they didn't lack players) – and even though he might be moving in less than a month, he still wanted to try out. Correction: He still wanted to be on the team. He liked being part of something. He liked the common goal, the inside jokes (even when the jokes were about the two points he scored for the rival team), and he liked going to bed tired – too tired to think about the dead bodies next door. Too tired to think about Abe.

So a week ago, he'd asked Sami to help him. Just went right up to her and said, "Will you teach me how to be a better batter?"

She'd studied him for a moment, and when she realized that he was serious, she nodded yes.

They'd met at the baseball field before school started on two different mornings. Sami showed him how to keep the bat straight and how to follow through. She helped him to judge the approach of the ball without ever saying, "Keep your eye on the ball."

Now that tryouts were here, he'd wished they'd started the lessons earlier and that he'd asked for fielding tips as well.

"Left field, Grover!" Coach yelled.

Lowen hustled out to his position. Was this field larger than what he was used to in Flintlock? He felt miles from the mound. He doubted any kid in middle school could hit this far. Might as well be on a different planet. No doubt Coach was sticking him in some no-matter position.

Wrong.

First hit by Dylan went well over his head.

"Back up, Grover! Follow the ball," Coach yelled.

The next two hits—one by a seventh-grader and one by an eighth-grader—were infield hits.

Then Sami hit a pop fly.

Lowen kept his eyes up, followed the ball, followed it . . . and . . . *smack!*

He had it!

He'd caught it!

Then he dropped it.

"Two hands, Grover!" Coach called. "Catch with two hands!"

How did you do that, when only one hand sported a glove? He'd have to ask Sami.

To everyone's surprise—but especially to Lowen's—Coach didn't make any cuts. They had all made the team! "Now, if you want actual playing time," Coach warned, "you'll have to show up at every practice and work hard.

No daydreaming in the outfield or doing your homework when you're on deck."

As they walked off the field, Sami motioned for Lowen to follow her into the dugout. She looked around to make sure they were alone, then sat down on the cement bench.

"I've been thinking about what you told me about your friend," she said gently.

He sat beside her. "My friend?"

"The one you sent to the store."

Lowen's heart stopped. She and Dylan hadn't brought up Abe since that day at the cemetery. Why was she doing so now?

"What did you usually do when he was bugging you? You know, when you were drawing?"

He kicked the dirt below his feet. "Why? What does it matter?"

"I have a theory."

"You mean B. F. Skinner has a theory, right?"

"Actually, yes. It is Mr. Skinner! Anyway, what did you do when Abe was bugging you?"

"I don't know." Lowen shrugged. "I usually tried to distract him. It was the only thing that really worked — though never for very long."

"Like how?" asked Sami, leaning closer.

"I'd give him candy and stuff," Lowen admitted. "Once I gave him a sketchbook."

"I knew it!" Sami smacked her glove on the bench.

"Knew what?" Lowen asked, totally confused.

"Don't you see, Lowen? You thought you were finding clever ways to get him out of your hair, but maybe he was bugging you so you would give him candy! Mr. B. F. Skinner would say that he was training you."

"*Training* me? Like a dog?"

"Or a pigeon. Think about it." She stared at him. Her face was so serious. So intense.

So Lowen thought about it. Maybe there was some truth to what she was saying. Maybe Abe had wanted Lowen to give him candy. But he suspected that what Abe had really wanted, more than candy, was friendship.

(Just like he told Oliver in his story.)

Lowen had tried so hard not to hurt Abe's feelings. Not to say to him, *Go away. I don't want you hanging around me all the time!*

But maybe he *hadn't* been thinking about Abe. Hadn't been protecting him at all.

He'd been protecting himself from feeling like a bad person.

And in the end, he hadn't protected either of them.

. . .

When Lowen returned home, Clem was trying to build the new front steps. He was measuring and sawing, hammering and swearing.

"What's your plan?" asked Lowen.

"My plan is to stay in Millville!"

"Because of Luna?" He regretted the question as soon as it was out; the last thing he wanted to talk about with Clem was Luna Muñoz.

"*What?* No! I like it here." Clem put the hammer down and shook out the tension in his wrist. "Besides, we broke up."

"You did? But she's so—"

"Pretty?" Clem finished.

Lowen nodded, blushing. "And talented."

Clem sighed loudly and plopped down in the grass. "Yeah. But she's also callous."

"What does that mean?" Lowen asked, sitting down on the ground next to his brother.

"Uncaring."

Lowen flinched, remembering how she'd treated him. "Is she that way with everybody?"

Clem looked at him. "Doesn't matter. She can't mess with my little brother."

Lowen stared. Was Clem saying that he'd broken up

with Luna *because of him*? He felt something hard, something solid, melt inside his chest.

"I'm the only one who can be mean to my brother," Clem added.

Lowen smiled.

"Now go get me some more nails—this size," said Clem, opening his palm to reveal two nails, "and help me with these steps. I got to meet my buds in an hour."

39.

Dylan sent Sami and Lowen a message, asking them to meet him at Field's after baseball practice—and after the two deliveries he had to make. On the walk there, they tried to predict the reason for the meeting. For a second, Lowen thought that Dylan might have prepared an ambush—some way to scare the wits out of them (moaning from the embalming room, a severed hand)—but he knew that wasn't Dylan's way at all.

Dylan was waiting for them at the back door when they arrived. "The Fields are away. I'm watering the flowers," he reported.

Sami looked back at the gardens, where annuals had just been planted. "Do you want some help?" she asked.

"Not with watering." Dylan motioned for them to come inside. He started to pace around the little serving kitchen, gearing up to tell them what this meeting was all about.

"Just tell us, Dylan," Sami said.

"My grandfather got a letter," he said.

"From your mom?" Lowen asked hopefully.

"From the bank. They're taking his house. Our house."

"What?" asked Lowen. "How can they do that?"

"It's called foreclosure," Sami said. "It's how most of us got our dollar houses."

"But a bank can't just take a house, can they?"

Dylan picked up a dish towel that was folded on the center island and began twisting it in his hands. "Gramps owes them a lot of money. When my grandmother got melanoma, the bills really piled up. And then my grandfather had his stroke and he hasn't been able to pay the extra loan on the house."

No wonder Dylan had been working at two jobs, skipping meals, paying with nickels.

"Can your dad help?"

"I'm not sure my dad would help him if he could. He'd rather I come live with him, anyway."

"What do *you* want?" Sami asked.

Dylan sucked in air. "What do *I* want?" he shouted. "I want my mom and Gramps to make up! I want my mom to come home! I want my family back!" Then he laughed. It probably felt good to let it out.

"What's going on?" It was Anneth. She must have heard them through the screen door.

Lowen looked to Dylan, who nodded. He opened the door and let his sister in.

As Dylan explained the situation to Anneth, Lowen grappled with mixed emotions. Here was the man who not only had done nothing to help any of the Dollar Families feel welcome, but had done everything he could to prevent their success. Lowen should be happy that Mr. Avery's house was being taken away from him. It was what he deserved.

Or was it?

He thought about how hard Mr. Avery must have worked to rise through the ranks at the mill—to make papermaker without a college degree. And how hard it must have been for him to lose his job.

Maybe Mr. Avery didn't always do the right thing or act in the nicest way, but he'd lived in this town his whole life and had seen it turn from a place of prosperity and beauty to a downtrodden shell of its former self. In that time he'd not only lost a wife, but he'd lost a daughter, too. And now he was losing his house—while others, like Lowen's family, were being given the opportunity to purchase houses for one lousy dollar. He was pretty sure Mr. Avery would like to buy his house for a dollar. Come to think of it, it's likely that Dylan's father would have given more than a dollar to stay.

Did one person's fortune always have to come at the expense of someone else?

"There's more," said Dylan.

"More?" Sami and Lowen said simultaneously.

"My mother called me. She's thinking of coming back home."

"Do you tell her about the foreclosure?" asked Sami.

Dylan shook his head. "I didn't want her to change her mind. Make other plans."

"But maybe she can help," Sami said.

"How?" asked Dylan. "She doesn't have money. If she moves back home, she won't have a job."

"He can't lose his house," Lowen said, the force of his conviction surprising everybody. "There has to be a way we can help."

"Unless any of you has a few thousand dollars lying around, there's just no way," Dylan said.

Lowen couldn't help but feel the frustrating irony of the situation. Maybe if Mr. Avery had supported the Dollar Families instead of undermining them, Mum's shop would be doing well enough that they *would* have a few thousand dollars they could loan him.

Everyone was silent for a while, thinking. Anneth curled a strand of hair around her finger. "Maybe we could crowdfund," she said at last. "Lots of fashion designers have gotten their start that way."

"What's crowdfunding?" Dylan asked.

The question surprised Lowen. He wasn't online that much, but even he'd heard of it. "It's when people explain their needs on a website and others donate to help them out. Friends, family—but sometimes strangers, too. Especially if you can get the word out."

Sami nodded. "My mom's friend raised money for her dog's vet bills," she said. "Mostly it came from her friends and coworkers, but it got shared a lot on Facebook, and strangers from different parts of the country chipped in, too. It makes people feel good to help those in need," she added, no doubt about to launch into the explanation of another psychological theory.

But Dylan cut her off. "Are you kidding? My grandfather would hate that! He would be furious if he even knew that I told you about the foreclosure notice. He hasn't even told *me* about it. I just happened to read the letter for myself."

"So we won't tell him," Lowen suggested. "Not at first. Seems to me he's going to feel lousy and embarrassed no matter what. We might as well try to keep the house for you and your mother."

"He's probably not on the Internet much. We can tell people that the crowdfunding is a surprise," Sami said.

Dylan snorted. "Fat chance keeping a secret in this town. And won't people be upset that my grandfather gets help but no one else does? There are still lots of peoples trying to hold onto their home."

"You may have a point there," said Anneth.

"No," said Sami. "It's not an organization helping Mr. Avery. We're just a bunch of kids doing something nice for—"

"... for a friend," said Lowen, completing her thought. "*Our* friend. Dylan. We're doing this for *you*."

Dylan shook his head vehemently. The idea seemed to scare him more.

"Think of it this way," Anneth said. "How are people in this town going to feel if one of their leaders—one of the town selectmen—loses his house? Won't they all feel like throwing in the towel, then?"

That justification seemed to sit better with Dylan. "Let me think about it," he said at last.

They agreed to wait a day or two. "In the meantime," Anneth said to the group, "think of incentives. People who donate to these sites usually get a little thank-you gift in return."

40.

TWO DAYS LATER . . .

They decided to go ahead with their plan. Lowen could tell that Dylan still had his reservations, but since no one had come up with a better idea, they went into action. They told a few of the older Dollar Kids (for help and better incentives) and swore them to secrecy.

Clem freaked when they told him.

"Avery's house? We're helping Avery?" Clem had said, slamming his hands down on the table. "Why haven't we been crowdfunding to get donations to fix up our own house?"

"I don't think crowdfunding would have worked for us," Anneth had said. "Only a tiny percentage of campaigns reach their goals, and most people would probably agree that we've already been given help."

"We're doing this for Dylan," Lowen said. He rubbed his hands on his thighs. "But, if you really think about it, it doesn't seem quite right. . . ."

Clem got it. "If we get a house for one dollar and Mr. Avery loses his?"

Lowen nodded. "I've been thinking about this. Why can't the town just give the house back to Mr. Avery for a dollar?"

"Banks agree to donate properties to a town"—Clem stopped to line up his thoughts—"so that others with more earning potential will move in and keep the town running. Once a homeowner has shown that he can't pay his mortgage, he's no longer considered an asset."

"An asset?" Lowen asked.

"Helpful," Clem corrected. It took Clem some time to agree, but in the end he said that he and Mason would come up with an incentive together.

They also decided to tell two adults: Mrs. Lavasseur and Coach. These adults could offer great incentives for large donors (paintings and handmade furniture), and Dylan—especially since he'd quit sports and started making deliveries—had already shared personal information with and trusted both.

At first, Coach, knowing full well how Mr. Avery might react, balked. But eventually he came around. "I suppose it's better to put his well-being before his pride," Coach said. "But, I can't promise not to tell Rena, if I see the need."

They had decided not to tell their parents—especially Lowen's mum and dad—for fear that they'd put an end to the campaign before it got started. Like Dylan, they would know that Mr. Avery would be mortified, and it could quite possibly make things worse than they already were for the Cornish Eatery. It was best to hope that the campaign was a big success and then ask for forgiveness.

So, on Anneth's orders, Dylan took on the task of searching for pictures to post with their plea. "Get some of the house, of course—especially the wishing well and the windmill," Anneth told Dylan. "And see if you can find good ones of your grandparents and maybe one of you as a little kid, playing in the yard. It's our job to pull at people's heartstrings," Anneth said.

"We should have a picture of the mill, too," Sami said. "In its heyday. That will remind people of what a hardworking man Mr. Avery has been all his life."

Lowen, Sami, Clem, Mason, and Luna (whom Sami had brought on board and who actually acted like a team player) gathered around Anneth and helped her compose their message.

"We can't exactly write this in Mr. Avery's words," said Anneth. "The last thing we want to do is make it seem like he's the one pleading for help."

"Maybe we write it from Dylan's point of view," Sami suggested.

Lowen thought for a moment and then shook his head. "Then it would seem as if this were all his idea. He could get in even *more* trouble."

"Let's tell people who *we* are, then," Anneth said.

Luna said, "You mean—?"

"Let's tell them that we're the Dollar Kids," finished Lowen.

"Why not?" said Anneth.

Anneth began typing:

Hello,

We are the Dollar Kids. Our families bought houses in the town of Millville for one dollar. We all have different reasons for moving here, but the one thing we all have in common is a desire to make Millville our home—just as it's home to many other people looking to live in a small community. One that prides itself on its history as a mill town. One that is determined to face hardship with grace, dignity, and optimism. One that is willing to welcome new families with open arms.

"That's a bit of a stretch, isn't it?" asked Clem, reading over her shoulder.

Anneth shrugged. "Some folks want us here. And they did decide to give the program a chance—at least in theory. I think we need to put Millville in the best possible light, to show people the best side of this town—and maybe to remind some of the townspeople themselves why they started the Dollar Program in the first place."

She continued typing:

But this isn't about us, or even about the town of Millville. This is about one man, Mr. Douglas Avery, who has lived and worked in this town his whole life and is about to lose his home.

When the mill shut down, Mr. Avery lost his job. Not long after, he lost his wife to cancer. The medical bills for his late wife

"Late?" Lowen asked.

"It means dead," Sami said.

Anneth continued:

piled up. And then Mr. Avery himself had to be hospitalized, with no way to cover the costs. As a result, the bank is threatening to foreclose on his home.

Mr. Avery's house isn't just the place where he started his family, the place where he watched his daughter grow up, the place where he celebrated (and here Anneth made an educated guess) more than forty years with his beloved wife, it's also the place where he's raising his grandson.

We're asking for donations to save Mr. Avery's home from foreclosure. Any amount, no matter how small, will help. Thank you.

Next they posted a list of incentives.

For small donations they were offering:

- Upstyling tips by Anneth
- A free subscription to Sami's advice column
- A humorous video of baseball tips from Clem and Mason

For larger donations:

- A recording of Luna's cello performance
- A personal caricature from Lowen

For VERY large donations:

- A painting by Mrs. Lavasseur
- A small end table or bench made by Coach

They clicked publish on the crowdfunding page and then waited.

41.

MID-MAY

At first nothing happened, which made sense. Keeping their campaign a secret meant that they couldn't tell people around town — the very people who would most want to help Mr. Avery, however modestly. But the Dollar Kids shared the link with their friends back in their former hometowns. Coach shared the link with other coaches in the area, particularly those who had grown up in mill towns. Mrs. Lavasseur shared the link with her grown children in other parts of the country, and they shared the link on their social media sites. And then people began to donate.

The donations were small at first. Anneth was regularly sending out her upstyling tips, and many subscribed to Sami's advice column (which she enjoyed writing and updated often). One woman who received Anneth's upstyling tips posted a picture of a jeans-pocket bulletin board in the comments section of the site. Then someone whom Lowen had drawn as a pan-wielding chef shared his caricature in the comments section, too. And then, much to their enormous surprise, an art collector donated a thousand dollars for Mrs. Lavasseur's painting of ladybugs clustered on a smudgy windowpane, and the site seemed to explode.

With school, baseball, and the crowdfunding site, the Dollar Kids became overwhelmed—but the Grover family suffered most. The Kellings and the Muñozes could afford to hire help to fix up their houses early on. Rena had Coach to help with repairs, and he brought a lot of skill. Dad was researching roofing material, petitioning the town council for more time to fix up the house, and also driving to Ranger to look at apartment rentals just in case, but he wasn't getting much help from Mum. To Mum's surprise, business suddenly picked up at the Cornish Eatery. Most of the customers were strangers passing through, and she decided that it must be a seasonal thing. Summer was coming, and Millville wasn't far from some beautiful lakes.

She thought that until one of the new customers asked about the crowdfunding site. When Mum looked puzzled, the visitor showed her the site on his phone.

A family meeting was called—IMMEDIATELY.

Lowen watched his parents' faces as they went from horrified (what would Mr. Avery say?) to angry (since when are you keeping secrets from us?) to amused (*how many paintings has Mrs. Lavasseur sent?*) to proud (you did all this on your own?).

Mum beamed at them. "The three of you have worked hard to help a family out, and that may be one of the very best results of this adventure."

"You make it sound like the adventure is over," Anneth said.

Mum and Dad exchanged a solemn glance. Lowen knew then that Anneth had been reading them correctly: something was wrong.

"What?" asked Clem.

Dad sighed. "As you know, Mrs. Corbeau is still acting as town councillor in Mr. Avery's place. She informed me today that we will not get an extension. The other Dollar Families have been able to meet their requirements, and rules are rules. No exception will be made for us."

It occurred to Lowen that when he and his mother applied for the house, they never considered the possibility that it would cause them more sadness, more regret, more missing.

Clem collapsed forward onto the table.

"It wasn't like we didn't try," said Anneth.

"We did try—you probably tried hardest of all, Clem," said Dad, reaching out to hold his shoulder. "I really admired your determination."

Lowen thought about the year and wondered if there was anything they could have done differently. He didn't think so. Sometimes, all the determination in the world won't make things go your way.

"This was a grand adventure," Mum said after a few moments of quiet, "and we learned a lot. We learned about ourselves, our persistence, and our creativity. Perhaps one day we can buy a house of our own."

Lowen fought back tears and lost. Anneth dropped silent tears, too. But they both nodded in agreement.

"Yeah. One that someone else doesn't mind selling to us," said Clem.

"One that doesn't require so much fixing up," Dad added.

And even though none of the Grovers was feeling particularly happy, they laughed again.

The next morning Mum announced that she, too, would like to contribute to the crowdfunding campaign. She researched food safety laws and decided that if Dad got the proper packaging, they could send frozen pasties. It would be her way of knowing that she'd made a contribution to Millville.

By the end of the day, the crowdfunding site had dozens of new donations and Mum was up to her ears in pasty dough. She asked the rest of the family and Dylan if they wouldn't mind helping her fill pie trays so they could be frozen overnight.

They were all sharing a Dad Chillin' and laughing at how it was still one of the most popular pasties at the Cornish Eatery when the door opened and in walked Mr. Avery, madder than anyone had seen him before. If Lowen were to draw him, he'd have smoke coming out of his ears.

"Sit down, Mr. Avery," said Dad, no doubt worried about the possibility of another stroke.

"Who do you people think you are?" Mr. Avery shouted. "What gives you the right to share my troubles with the whole damn world?"

"Gramps," said Dylan.

"You think you know everything about everybody. That everyone's willing to take a handout, just like you. You come in here all high and—"

"Gramps!" Dylan banged the rolling pin on the counter. "Who do *you* think you are?" he shouted at his grandfather.

Mr. Avery stared at Dylan, mouth agape.

Mum reached over to put her hand on Dylan's shoulder, but he moved out from behind the counter. "What do you know about anything?" he shouted at his grandfather. "You can't take help from anyone! And you know what? You can't give help, either! You didn't help Dad when he was depressed. You didn't help Mom when she needed money to keep things going. I've lost both my parents and one home and I'm about to lose another, and you still go on about people minding their own business! What about *my* business, Gramps? Who's minding my business?"

Seconds passed. Mr. Avery took a deep breath. "You're right," he said at last. "I'm no good to anyone."

He turned and walked out the door.

42.

THAT NIGHT . . .

Dylan slumped over the counter. "I shouldn't have said that."

"He'll likely come around," Dad said, but Lowen didn't think Dad was necessarily right. Mr. Avery seemed especially good at holding on to bad feelings.

"I better get home," said Dylan, untying his apron.

"Are you sure you want to do that?" Mum asked. "You can stay with us tonight."

Dylan shook his head. "Naw, I need to be there for him. Not many people are."

Later Lowen texted Dylan: Everything OK?

Return text: He said three words to me: Go to bed.

Lowen, Anneth, and Clem couldn't go to bed. The crowdfunding site had exploded. Links to the site had gone viral—everyone was talking about the Dollar Kids and their attempt to help someone in their new community. Loads of people were leaving comments on the site—praising the Dollar Kids, calling out the cool incentives (Coach would need to hire help to make tables), or discussing Mrs. Lavasseur's extraordinary talent. It seemed she had been discovered.

The next morning, they had far exceeded their goal of saving the house. "This could go a long way toward paying down his debt," Mum said, marveling over the money the kids had raised. "Once he gets over being furious with everyone, I hope he'll start to feel some peace of mind."

Ms. Duffey dropped by the Albatross to tell them that several reporters had contacted the town council—they were on their way to do a story about Millville, the Dollar Kids, and Mr. Avery.

"I hope you don't mind," said Ms. Duffey. "I told them that your kids—as well as Sami, Mason, and Luna—could be interviewed at the Cornish Eatery this afternoon. Dylan may want to be there, too," she said as an afterthought.

"That will work," Mum said. "I could use the kids' help today."

Dad cringed. "How's Mr. Avery reacting to that news?"

Ms. Duffey shook her head. "He didn't answer the phone last night. I'm heading over there to talk with him now."

"And I'm heading to the shop," said Mum. "I don't know how we're going to fill all the orders."

"Do you need even more help?" asked Ms. Duffey. "I could spread the word."

"Yes," Mum said without hesitation. "I'll take all the help I can get."

That morning, the Kellings and the Muñozes came by with their younger kids to help fill orders—and to be there when the older kids were interviewed.

At one point Rena popped in to borrow Kate Kelling for a little while. Apparently, she and Kate had been working on a website for Restored Riches—a website where people could order one-of-a-kind clothing—and she wanted it up and running before the Millville story ran all over the news that night.

Despite the celebratory atmosphere and the excitement of the impending interview, Mum seemed a little down. Lowen wondered if she was facing the fact that they'd be leaving just at the point when her own shop was getting so much business. "Are you OK?" he asked her.

"You want to know the truth?" she said. "I really thought that when Ms. Duffey put the word out that we needed help, that we'd see more Millvillians here. It makes me sad that they still don't think of us as one of them. That they don't realize that our efforts will not only save Mr. Avery's house, but shine a little light on their town."

Even more surprising, at least to Lowen, was that Dylan never showed up—not to help with the pasties, but also not for the interview. Was his grandfather keeping him away? Was Mr. Avery still mad, even knowing that they'd saved his house?

When the reporters arrived, they interviewed Anneth, Sami, Clem, Mason, and Luna. When it was Lowen's turn, he said that moving to Millville had taught him a lot about friendship and that he had wanted to do whatever he could to help his friend Dylan. (All the while, he hoped Dylan was OK.)

At the dinner hour, the Grovers took a break and headed home to watch the evening news. Mum had sent the volunteers home after the interview, thanking them profusely for their help but saying that the family could handle the rest of the work on their own. Lowen guessed the real reason was that she needed some space and didn't want her sad mood to bring everybody else down.

Lowen was excited to see the Dollar Kids on TV, of course, but he couldn't help wondering how Mr. Avery was reacting to all of this. They hadn't seen him since his angry outburst. What if the television interview made him even more furious? Lowen didn't know what they'd do if he flat-out refused to accept the money.

"What the—?" Clem blurted out as they turned the corner and saw their house.

It was as if elves had been there during the day! The house had a new metal roof, fresh paint, and Clem's steps were now attached to the porch. The front lawn had been mowed, there were freshly planted flowers in the front, and the honeysuckle bush had been trimmed back.

Just then, Rena approached them from the back of the house. "Come on in, you guys! Everyone's waiting!"

"Rena, what on earth—?" Mum began, but Rena just laughed and tugged on Mum's arm.

"We have to go in through the back; the paint's still wet on the front door."

As they walked around their house—Lowen still couldn't get over how different it looked with a coat of fresh paint; it was as if the house had gotten a face-lift—they could hear voices inside. *Lots* of voices.

They walked in the back door and Mum gasped. The kitchen was as dramatically transformed as the exterior of the house. The floors had been sanded and polished till the wood glistened. There was a new tile backsplash and new countertops. And there were brand-new kitchen cupboards.

"Wow. I bet Coach built these," Lowen said, running his fingers over the smooth wood.

"Rena! How long have you known about this?" Mum asked. But again, Rena just smiled and pulled Mum along.

There wasn't an inch to spare in the living room. The Kellings, the Muñozes, the rest of the Doshis, Mrs. Manzo, Coach, Ms. Duffey, Rutabaga Dave, Mr. and Mrs. Field, Mrs. Lavasseur, most of the guys from the high-school baseball team (who were sitting on the stairs), and all of Lowen's and Anneth's classmates—including Dylan—were crowded into the little room, and in the center of the crowd, sitting in the corduroy chair, was Mr. Avery, wearing grubby paint clothes. The TV was blaring.

The Grovers looked at one another, stunned. "How did all this happen?" Dad asked.

"Shhh," said Mr. Avery. "It's starting."

One of the reporters who'd interviewed them was standing outside the Cornish Eatery, explaining about the town of Millville's Dollar Program and touching on the situation with Mr. Avery's house. Then clips of the Dollar Kids' interviews aired, which was simultaneously embarrassing and really, really cool.

Then the reporter broke away from the shop and climbed the hill to the Albatross, where, "Unbeknownst to the Grover family," the reporter said in hushed tones, "a very appreciative Mr. Avery has organized a work party." As they watched, the reporter approached the house. Folks in the room started calling out to one another: "That's you with the ladder, Dave!" and "Hey, that's Sara painting the porch!"

And then the camera zoomed in for a close-up of Mr. Avery and Dylan. "Our community's been through some tough times," said Mr. Avery. "But I realize now that at one time or another, *everyone* needs help—and *everyone,* at one time or another, can find a way to be helpful." He turned to Dylan. "My grandson taught me that."

The room cheered—and then cheered even louder when the reporter wrapped up the story, announcing, "Not only has Mr. Avery's house been saved, but, from the looks of it, the Grovers' house has been saved, too."

43.

JUNE

A very sad thing happened in the first week of June. Mrs. Manzo came over to tell them that Mrs. Lavasseur had died in her sleep. She'd had a very successful day painting a single mill smokestack. Then she went home to bed. She never woke up. If Abe had had the worst kind of death imaginable, perhaps Mrs. Lavasseur had one of the best.

The Grovers—even Lowen—attended the visiting hours at Field's. Lowen dressed in his best clothes, though he didn't wear a suit jacket; over the year his arms had grown another three inches and his jacket no longer fit.

When it came time for the family to walk up to the open casket and say their good-byes, Clem hung back for a moment, but not Lowen. Since drawing his Abe comics, he felt calmer, braver. This time he would look at the body. He would look death straight in the face.

It wasn't as scary as he thought it would be. In truth, the body in the casket looked like Mrs. Lavasseur, and it didn't look like her. It was like viewing the discarded skin of a snake. The energy that made Mrs. Lavasseur Mrs. Lavasseur was gone.

He wondered what her artistic soul was seeing now.

The Corbeaus were at the funeral, too. While standing graveside, Lowen overheard Mrs. Corbeau say, "You wait and see what that family has set off. There'll be so many tourists trampling through Millville that we won't even recognize our lovely town."

Sami rolled her eyes at Lowen.

"She doesn't know what she's talking about," he said.

But in a way she did. What none of the Dollar Kids realized on that bright June morning was that their crowdfunding efforts set actions in motion that would affect the town for years to come. Folks would travel to Millville to taste Mum's pasties and to visit Restored Riches. Artists would bring their art to be exhibited in Rena's expanded shop. Many, realizing that houses cost very little in Millville, would stay. With so many artists in town, other businesses would come too: a coffee shop, an art supply store, a bookstore, even a greengrocery that sold rutabagas. Eventually, Ms. Duffey and a group of artists would convince the company that owned the old mill building not only to leave it standing, but to turn it into studio space for painting and sculpture. (She would no longer regret her decision to turn down a marriage proposal and stay in Millville.) More folks would come to Millville to see the extraordinary art that was being produced. More houses would be built to accommodate all of the folks who wanted to live there. A wing would be added to Central School.

On the day they stood in the cemetery, none of the kids could know that visitors to the mill would be greeted by large comic panels—panels that told the history of the town from its early days of papermaking to the present.

As for Mrs. Corbeau, she wouldn't stick around long enough to realize that selling dollar houses had been good for Millville.

Just a few months after the funeral, she and Mr. Corbeau would sell their shops, move to Florida, and complain about the traffic.

44.

LATER THAT DAY . . .

When the funeral was over, Lowen headed to opening day at the town pool with Sami and Dylan. Dylan warned them that the pool was always freezing on opening day, and it was. Nevertheless, most of the town's kids—who no longer differentiated themselves as Dollar Kids or Millvillians—were there. After doing a few cannonballs into the ice-cold water, the three of them lay down on their bellies on the hot cement. They soaked up the heat and breathed in the smell of chlorine rising from their wet skin. Lowen turned his head to the left. Dylan had his eyes shut. Then he turned his head to the right to look at Sami. She opened one eye and smiled at him.

Shazam!

The snake inside him seemed to be replaced by an electrical current.

That very same day, when Lowen returned home, a letter was waiting for him on the kitchen counter. It was from Mrs. Siskin. He started to tear open the envelope but stopped himself. The day had ended so sweetly. He'd read it tomorrow.

Only, that night, he couldn't sleep. Not with something explosive sitting there.

Finally he got up and opened it.

Dear Lowen,

Thank you for writing to me. That act took much courage. As you predicted, it was hard for me to read your letter. A thousand times or more I have wished that I could turn back the clock. What if I had made him clean up his room before leaving the apartment? What if I had held him in a hug for just a moment more? What if, when he peppered me with questions while I was trying to clean up, I didn't suggest that he go play with you?

Don't get me wrong, Lowen. I am not angry with you for sending Abe to the store. You see, I did the same thing. I shooed him away.

What pains me most (when I am not thinking about how angry I am at his killer or the fact that this seventeen-year-old had access to a gun) is that I didn't realize that the very thing that annoyed me when Abe was living is the thing I desperately want now that he's gone. I want my little boy glued to my side, asking me questions.

In truth, Abe's voice continues to follow me around, asking questions. Only now, I stop to think about them. As you pointed out in your letter, he was curious about everything, and his curiosity forced us to see the world differently. Time and time again, he brought me back to the moment.

Yes, your letter caused me sadness, but what I want you to know is that it also offered me solace. It is a great comfort to connect with someone who knew Abe so well, who loved him as I did.

I know you cared deeply for Abe and you must forgive yourself for all of the complex feelings that come with a true friendship. There was frustration, but there was also happiness. Remember the happiness, because you did, indeed, make Abe's short life very happy.

I hope you will write me again.

With love,

Rachel Siskin

That night, Lowen drew this strip:

"You are, Abe," Lowen whispered to the dark, and drifted off to sleep.

Lowen finally told his parents about what had happened on the day Abe died. He figured that if his friends could forgive him, and Mrs. Siskin, probably his parents would, too. And they did. Of course they did.

That evening, Lowen pulled out his sketchbook. He had been thinking about Abe, thinking of a way to end his story. In the first frame he drew Abe standing, looking out, saying, "Is that you, Lowen?"

"Yeah," Lowen said aloud as he filled in Abe's features. "It's me."

"He's all yours, Abe. He belongs to you now."

Lowen laughed and adjusted Globber Dog's ears.

Lowen closed his sketchbook and went downstairs to be with his family. They could hear the *pound, pound, pound*-ing of a basketball out back.

"Part of me wants to go out there, but part of me is too tired," Clem said. He'd worked hard that afternoon to dig an herb garden for Mum.

"Too tired to shoot some baskets with your old man?" Dad asked.

Mum looked at Dad with astonishment.

"*What?* I know I'll stink, but I thought Clem could share some of his knowledge."

Clem hesitated and then grinned. "OK," he said, standing. "Do you want to come, too, Lowdown?"

Lowen smiled. His brother had called him by his nickname. "Sure."

"Me too?" asked Anneth.

Clem nodded.

"Wait," said Mum. "I'll change into trainers."

The Grover family joined the Fields on the blacktop and passed, teased, encouraged, dodged, and laughed. At one point Dad fell, but he quickly got back up again.

The sky turned from blue to royal purple. The air cooled, and the day stilled. Fireflies began to flicker in the tall grass around their house.

Lowen stood still for a moment and watched for each new sparkle of light.

He felt incredibly peaceful, as if the expansiveness of the night were sharing a secret.

A secret from an unseen force.

There might very well be a heaven, he thought.

And for now, it was right here in Millville.

ACKNOWLEDGMENTS

Enormous thanks to my agent, Alyssa Eisner Henkin, for enthusiastically embracing *The Dollar Kids* when it was little more than an ember. You carefully tended this story—simultaneously fanning it and containing it—as needed. Your editorial and professional guidance has been invaluable. Thanks also to Meagan Cohen, Alyssa's assistant.

Thanks to my husband, Don O'Grady, who introduced me to East Millinocket and patiently answered my 1,265 questions. I have loved getting to know your hometown! Thanks, too, to my grown children and stepchildren, who were willing to grapple with logistical, philosophical, and political questions as they related to this story.

Thank you to my readers Mary Atkinson, Jane Kurtz, and Holly Jacobson for your insightful feedback. You know how much I depend on your knowledge of story, your deepest reactions, and your analytical superpowers. (I never tire of your input.)

Thanks to my friend Frank Crosby, who shared his knowledge, literature, and videos on the Millinocket region. And thanks to (then) fifth-grader Audrey Murray, who taught me about "left foot day."

Huge thanks go to my brilliant editor, Kaylan Adair, who in asking all the right questions in all the right ways led me to create a richer, more connected world. You have been my cheerleader, my writing coach, and my editor extraordinaire. I know how lucky I am to have you as a creative partner.

And thanks to the rest of the Candlewick tribe: Mary Lee Donovan, Hayley Parker, Sherry Fatla, Jessica Saint Jean, Chris Paul, Angie Dombroski, Kate Schwartz, Maggie Deslaurier, Emily Quill, K. B. Mello, Jamie Tan, Susan Batcheller, Katie Ring, and Kathleen Rourke, who helped design, publish, and promote this book. You rock!

Finally, thanks to the incredibly talented Ryan Andrews, whose art makes the heart of this story beat brighter.